HOPE AND A FUTURE

PAMELA BROWN

"For I know the plans I have for you," declares the Lord, "plans to prosper you and not harm you, plans to give you hope and a future." (Jeremiah 29:11)

"**D**oomed. Doomed. Doomed."

"See, in situations like this, I think it's important that we stay optimistic."

"Doomed."

"Let's be positive."

"Doomed."

"At least we aren't being melodramatic."

"I'm doomed. Tell me I'm not doomed."

Luke Castleman looked at his twin sister, Lacey, and then at the pathetic display before her on the counter.

"I'm doomed!"

"Well, if you don't look at them directly, they kind of look like brownies," Luke lied.

"They're not even brown, they're purple," Lacey wailed.

Luke was actually thinking that they looked blue, but he didn't bother correcting her. Besides, he couldn't fathom how she'd managed the feat, considering she hadn't used any food coloring. He was also stumped on how she could have burned the brownies when they still had the texture of uncooked batter.

Luke sniffed the air and caught another whiff of burnt brownie odor. Yep, she'd burned them alright. If the fire alarm hadn't stopped working months ago, it would be beeping right now. He shook his head in bewilderment. She really had no cooking skills at all.

Not for the first time in his life, Luke marveled at how he and his sister could look so similar, yet have such differing personalities. Born only two minutes apart, they were identical in every way, from their dark brown hair and light brown skin, courtesy of their Native-American mother, right down to the smattering of freckles across the nose. Yet, when it came to their individual abilities, they were as different as night and day.

The proof of this was Luke's own home economics project sitting on the worn countertop in front of him. A tray of moist chocolate brownies sat there cooling, guaranteeing Luke a passing grade.

It was mindboggling to Luke because they had used the same ingredients and followed the same recipe. But while Luke had produced a delectable treat, Lacey had somehow created the science project that was currently stinking up their small apartment.

"What is that smell?" Stephen Castleman walked into the kitchen area, his wife right behind him. "It smells awful. The neighbors are going to start to complain."

"Is something burning? What's burning?" Anna Castleman, his wife, entered the now crammed kitchen and stopped short when her eyes fell on the brownies sitting on the counter. "Oh," she said, "your brownies."

"I thought the assignment was to bake them, not burn them," Mr. Castleman said with a chuckle. He was tall, lanky and blonde – the only member of his family to claim those features – and when he laughed, he placed his hands on his hips and threw his head so far back that his upper torso leaned back as well. This was also a unique trait within his family.

Mrs. Castleman, whose petite frame and deep brown skin more closely resembled her children, did not find her husband's joke funny. She nudged him and he lifted his eyes from the burnt concoction to his daughter's face.

"Lacey," he said, the laughter gone from his voice. "I'm sorry honey, I didn't mean-"

Mrs. Castleman rushed over to console Lacey, who looked on the verge of crying. "They're just brownies sweetheart," she said as she pulled her daughter into a hug. "No one cares about burnt brownies. It's not a big deal, I promise."

"But-" was all Lacey could manage before the first tear fell.

"Don't pay your father any mind." Mrs. Castleman wiped the sole tear away from Lacey's face. "He can't help but say stupid things."

"It's true," Mr. Castleman said sheepishly. "I think I was born with my foot in my mouth."

Lacey gave a half smile at his joke.

"In any case," Mr. Castleman added, "don't worry about the brownies or your grade. You tried your best and that's all we care about." He leaned over and kissed her on the forehead. Then, seeing Luke's beautiful creation, he gave his son a smile and a hi-five. "And," he continued, "when we finally save up enough money to travel the world, you'll get to taste the finest cuisines all around the globe and learn how to cook even more dishes. You'll be international chefs."

"Yes," Mrs. Castleman agreed, "and now we are going to leave the kitchen before your father says something else he regrets."

They both exited the kitchen, leaving Luke feeling validated for his accomplishment, Lacey feeling a bit better about her failure and both twins feeling like they had the best parents in the world.

Then Lacey's eyes fell back onto her project. Her shoulders slumped and her face crumpled.

Luke looked over at Lacey to try and convince her it would be okay, but when he saw that she was near tears again he couldn't bring himself to utter the words. This was a failing grade and they both knew it.

The two of them had taken home economics together with the intention of learning how to cook. However, while Luke had soared, discovering a talent for all things culinary, Lacey had plummeted, struggling through the entire semester.

Lacey had tried. She really had. But it seemed that she just wasn't cut out for home or economics. Now, after a string of failing grades in the class, Lacey had desperately needed this baking project to turn out well. Burning the brownies meant that she was sure to get a poor grade in the class, if she didn't fail it altogether. And it would be a devastating blow to have her 3.5 GPA that she'd worked so hard to maintain lowered because she couldn't cook.

Seeing Lacey about to cry broke Luke and it made it easy for him to decide what to do.

.....

"LUKE. LACEY. COME IN."

Principal Forrester ushered the two of them into his office where the school psychologist was waiting, and closed the door behind them. If one listened closely, it almost sounded like Lacey gulped at the sound of the door closing. It didn't take quite as much effort to see the nervous twitch she was displaying.

Lacey didn't like getting into trouble. In fact, she was against trouble of any kind. The thought of punishment frightened her severely. Thus, she had devoted her entire 14 years of life to developing into an obedient daughter, a model student, and an honest person. Until now.

Lacey hadn't even wanted to go along with Luke's plan to switch brownies. She had adamantly refused when he'd first suggested it. But with no money to buy more ingredients to bake another batch, and the very real threat of failing Home

4

Ec., Lacey had eventually agreed to let Luke take her failing grade for her. After all, as Luke had reasoned, with all A's in that class, he could afford to take one bad mark. Lacey, however, could not.

The plan seemed to have worked too, as the Home Ec. teacher had praised Lacey for her excellent work, and frowned and shook her head in disapproval as Luke tried to explain that he had fallen asleep with the brownies in the oven.

Lacey's optimism about finally receiving a good grade in the class had lasted right up until the moment the guidance counselor had appeared in her science class to escort her to the principal's office.

Lacey had never in her entire school career been summoned to the principal's office. Call her paranoid, but the fact that this inaugural event occurred on the same day that she had cheated for the first time, did not seem like a coincidence to her. Then, seeing Luke waiting at the door of Principal Forrester's office, had solidified in her mind what this impromptu meeting was about.

As the principal and school psychologist both sat down and pointed the twins to the two remaining empty chairs, Lacey spared Luke a panicked glance. Luke looked as terrified as she felt. He must have deduced the obvious as well. They were cornered and there was no way out.

Still, Lacey reasoned to herself. They had baked the brownies at home. There were no witnesses. There was no way that anyone could prove that they had switched. All she and Luke had to do was deny everything.

"Alright! Alright! We did it!"

To the shock of everyone in the room Luke jumped from his chair and began confessing.

"We switched brownies, it's true. But it was all my idea. Lacey didn't even want to do it, so if you're going to punish anyone, it should be me, not her."

Lacey groaned. As terrible as she was with handling punish-

PAMELA BROWN

ment, Luke was even worse. She should've known he couldn't hold out under the pressure. Now they were done for.

Much to the surprise of Lacey, the two adults looked bewildered by Luke's outburst. They looked to each other as if trying to get clarification from one another.

Principal Forrester said, "Run that by me again."

"We both baked brownies for Home Ec. and Lacey burned hers. I let her turn mine in so she wouldn't fail."

"Oh," Principal Forrester said, finally understanding. Then he waved away Luke's confession, "Don't worry about that. That's not important now."

"Oh." Luke sat back down.

Lacey was relieved, but more than a little confused. Luke had just confessed to cheating on a school project and he was told that it didn't matter. She exchanged a look with Luke, and he looked just as thrown off as she was.

It's a peculiar thing – how tragedies occur. The way they sneak up on you in the most unexpected way. No one ever wakes up in the morning expecting a tragedy on that day. They just happen. For example, neither Lacey nor Luke got dressed that morning with thoughts of trouble on their mind. As they went through their morning rituals, said a hurried goodbye to their equally rushed parents, and ran to catch the school bus, they had little more on their minds than the highs and lows of high school life. And that's how tragedy found them, completely unaware.

They had no idea that their parents, who shared a carpool to work, would be speeding on that particular day, trying to make up for lost time. Luke and Lacey certainly couldn't have known that the other driver wouldn't look both ways before driving through the intersection. Therefore, they were completely unprepared when Principal Forrester told them that when the two cars collided, neither their mother nor father had survived the accident.

As the principal looked upon them with pity in his eyes, and their school psychologist looked close to tears and more in need of consoling herself than able to console, Lacey and Luke became intimately familiar with the unexpectedness of tragedy. Then, escorted from the school by the social service worker they found waiting for them just outside the principal's office, Luke and Lacey began their new lives as orphans.

L uke and Lacey had been silent all morning. From the time their caseworker, Miss Abigail, had shown up unannounced at the children's shelter, to the point where they had been hustled into the backseat of her blue Chevy Cruze, dragging along the few belongings they had left in the world in black plastic garbage bags, they had remained mute. They hadn't even spoken to each other, both locked inside their individual misery.

Now, as they were being driven along to an unknown destination, they were each absorbed in their own thoughts, which were eerily similar. From the moment the nightmare had begun in Principal Forrester's office six months ago, they had been given little information, only expected to mindlessly obey as they were shuffled from shelter to foster home to shelter. Now, they were both being eaten up with anxiety over where they were being sent next.

Lacey tried to comfort herself by thinking that wherever they were headed, it couldn't be worse than the shelter they had just left. An involuntary shudder went through her, but whether it was from the memory of the place that they'd left or apprehension over where they were going, she wasn't sure.

Luke, however, was on the edge of his seat. He was feeling just as anxious and worried as Lacey, but nowhere near as optimistic about the outcome. Luke was convinced that they were being transferred to somewhere far more heinous than the place they were leaving. After several weeks in that depressing place that they were told to call home, his optimism had all but vanished.

They had been driving for at least an hour on the highway, heading east, and that was about as much as Luke knew. He was guessing at an hour. He didn't know for sure how long it had been, because the watch his parents had given him for his last birthday had been stolen from him in the first foster home where they'd been placed. Regardless, he knew that there was nothing good in store for them, and he just wanted to know their fate.

"Where are you taking us?" Luke asked, with a little more edge to his voice than there had been six months ago. A little more anger. A little more distrust.

Miss Abigail seemed unable to hear him though. She was a middle-aged mousy brunette, who at times seemed scatter-brained and at others aloof. At the moment, she was dividing her attention between the road and her phone and seemed oblivious of the two teenagers riding in her backseat, or perhaps just disinterested.

"Where are we going?" Luke asked again, louder and even more gruffly than before.

Lacey looked over at the harshness in his voice, but then lowered her eyes back to the floor. She had changed over the past six months as well. A little quieter. A little more reserved.

Luke's harsh tone seemed to grab the attention of Miss Abigail though, as she acknowledged her charges for the first time since she'd corralled them into her car.

"Hmm?" she said, tearing her eyes away from the phone, momentarily sparing them a glance through her rearview mirror. "Oh, I'm sorry. Did you ask me where you're going? Of course, you did. You two always ask me that when I pick you up. You're going to your new home."

Luke regretted asking her. She called every placement their "new home," so he should've known that it would be pointless to ask where they were headed. Also, he had forgotten about her tendency to ramble, and he wasn't in the mood to hear her carrying on today. However, her next statement grabbed both of their attention and kept it.

"Yes, we should be arriving there soon. It took forever, but we finally located your uncle and he agreed to take you in. The local Department of Children and Family Services have already run the background check and interviewed him, so all I have to do is get you there. He lives in some little town called Port St. Annie, or something. I don't know. My GPS keeps acting up..." she trailed off, as she went back to her phone to try and locate the elusive town.

Luke and Lacey barely noticed that she seemed to have gotten them lost. Instead, they were staring at each other in disbelief. An uncle? Neither of them had ever heard of an uncle. As far as they knew, both their parents had been only children, and their grandparents had died long ago. That was how they'd wound up as wards of the state in the first place. They had no other family.

"Finally!" Miss Abigail breathed a sigh of relief as they reached the sign indicating that the exit ramp for Port St. Annabelle was a mere 5 miles away.

Luke and Lacey's earlier fears were abated as new questions arose in their place. Who was this mysterious uncle? Why had they never heard of him? They both squirmed in their seats, filled with apprehension. What exactly was in store for them now?

A short while later Miss Abigail exited the highway, and they were driving through the town limits of Port St. Annabelle. She let down her window, getting a better view of the scene around her. Small businesses and local shops with bright banners and colorful names (Meryl's Make-up Madness, MacPhearson's Hardware House) lined the street. Pedestrians, shoppers and sightseers ambled along the sidewalks, enjoying the warm season. As Miss Abigail eased the car down what appeared to be the town's main road, she gasped and oohed and aahed.

"Look how lovely it is here," she gushed. "Can you believe you get to live here? Aren't you two the lucky ones?"

Lacey stared at her in shock. Luke glared at the back of her oblivious head and then shook his own head in dismissal. He couldn't waste his time worrying about insensitive adults, even one as clueless as Miss Abigail. No, he had more pressing concerns, like what new horror would await them at the end of this road trip.

"You know," Miss Abigail continued conversationally, not taking the hint from the silence that followed her last remarks, "this town is listed as one of the best places to live in Florida. It's so isolated and remote that none of the big city people have come to destroy it yet. It's a hidden gem. Just look at the architecture of these buildings."

Miss Abigail rattled on about the wonderful aspects of Port St. Annabelle but neither of the twins listened or cared. Lacey watched the shops and people float by as they continued down the main thoroughfare. It was a picturesque scene, but she was too much of a nervous wreck to appreciate any of it. How could they have an uncle and not know about him? Was he really their uncle, or some creep pretending to be related to them? And most importantly, what kind of nightmare would he put them through?

In what seemed like no time at all, they were through the main part of the town and driving through a residential area with quiet streets dotted with storybook houses and perfectly manicured lawns. With the window down, the smells of spring filled the interior of the car. The scent of fresh cut grass and the promise of afternoon rain surrounded the three of them.

"So peaceful," Miss Abigail commented. "So charming."

The GPS then led them onto a dirt road where the houses became more scarce and the woods grew more freely. In fact, it wasn't long before they were entirely surrounded by trees with no sign of human life.

"Hmm," Miss Abigail mused, as she carefully navigated her car along the road, trying to avoid the bumps. "He didn't tell me he lived out in the woods."

If Lacey had been nervous before, she was close to panicking now. She had seen this movie before. They would be out in the woods where he could get away with anything. No one would see what he did to them.

Luke's thoughts weren't far from his sister's. He mentally prepared himself for what they were about to face. He would fight if he had to. No matter what, he wouldn't let this psychopath hurt them.

Sooner than either Lacey or Luke would have liked, they came upon a break in the trees. Miss Abigail slowed the car and turned down an interminable driveway, the end of which opened onto a large clearing containing an impressive log cabin that stood two stories high and had a grand wraparound porch. Nestled into the woods the way it was, the setting would have been lovely if a suspicious character (possibly a psychopath) didn't live there.

The moment they arrived, before Miss Abigail even had time to turn off the engine, the front door opened and a Native-American man exited, followed by a hyperactive Basenji dog. They both went out to meet the newcomers and Miss Abigail squeaked. She actually squeaked, like a small child or a mouse.

"He has a dog," she pointed at the barking creature racing toward the car. "I don't like dogs," she said, and then began fanning herself as if she were going to pass out. "I'll just stay in the car," she announced to the two of them. "Dogs are not good. Dogs bite."

Luke shrugged and exited the car. He didn't care if she stayed locked in her vehicle. She was never much help at this point in the transition anyway. She usually just dropped them off, chatted with the new guardian for a few minutes, and then sped away, leaving the two of them to get adjusted on their own. Lacey followed Luke's lead and got out as well.

Neither of them shared their caseworker's view on the animal which had reached them and begun sniffing away at the foreigners. To be honest, the sight of the dog had given them both second thoughts about their new guardian. Psychopaths didn't typically have cute dogs that sniffed and licked you relentlessly. They didn't think. They hadn't actually done research on the subject matter.

The owner of the dog was the most average looking man either of them had ever seen. He stood at an average height and had an average build. There was nothing remarkable about his features whatsoever. He didn't have large ears, no tattoos, no crooked nose. There were no scars or marks on his face, no cuts or bruises, no interesting features to hold the eye. There was absolutely nothing about him that made him stand out. He was the very definition of the word plain.

The plain man reached the car and approached the driver's side where Miss Abigail was still barricaded inside with the window barely cracked by which to communicate.

"Are you Miss Abigail?" he asked.

"I am," she answered, her voice slightly muffled, despite the crack. "You're the children's uncle, right? We spoke on the phone."

The man produced his wallet from his back pocket and showed her his ID. She nodded in approval, and he returned it to his pocket.

"If you don't mind, I'll just stay here while the children grab their things," Miss Abigail said.

"What?" he looked confused by her answer. "Aren't you going to come inside and look around? Help them get settled?"

This drew the twins' attention. He was inviting her inside?

He wanted her to look around? Then he most definitely probably was not a psychopath. Hopefully.

Miss Abigail waved away his offer. "I don't really do that," she explained. "Besides, they've moved enough times by now. They know the ropes."

The man didn't look pleased at her response. His brows furrowed and he looked at her dubiously. After a moment he asked her, "How many?"

"What?"

"How many times have they been moved about?"

"Well," she began searching through the bag on the front passenger seat of her car, presumably for something that would help her answer his question. "You see," she tried to explain while pulling paperwork from her bag, "I have to keep moving them because they just can't adjust. The boy fights and he's always angry, so no one wants to keep him." She browsed through the paper before declaring, "Five. They've been moved five times. It was getting difficult to find anyone to take them, considering how the boy fights all the time."

"Gee, I wonder why," the man muttered.

Miss Abigail continued as though she didn't hear him. Considering there was a window between the two of them, she may not have heard him. "I have to say, it's a good thing you showed up when you did. I've been trying to keep them together, but I've run out of places to put them. If I have to move them again, then they'll be separated. Really, they could end up anywhere in the state."

Both Luke and Lacey, who had all but forgotten about their bags in the trunk, and were busy petting the dog, froze in place. Luke felt like the air had been sucked from him. He had been punched in the gut before, many times in fact, and never had it rendered him as helpless as Miss Abigail's words just had. Lacey's eyes filled with tears and she began wringing her hands. They both stared at each other helplessly.

The past six months had been unkind to the two of them.

No. They had been cruel. And in that time, they had both learned that there were no certainties in life, and that nothing should be taken for granted. Because nothing remained forever. At least they had thought they'd learned this. But it seemed that life had one last trick to play on them, one more malicious spin of the wheel of fate. They had already lost everything – their parents, their home, their peace of mind, their sense of security, and now they were in danger of losing the only thing they had left – each other.

Miss Abigail carried on with her task, unaware of the tornado of emotions that they were feeling, which her words had caused. "I just need you to sign some paperwork," she said to the man.

She slid a clipboard and pen through the slit in the window and waited while he signed. Once he'd returned the clipboard to her, she glanced at his signature and then announced, "Okay, so that's everything. I'm sure you will all get along well."

"Wait a minute," the man called out. She had rolled up her window and was reaching for her keys to start the car. Now she looked less than pleased that he had halted her departure. "What about–"

"Oh, right," Miss Abigail cut him off. "I'm so sorry. I completely forgot. Of course, you want to know about the money you'll get for taking them in. You'll get a deposit from the State of Florida into your account the first of every month. And you'll get double because there's two of them."

Luke, who had hoisted Lacey's bag from the car, and was in the process of grabbing his own bag, rolled his eyes. Of course, he wanted to know about the money. That was what they all wanted to know about. It was the only thing that mattered to them.

"That's not what I was asking about," the man said, impatiently.

"Well, the exact amount you'll get–" Miss Abigail continued anyway.

"I don't care about the money," he cut her off.

Luke dropped his bag and banged his head on the trunk door at the words he'd just heard. Lacey, who had been kneeling over and petting the dog, stood up quickly. They both peered around the car to stare at the man in disbelief. They had never heard a guardian say anything remotely close to those words before.

Miss Abigail seemed to be just as shocked as they were. For once, she had no words. But the man had something to say.

"Where are their belongings?" he asked her. "Will they be shipped here? Do I need to go and pick them up?"

"Oh no, nothing that complicated," Miss Abigail answered, still sounding a bit flustered. "They have everything with them. They're getting their things now." She pointed towards the back of the car.

"Thank you," he said.

He turned to see them making a small train from the trunk to the side of the car where he stood. Luke was in the front, holding his bag in both arms. Lacey followed, dragging her bag along behind her. Last was the dog, barking happily the whole way.

The man did a double take at the scene. "What?" he asked in confusion. "Is this a joke? Where's the rest of their things? And why are they in garbage bags?" His voice raised an octave with every question, as his confusion was clearly turning into anger.

What was unclear was why he was angry. Luke stared at the man bewildered. Why should this stranger care about their belongings? No one had ever cared before. Not even Miss Abigail. And it was her job to care.

At the moment, Miss Abigail was demonstrating her level of concern over her charges' personal items as she was backing out of the driveway. She apparently chose to ignore the angry questions that had been aimed at her, instead yelling in her retreat, "I'll just leave you to get acquainted," and then disappearing the way she had come.

.....

"Unbelievable." The man shook his head at the dust cloud the social worker left in her wake. Then he turned his attention to the barking dog that was jumping about in excitement and circling the new strangers. With a snap of his finger and a short command, the dog calmed down and sat at attention, leaving only a wagging tail and an alert gaze to betray his excitement.

Finally, he looked at the two teenagers that had just been left in his care. They were the same size, which was small. Very small. In fact, underneath the baggy clothes, which had probably been donated to them as they were at least two sizes too large on both their bodies, he wouldn't have been surprised to find that they were undernourished. They were dressed in exactly the same t-shirt, shorts and sneakers, the only difference being in the color of their shirts. They both had the same haircut, stopping just below their ears – short for a girl, long for a boy. It was the same shade of brown as his own hair. The twins shared a dollop of freckles scattered across their noses and the same brown eyes – hers widened in fear, his narrowed in anger. Clearly their 'fight or flight' responses had been activated. He looked prepared to fight, while she looked as though the slightest sound would make her run. The boy also had the remnants of a black eye and a crooked nose that had obviously been broken at least once. Apparently, he was used to fighting. Or, considering his tiny size, used to getting pummeled.

"Well," the man said, and the girl jumped while the boy took a fighting stance. They were definitely skittish. He pretended not to notice their odd behavior and continued his sentence. "Let's go inside."

He reached down and grabbed the bag from the girl who was never going to be able to carry it all the way to the house. Not without leaving a trail through the grass on his front lawn. Then, after glancing over at the boy, who was struggling with his burden as well, he grabbed the second bag too, and began marching back toward the house.

The dog followed its owner. The siblings, not knowing what else to do, followed too. When he reached the front door, he stood there for a moment and waited. When nothing happened, he turned around to look at the teenagers, expectantly.

After a moment, the boy rushed forward. "Oh, sorry," he said. He opened the door and stood back for the man to enter. "Here you go Mister or Sir."

Instead of entering, the man stared at him, looked back at the girl, and then looked at him again.

"Let me guess," he said. "your social worker never told you my name."

The girl stared at the ground, but the boy spoke up. "She said you were our uncle. So, you want us to call you Uncle?"

The man sighed deeply, his distaste for the flighty social worker growing by the minute. "My name is Owen Stillwater. You can call me Uncle or Uncle Owen if you prefer. You're Luke and Lacey, right?"

At the sound of the man's name, the girl's head shot up and the boy gasped.

"What is it?" Owen asked.

Still, the girl couldn't speak, but the boy found his voice. "That–" He stumbled and started again. "Stillwater was our mom's name. Her maiden name. You have the same name as our mom."

"So?"

The two twins shared a look before the boy spoke again. "So... then it's true? Miss Abigail was right? You really are our uncle?"

"Of course I am," Owen said as he walked into the cabin. "Anna was my older sister."

❧ 3 ❧

Once inside the cabin, the twins received a short tour of the largest home they'd ever seen. Certainly, it was the largest one they'd ever lived in. Owen walked them through the foyer, into an expansive great room with sparse furnishing. It boasted a high ceiling, a working fireplace (working but unnecessary, because it was Florida) and a massive window looking out onto the front lawn. Owen spoke very little along the way, but pointed and murmured brief statements that they barely heard.

"This is the great room," he mumbled. "Through there is the dining room and kitchen." He pointed straight ahead towards the mentioned rooms but didn't head in that direction. Instead, he headed to the left where a large staircase with an ornate wooden banner was located. "You can look around later if you want," Owen muttered as he climbed the stairs, a black trash bag slung over each shoulder. Luke and Lacey followed mutely, eyes darting about, taking in everything.

At the second-floor landing, he stopped and pointed again. "There's one room. There's the other room. My room's at the end down there. Each room has a bathroom. I'm going to take my dog, Nosey, outside for a bit. He's been cooped inside all day waiting for your caseworker to show up."

Nosey, who had followed them through the cursory tour, affirmed this statement with a bark.

Owen dropped both trash bags to the floor and stared at them for a moment, as if the bags had personally offended him. Then he said, "While I'm gone you can get settled in. Go through your things and come up with a list of items you need. We can head into town when I get back. I need to stock up on some stuff myself."

With that he turned and went back down the stairs. Nosey hesitated before following, a bit reluctant to leave his new friends.

Left alone, Luke and Lacey were both unsure what to do. The man, Uncle Owen, had told them to settle in. What did that even mean? He'd pointed out two separate bedrooms. But surely they were meant to share a room. A very small, cramped room with bunk beds, peeling paint, and stained carpet. That was the way it had been everywhere else they'd been placed. In fact, at the last home they'd had to share a room with two other kids. So, which room was theirs? He'd also said to make a list of what they needed. As if he cared about what they needed. No one cared about what they needed. Certainly not adults. Confused about what was expected of them, they both stood silently at the landing, the hallway stretched before them and their bags at their feet.

They took in their surroundings, their new home. The walls were bare – no paintings, no portraits. The wooden floorboards beneath their matching sneakers looked worn but polished, their quality craftsmanship having stood the test of time. There was an eerie silence that stretched throughout the hallway, a stillness that echoed off of the empty walls.

"This place is really big," Lacey finally said quietly, more out of a desire to break the silence than to comment on the space.

Luke snorted. "The dude's loaded. Maybe he's a drug dealer or something."

Another stretch of silence, then Lacey asked, "What are we supposed to do?"

Whether she was asking about the bedroom situation, or their hopeless orphan situation, Luke's answer was the same. He shrugged his shoulders. That was the best he had for her.

Without anything left to say, they went back to silence. That was how Owen found them – standing where he'd left them, with bewildered looks on both of their faces.

"Is something wrong?" he asked. "Why didn't you go to your rooms? Get settled in? Go through your things? I know I was gone long enough."

Luke hesitated slightly, but then spoke up with as much bravery in his voice as he could muster. "We don't know which room is ours. You didn't tell us."

"Oh," Owen frowned. "You're 14. You don't need me to pick out your rooms for you. There's two of you. There's two rooms. Decide amongst yourselves."

"We–" Luke stumbled and then tried again. "We get our own rooms?"

Owen looked from one confused face to the other and then sighed. "Of course you get your own rooms. Your own bathrooms too." He pointed to the bags still on the floor. "Now take your things, go to your rooms, and make a list of what you need."

He walked past them, down the hall, headed to his room. "I'm taking a shower," he said as he left them. "Meet me downstairs in 20 minutes so we can go get the items on your list." With that, he went into the main bedroom and closed the door.

.....

HALF AN HOUR LATER, THE THREE OF THEM WERE SITTING IN Owen's pristine Ford F-150 (Owen in the driver's seat and the twins in the backseat) riding down the same dirt road that had brought the twins to their new home. The twins were silent while Owen hummed along to a 90's song on the radio. Once the song ended, he turned the volume down and spoke.

"So, where's the first place we're headed?"

Silence.

The moments ticked by and no one spoke. Owen looked at them through his rearview mirror.

"Well?" he asked.

They looked back at him with the same confused expressions he had seen on their faces since the moment they'd been left in his care.

"What's the first item on your list?" Owen asked. He thumped his fingers on the steering wheel, waiting for a response, but he received none.

Lacey and Luke merely exchanged a look and then turned their bewildered faces back to him.

"The list I told you to make," Owen explained further. "You can't possibly have everything that you need in those garbage bags. So, what items are you missing? What do you need?"

Once again, Luke was the spokesperson for the two of them. Owen was beginning to wonder if Lacey was mute.

"Sir, I mean Uncle. Um..."

Owen waited for the end of the sentence which never came. He gave another look into his rearview mirror and saw that they were looking at each other, engaged in some kind of silent conversation.

"Am I missing something?"

The spokesperson responded. "We... we didn't make a list."

Owen frowned. "You didn't? Why not?"

"We didn't think you really meant it."

"Of course I meant it. I wouldn't have said it if I didn't mean it."

"You're-" Luke started, then faltered as if afraid to even allow the words to leave his mouth. Owen gave him a moment to collect himself and was rewarded with Luke's full sentence.

"You're going to buy us stuff?"

Whatever he thought Luke would say next, Owen certainly hadn't expected that question. He glanced once more into his mirror and saw two identical faces staring back at him in utter disbelief.

"Of course I am," he responded. "How else will you get the things you need? You don't have any money, do you? I mean why wouldn't I get you what you need?" He had somewhat meant these to be rhetorical questions, so he was surprised when he heard a response. It was almost a whisper, but the words were clear.

"None of our other guardians ever bought us anything. Just food... sometimes."

This elicited a long sigh from Owen as he tried to think of the best way to proceed. He decided to go about it the way he approached everything in life – by being straightforward and direct.

"Listen, I'm only going to say this once, so I hope it gets through to you. I'm not your foster parent and this isn't your foster home. I'm your uncle and this is your home. We may not have been in each other's lives before now, but we're family. That means we take care of each other. Now, I may not have kept in touch with my sister, but I know she would've taught you that much. Family looks out for one another, and that's what I'm gonna do for you. So, from now on, no more secret twin looks. If you need something, then tell me. If you got a question, just ask it. I'm not gonna know what's going on in your head unless you say it."

By this point they had reached the main part of town and Owen pulled his truck in front of a diner and parked. He turned around and pinned the two of them with his gaze. "Did I make myself clear?"

They both nodded silently, which Owen took to mean they understood him or were too terrified not to agree with him. Judging by how big their eyes had gotten and the way Lacey's lower lip trembled, he was betting on the latter.

"Okay then," he said to himself, "just one step at a time." Then, to the twins he said, "Alright, everyone out."

They obediently clambered out of the truck and stood waiting for their next instructions.

Owen reached into his wallet and pulled a couple of bills out. He divided them evenly and placed them into each of his charges' hands. The two teenagers' mouths hit the ground as they both looked at the crisp bills their uncle had just given them. Luke swiftly counted the money, while Lacey was content to hold her share and stare at it.

"We can just start with clothes for now," Owen said. He gave another look to the faded and oversized garments they were wearing, noticing a rip along the collar of Luke's t-shirt and several holes along the hem of Lacey's shorts. "Yeah, we should start with clothes. There's a clothing store right across the way." He pointed it out, but neither of them looked, both still transfixed by their newfound wealth. Lacey had finally gotten around to counting her wad of cash, while Luke was now holding each of his bills up to peer at in the light, presumably checking to see if they were counterfeit.

"Anyway," Owen continued, "they may not carry all the latest styles, but their clothes are pretty nice and should do just fine for now. Why don't you two go on over and buy yourselves some clothes. I'm going to get a few groceries and supplies from a couple of these stores. When you're done shopping, just come and grab a booth in this diner. Got it?"

They had finally both pocketed their stashes and looked up at him with what appeared to be a bit of excitement. At least that was what Owen chose to believe it was. So, having given them their mission he shooed them off, before abruptly stopping their departure and calling them back to him.

"I don't want anymore miscommunication," he said to them, knowing that they'd been so distracted by the money that they'd barely heard his instructions, "so you tell me what you think you're supposed to do."

They shared their silent look again, before Luke answered him. "We're going to buy some stuff," he said.

Owen corrected him. "Buy some stuff in that store," he pointed again to the clothing store. This time, they turned around to see where they were meant to shop. The look of revelation on their faces was proof that they hadn't taken in that bit of information the first time. "Then what are you going to do?" Owen prompted.

"Meet you here?" Luke's response was more of an uncertain question than a definitive answer.

"Meet me *in* the diner," Owen amended. "Got it?"

They both nodded and Owen felt more assured that they understood the assignment this time. He let them go a second time and went about completing his own errands.

❧ 4 ❧

Their first impression of Franco's Fab Fits could be summed up by Luke's statement.

"This sure isn't Wal-mart."

Lacey could barely hear him over the classic R&B music blaring throughout the store. She simply gazed at the neon blinking signs hanging from the ceiling, pointing out the different sections of the store. Luke hadn't noticed the signs. He was staring at the neon-colored mannequins – all undressed and all posed as if attempting different dance moves.

They stood just inside the entrance overwhelmed by the cacophony of sights and sounds assaulting them until an employee (they assumed) yelled out to them over the music.

"Hey yo kiddos! Kids and teen clothes are over there!" He pointed to the far left where the blinking neon pink Kids sign and neon green Teens sign were hanging from the ceiling. Then he moonwalked away across the orange linoleum floor.

Luke and Lacey headed towards the Teens sign, maneuvering around the racks of clothing and the other shoppers, many of whom were dancing more than shopping. When they reached their destination, they discovered that not only didn't this store look like Wal-mart, but it didn't have Wal-mart prices either.

"You could get these," Lacey said, holding up a pair of baggy jeans in Luke's size.

Luke could barely hear her over the music, but he figured out what she was trying to say by the way she was shaking the jeans in his face. He grabbed them from her and looked them over. They looked to be vintage. In fact, Luke noticed that all the clothes had a retro 90's look to them. Maybe that was the reason for the old music playing overhead. Fiona's Fab Fits must be a vintage clothing store. Luke had to admit that he was impressed with the clothes. He wouldn't mind wearing any of the pieces he saw on display. He examined the jeans he was holding and turned the price tag over.

"Is that the price of the jeans or the whole store?"

Lacey looked at the price tag, snatched the jeans from his hands and quickly returned them to the clothing rack, backing away as if they had personally offended her.

"Everything in this place is overpriced," Luke yelled over the music. He checked the price tag on a t-shirt with the logo of a television show printed across the front. "30 bucks for one shirt? No way."

"He did give us a lot of money," Lacey pointed out.

"Yeah, but we can't just blow it all. He's gonna want his change back, right? We don't want him thinking we spent up all his money. Especially on expensive clothes."

"That's true. Well, how much do you think we should spend?"

Luke shrugged.

"Maybe they have a clearance section," Lacey suggested. "Every store's got a clearance section."

A brief scan of the blinking neon signs produced results.

"Bingo!" Luke shouted. He pointed to the wall in the back of the store and the blinking neon yellow sign hanging in front of it.

"Thant says Changing, not Clearance. Those are the changing rooms."

Luke squinted, then said, "I can't read these signs. They're too bright."

"It's over there!" Lacey pointed to the wall on the right.

They made their way over and began examining the meager offerings on Clearance.

"Hey," Lacey said after a moment, "why do you think he gave us so much money?"

Luke shrugged. "I just know we better not spend it all."

"Wait a minute. What if we're not supposed to spend any of it?"

Luke's eyes got big at the idea. "You're right," he said. "It's a test. He's testing us to see if we're greedy or thieves or something." He backed away from the clothing rack and folded his arms, as if afraid that even touching the clothes would be proof of his thievery.

"Wait," Lacey chewed her lip worriedly.

Luke waited for her to continue, hoping she had some further insight. He shuffled on his feet, feeling just as anxious as she did. They couldn't mess this up, not on the very first day.

Finally, Lacey voiced her idea. "What if he thinks we're ungrateful? I mean, he gave us all this money, and then we don't even touch it. Like, we think we're too good for his money and stuff."

"Yeah, you're right," Luke said, brows furrowed in concentration. This was a perilous situation indeed.

After a moment of silence between them, during which they both brainstormed the solution to this problem, Luke hit upon inspiration.

"Okay," Luke said, "we're gonna buy stuff, but like only a little bit, not a lot." Then he nodded his head, and said confidently even though he felt anything but confident in this plan, "Yep. That's what we're gonna do."

So, that's what they did, and an hour later, they entered the diner that Uncle Owen had parked his truck in front of. They stood just inside the entrance, each holding a shopping bag, and took in the sight of small town life at its finest. The place was crowded and noisy and a perfect cliché.

"Have a seat wherever you like," a busy waitress called to them as she passed by, her hands full with plates of food. "That is if you can find a seat," she added over her shoulder.

"The booths are full," Lacey said to Luke, and he somehow heard her above the clamor of plates scraping, gossip spreading, and food cooking. He looked at the row of booths lining the storefront window and indeed they were all packed. Clearly this was the place to be on a Friday evening.

"He told us to sit in a booth," Lacey said, a bit of worry creeping into her voice. "Now what do we do?"

Luke took charge. "Come on," he said, and guided Lacey to the bar along the left side of the diner where there were a few seats still vacant. "We'll have to sit here," he decided. "There's no place left."

Lacey followed his lead and they both settled themselves on stools along the bar which were surprisingly comfortable given that they appeared to be decades old. They placed their bags on the formica bar in front of them and looked at each other.

"Now we wait," Lacey said.

"Now we wait," Luke said.

Their wait proved to be short. Not the wait for their uncle. It took him quite a while to arrive. But they didn't have to wait long before they had company at the bar. First was the waitress that had called to them when they'd walked in. She appeared at the bar and began telling them the specials as she offered them each an oversized laminated menu to read.

Luke interrupted her before she got through with her speech. "Oh no, we're not ordering," he said. "We're just waiting for our uncle."

The waitress, a thin African-American woman with short brown hair and intelligent brown eyes, abruptly stopped speaking. Her eyes lit up and a huge grin formed on her face.

"I was so busy that I forgot you were arriving today," she said.

"It's all anyone's been talking about. Oh, and you look like him too." This was directed at Luke, who was becoming more terrified by the moment. The waitress had seemed normal at first, but now she was rambling nonsense and grinning at the two of them in the most unsettling way.

Then she said, "Stay here. I'll be right back," and left the bar area where they were seated.

Luke had no intentions of waiting for her to return with a gun or knife or who knows what. He'd heard about small towns and crazy people and neither he nor Lacey would be kidnapped today, or worse. Nope. Not if he could help it.

"Let's get outta here," he said to Lacey, who was only too happy to agree. She had been just as put off by the crazed woman as Luke.

They grabbed their bags and were about to leave when the waitress returned with a blonde woman by her side, grinning even more than the waitress.

"Man, she's fast," Luke said under his breath.

Both women stared at Luke and Lacey with matching grins and the blonde one gave an enthusiastic wave.

Luke eyed the door, wondering what their chances might be if they made a run for it. They were rather far away and there were a lot of obstacles in their way – tables, chairs, people, but it might have been their only shot of getting out of there alive.

"Knock it off you two!"

Luke whipped back around to see where this had come from, and found a tall older woman had joined the welcoming party. Only she was yelling at the two psychopaths that had been standing in front of him and Lacey.

"I mean it." The older woman had her hands on her hips and was glaring at the two younger women who didn't seem as frightened as Luke would've felt if the woman had been yelling at him.

But she wasn't done admonishing them. "Can't you see you're scaring these poor kids to death with your crazy behavior?" She gestured toward the twins who were both clutching their belongings to their chests, Lacey halfway off her seat in full flight mode.

This took the grins off the two women's faces, who now looked remorseful.

"Like you have nothing better to do than harass a couple of innocent kids," the woman continued. "I mean, it's not as if it's our busiest night and the place is packed."

To accent this point, the cook yelled "Order up!" from behind the partial wall that separated the kitchen from the dining area. He even hit the little bell, just like in the movies.

"We didn't mean to scare them," the waitress said.

"Yeah," agreed the blonde. "We just wanted to meet them."

"Well perhaps now is not the right time?" The older woman pointed toward the food getting cold on the counter where the cook had placed it. Then she pointed towards the end of the bar, where a line of customers was waiting at the cash register, presumably to pay for the meals they had just eaten.

Both women nodded their understanding to the older woman, and then returned to work, their heads a little low after their reprimanding. Luke almost felt sorry for them. Almost.

Once they had dispersed, the older woman then turned her attention to Luke and Lacey.

"I'm Shirley," she said, "and this here's my diner. The blonde one is the cashier. Her name's Regina. And the waitress is Annika. Don't mind either one of them. I promise you, they're harmless. Sit down sweetheart. No one here's going to hurt you."

This was directed at Lacey, who was still halfway off the stool, unsure whether she should run. At Shirley's command, however, she reclaimed her seat, though she still looked like a deer in headlights. Luke was wary as well, dubious to Shirley's claims about her staff's sanity.

So," the older woman said, "you're Owen Stillwater's niece and nephew?" Then, noticing the shocked looks on their faces, she explained. "Oh, you're wondering how I know about you. Well, your uncle's been telling everyone with ears to listen that his niece and nephew are coming to live with him. He's just been so excited about it. Oh, and don't worry about Annika and Regina. They're not crazy, they're nosy. Just like everybody else in this town. You see, we don't get a whole lot of new faces around here, so whenever someone new shows up, they become the talk of the town. And the fact that you're related to Owen Stillwater, well that just made you the most interesting bit of news this town has had in weeks. Those two busybodies won't be the only ones you'll have to deal with. But if any of these locals gets on your nerves, you just tell them to mind their own business, or you'll sic Shirley on them. That oughta get them off your back."

During her speech, both Luke and Lacey had visibly relaxed. No longer did they appear panicked and ready to bolt at a moment's notice. Instead, they were hanging onto her words and when she told them to sic her on nosy people, Lacey smiled and Luke gave a quiet laugh.

That was the scene Owen walked into, and it gave him just a glimmer of hope. He had just spent the past hour buying groceries and other things needed around the cabin. And during the entire time he had fretted and worried and anxiously thought over the precarious situation he was now in. He had been provided with precious little information prior to the twins' arrival. Although he had asked for more details, few answers had been given. Therefore, he'd had no idea what to expect.

The moment he first saw them, his heart had been torn from his chest. Although, their skin tone was a much lighter complexion, they still looked exactly like his sister, Anna. They had the same cheekbones, the same eyes. There had been no doubt that they were her children. That had been his first thought. His second thought was, what had they been through in the months since Anna's death. They were ragged, frightened, and much too thin, indicating that they had missed a few meals at some point. Or more than a few. He may not have kept in touch with Anna through the years, but he knew without a doubt that they had not gotten that way while in her care. He knew it just as he knew that she would be enraged that her children had been so poorly cared for.

The third thought that had popped into his head was more of a re-commitment to the silent promise that he had made when he'd first gotten the phone call from the caseworker, telling him that his niece and nephew were now orphans, and asking him if he would take them in. He'd sworn to himself that he would help them through this. Owen had meant what he'd told them in the truck – they were family and that was all that mattered.

But this was easier said than done. From the short time that they'd spent together, Owen could see that he was in over his head. The girl looked like she would burst into tears or run for her life at any moment. And the boy clearly didn't trust anyone. Maybe he had at one point, but not anymore. So how on earth was he going to get through to them?

This was what he was wondering when he was rewarded by the sight of the two of them not only relaxing, but also smiling. It was almost too good to be true. He walked over to the bar and sat next to Lacey, claiming the last remaining empty seat.

"Did I miss something?" he asked, grabbing the menu that had been left sitting on the bar by his seat's previous inhabitant. "You weren't laughing at me, were you?"

"Oh," Shirley said. "I was just getting to know your delightful niece and nephew." She winked at them as she said this, which garnered her another smile from Lacey, this one bigger than the first. "And I was telling them that folks around these parts are pretty much harmless, just a little too friendly for their own good." At the last part she raised her voice and looked meaning-fully at the waitress, who had returned to take their orders.

For her part, the waitress did look properly chastened for her earlier behavior, and both of the twins began to feel a bit of sympathy towards her. Owen, however, harrumphed, twisted up his mouth, and then pulled his menu up as if deliberately trying to block his view of her.

Shirley ignored Owen and directed her attention to the twins. "This is Annika," she said. "She'll be taking care of you, and she won't be harassing you any further. Now, I'll leave you three to enjoy your dinner. I've got to get back to work." She left and did just that.

After Shirley's departure, Annika went into apology mode. "I'm so sorry. I didn't mean to upset you two. I was just so excited to meet you that-"

"Oh, for crying out loud. Are you going to take our order or just keep blabbering?" This came from Owen, who had lowered his menu enough to complain.

Annika met his rude outburst with a death glare. She then turned back to the twins and gave them a friendly smile. "As I was saying before I was so rudely interrupted by an ignoramus, I'm very happy that you came to live in Port St. Annabelle, and I didn't mean to make you uncomfortable-"

"Well, you're making me uncomfortable. I'm hungry and I'm pretty sure they're hungry too. How's that for being uncomfortable?"

She shot daggers at Owen, who returned her stare with a steely gaze of his own.

"Annika, just take his order." This came from the cook, who had heard the entire exchange from the kitchen area. It wasn't as if the two of them had attempted to keep their voices down. "Honestly," the cook said, "you can't argue with him every time he comes in to eat. Just serve him and move on."

Annika reluctantly retreated from the staring match, and once again turned her attention to her two young customers. For their part, the twins had found the entire exchange between the waitress and their uncle to be quite comical, and they were disappointed when it came to an end.

"What would you like to eat?" she asked them, with all the kindness in her voice that she hadn't shown Owen.

This caused a problem for Luke and Lacey, as neither of them had even picked up the menus that she'd delivered to them earlier, much less opened them, so they had no answer for her.

"Umm," Luke said, as he and Lacey grabbed the forgotten menus, thinking to rush through them or pick something at random.

Annika, seeing how flustered they both were, offered up a solution. "How about a couple of burgers and cold cokes? That's what all the kids around here order. And," she leaned in and whispered conspiratorially, "if Dave likes you, he'll throw a couple slices of bacon on it free of charge." She gestured towards the kitchen, where the cook wasn't visible, but the sounds of his work were loud and clear. The frying and sizzling of fresh food being prepared, and the delicious aromas of sugar, salt and grease wafted from the kitchen, towards the bar and out through the dining area.

Luke and Lacey agreed to her suggestion, and Annika wrote their orders on the notepad that she'd pulled from the pocket of the apron tied around her waist.

"So that'll be two burgers with cokes," she said as she wrote.

"I want the meat loaf," Owen told her.

"Two burgers with cokes it is," she repeated. "Nothing else. Just burgers and cokes. Your order will be up shortly." She turned on her heel and left.

Once she was gone, Owen said, "This place has really good food. That's why it's so packed. But the employees," he shook his head. "They've got the worst servers you've ever seen."

Luke put his head down in an attempt to hide what appeared to be a smirk. Lacey, sitting closest to Owen, covered a small laugh behind her hand. Owen chose to believe that they were amused by something that had occurred earlier, and that they weren't laughing at him. A change of subject was needed.

Owen cleared his throat. "So, I enrolled you both in the local high school. But since Spring Break starts soon, I was just think-ing, and the principal agreed, that you may as well wait until after Spring Break to attend. That way, you'll be starting when the new semester begins. So, you basically have two weeks free before you start school."

During his announcement, Owen watched the two of them as the light that had just begun to spark behind their eyes, slowly went out. With each word he spoke, their faces dropped, and their shoulders drooped a little more. It was as if being in the diner and interacting with the employees had allowed them, just for a moment, to forget about their lives. But with Owen's statement about school, they were ripped back to earth, and the reality of their situation came crashing down upon their shoulders once more, making them bow under the weight of the burden that they carried.

Owen regretted even speaking. But it wasn't as if it was something they could shy away from or ignore. This was their reality, and it was better to face it head on and learn to deal with it.

Before Owen had time to think on this any further, Annika reappeared, this time holding three plates loaded with food in her arms. She carefully set Luke then Lacey's meals in front of them with a flourish and a smile.

"Bon Appetit," she said to them, and then leaned in and whispered, "I think Dave gave you extra fries as well as bacon. He must like you already."

Then she hastily dropped Owen's meal in front of him, turned her back and walked away without a word in his direction.

"Lousy servers," Owen mumbled to no one in particular as he picked up his fork and settled into his meal.

Luke and Lacey followed his lead and started on their dinners as well. It wasn't long before the three of them had eaten their fill and were headed back to the cabin in the woods.

Once they'd returned, there was the business of bringing their purchases inside and putting everything away in its appropriate place. Owen directed them both to help in these tasks, instructing them on where everything should go. In fact, they were so busy with this, and Owen was so preoccupied with ensuring that everything was put away neatly in its rightful place, that he hadn't noticed until they were done, that there was a distinct lack of bags from the twins' shopping.

"Wait a minute," he said, looking around in case he'd somehow missed something. They were in the great room, having just sorted through the last of the supplies Owen had purchased. After such an eventful day, Owen was exhausted and ready to retire to his study to complete the day's crossword puzzle, which he hadn't gotten around to doing yet. Or perhaps he would even call it a night and go to bed early. He really was quite tired.

But the fatigue was now masked with confusion. He had sent them to the store. He had given them money. He had instructed them to buy clothes. So where were the clothes?

"Wait a minute," Owen repeated, "where are your bags? The things that you bought?"

Each twin held up one bag, a tentative smile on their face.

"Thank you," Luke said, and he handed two receipts to Owen.

Owen looked at both receipts, then looked at both twins, and then looked at both receipts, willing them to say something different.

"Did we spend too much?" Luke asked, worry creeping into his voice. "We didn't know how much to spend. You didn't say. We're sorry. We'll take it all back. We didn't mean to spend so much money. We're sorry."

His rambling only stopped when Owen looked up at him.

"You bought a t-shirt and flip flops."

Lacey and Luke shared a worried look, but neither said anything.

"I sent you to buy clothes."

Another worried look. Silence.

"And you bought a t-shirt and flip flops?"

Owen squeezed the bridge of his nose. He could feel the headache brewing in the back of his head. He gave a deep sigh and tried again.

"I gave you $200 each."

Still silence, but this time with a little fidgeting and digging in pockets. They both produced a handful of cash which they shoved into each of Owen's hands. For a moment, Owen stared dumbfounded at the money in his hands, and then he made a decision.

"Okay," he said. "It's late and I'm tired. So, we'll deal with this tomorrow."

"We'll return our stuff first thing tomorrow," Luke promised.

Lacey nodded her agreement.

"No, you don't have to return anything. Look, I meant for you to spend all the money. You need new clothes. Clothes that fit." Owen tried to explain, but seeing their faces he wasn't so sure that they understood. "Never mind," he said. "We can talk about it in the morning. I'm going to take Nosey out one more time, and then I'm going to bed. I'll see you both tomorrow."

.....

Just a short while later, Lacey and Luke were holding an impromptu meeting in one of the bedrooms they'd been assigned. The room was massive in size, with a mahogany wood dresser on one wall, a large window with Venetian blinds on another wall, and a paisley patterned rug stretching across the wooden floor. In the center of the room sat a Queen-sized bed with fluffy bedding and a great number of pillows in a variety of shapes and sizes.

It had been decided early on that they would be sharing a room. They were living in a log cabin with a complete stranger in the middle of the woods with no one else around for miles. Yeah, there was no way they would be splitting up. That's how people died in horror movies.

Currently though, they had important things to discuss that couldn't wait for the morning. So, as they prepared for bed, they addressed the matter at hand.

"So? What do you think?"

This was from Lacey, who was sitting on the bed, cushioned by all the pillows with her legs tucked underneath her. She was wearing the same shirt she'd worn all day, as it was doubling as her pajamas. Her shorts were neatly folded and sitting on the floor, ready to be worn again tomorrow. She had a couple of other shorts, but they were far too big and didn't fit her comfortably. So, she usually just stuck with the one pair, washing them whenever she could.

Luke exited the adjoining bathroom, where he had been brushing his teeth. He was wearing his own version of pajamas, which was the same shorts and shirt he'd been wearing all day. Unlike Lacey, he did have another pair of shorts he could wear. Just one more pair. He only hoped that they were clean when he'd stuffed them into the black trash bag. He honestly wasn't sure.

They both had their belongings sitting by the door, fancy dresser ignored. They were also avoiding the walk-in-closet they'd discovered upon inspection of the room. Without discussion, they both knew that there would be no utilizing the ample storage provided. After their second foster home they had developed a rule – no unpacking, no settling, because we're not at home.

Luke turned the light off behind him and sat across from Lacey on the bed. "What do I think?" he repeated her question. "I think the guy's a freak. That's what I think."

"A freak?" Lacey knew from experience that Luke wouldn't take to their guardian. But she hadn't expected this answer.

"Yeah, he's a freak," Luke said, crossing his arms. "He's living alone out here in the middle of the woods in this big ole cabin all by himself. Who does that?"

"Maybe he just likes to be alone or something. Maybe he likes privacy."

Luke snorted. "Yeah, privacy to do what? And answer me this. Where'd he get all this money? Look at this place. The guy's loaded and he just hands out cash like it's nothing." Luke surveyed the pillow collection on his side of the bed for a moment, then chose one at random to sleep on and tossed the others onto the floor.

"It was nice of him to buy us stuff." Lacey mimicked Luke's actions, selecting a pillow for herself, but moving the rest aside with much more care than he had, placing them gently on the floor beside the bed.

"Yeah, maybe. But I'm telling you there's something off about him."

"Why didn't mom ever mention him?" Lacey asked.

"That's another thing I'd like to know. Where's he been all our lives? If he cares so much about us like he claimed, then where was he when mom and dad were working their tails off just to pay rent on our tiny apartment? All the while, he's out here living like a king. Where was he when we needed him?"

Luke was starting to get worked up just thinking about the disparity in their situations.

"Well, he's here now," Lacey offered.

This was met with another snort of cynicism from Luke. He shrugged his shoulders, pulled the covers back and laid back onto his chosen pillow. Lacey got up and turned off the bedroom light before copying Luke's movements and snuggling herself onto her own pillow next to her brother.

Luke turned to face the wall and get comfortable before saying, "It would've been nice if he'd shown up six months ago."

Lacey couldn't argue with that fact.

"Besides," Luke said, "we don't even know if this is going to work out. He'll probably get rid of us at the first chance, just like everyone else did. So don't get comfortable. We probably won't be here long."

"But this has to work out," Lacey said in a small tremulous voice. "Miss Abigail said-"

"Yeah," Luke said, suddenly remembering. How could he have forgotten?

"We gotta make this work Luke," Lacey repeated softly, almost as a wish spoken into the dark.

"We will," he promised her. "We'll make it work." And he didn't know how he would manage it, but that was a promise he would keep.

5

L uke woke early, well before the sun rose. This was very unusual for him. He normally slept in late, but on this occasion, he found himself wide awake at an ungodly hour. This may have been due to the unease over the intentions of their new guardian. He knew his early rise had nothing to do with his surroundings, as he was accustomed to sleeping in strange new places. In fact, it was Lacey, who often had trouble sleeping soundly in new environments.

Lacey turned over onto her side and her light snores turned into a deep guttural noise that could wake the dead. Clearly, she wasn't having any trouble sleeping in this house. As he thought this, Lacey elbowed him in the rib cage as she, amazingly, began snoring even louder.

Luke yelped and jumped from the bed. Safely out of his sister's reach, he rubbed the tender spot that she'd just tried to pulverize and imagined that she was probably the reason he had woken so early. With a sigh, he realized it didn't really matter the reason, the fact was that he was awake and wouldn't be falling back to sleep anytime soon.

He wondered what time it was. He no longer owned a watch, so he couldn't be sure, but he hoped the sun would be rising soon. In the meantime, he couldn't just stand there staring into the dark. He decided to get ready for the day. After he showered and got dressed, it was still dark outside of the large window on the far wall. He could see the faint light of the moon shining through the Venetian blinds.

Luke decided that he wouldn't waste this time that he had alone. No, with the house silent and everyone asleep, now was an ideal time to do something that he loved – investigate.

Not wanting to turn on a light and wake Lacey, Luke fumbled his way through the dark to the corner where he had left his trash bag of belongings. He reached inside of it and felt around for his most treasured item. After a moment he found what he was searching for. His fingers brushed over it and he recognized it instantly by its cylindrical shape. Pleased with his success, Luke rescued the pocket-sized flashlight from the bag and turned it on. Now he was ready to start investigating this house. He would find out what secrets this guy was hiding.

Luke thoroughly searched the place and he now knew that besides the great room they'd passed through the day before, the first floor also held a utility closet, a half bathroom and a den. The latter even looked cozy and Luke found himself lingering there. Bookshelves piled high with books lined one of the walls and a large fireplace occupied the adjacent wall. The brown leather furniture darkened from age and use helped make the space look comfortable. Luke noted the crotched throw blanket draped across the back of the recliner and could almost imagine himself relaxing there, but he quickly came to his senses and returned to the job at hand.

Half an hour later, Luke's investigation had led him into the kitchen. He hadn't uncovered anything scandalous yet, but he had memorized the layout of the house and no longer felt like he was trapped inside of a labyrinth. All in all, it had been a productive use of his time.

When he entered the kitchen, however, he was shocked to

discover that the light was already on and standing at the stove, was the subject of his investigation.

He was cooking? This early in the morning? (Although technically, Luke had no idea how early it was.)

For his part, Uncle Owen looked just as surprised as Luke to find that he was no longer alone. "You're up already? Did you have trouble sleeping?"

"No, I'm fine," Luke said defensively. He left his answer at that, not wanting to tell his uncle that he had been roaming about his house, looking for clues that he was a creep. "I just woke up early."

Uncle Owen noticed the flashlight in Luke's hand. "Oh," he said. "Were you exploring?"

Luke bristled. He hated when Lacey accused him of exploring when clearly he was an investigator. "No," His response was curt. "This place is big, so I was just trying to find my way around."

Uncle Owen shrugged. "Whatever." Then he added, "Why don't you help me finish cooking breakfast?"

"Isn't it too early for breakfast?"

"It's 6:30. We start cooking now it'll be ready by 7. How late did you want to eat?"

"I didn't realize it was that late."

Uncle Owen began issuing directions, which Luke obediently followed. Despite himself, Luke found that he enjoyed this basic routine with his uncle. Uncle Owen didn't speak much except when giving instructions and Luke, who had never been particularly loquacious himself, appreciated the silence. Besides that, they worked well together.

The quiet also gave Luke a chance to examine the kitchen. His first view left him momentarily speechless. He was certain that the entire apartment he'd grown up in could fit inside of this one room. It was fancy. Like the kitchen of a cooking show on television type of fancy. Like the kitchen of a celebrity who doesn't actually cook but likes to be photographed inside their kitchen while they pretend to cook type of fancy. There was a six-burner stove and an enormous fridge with two freezers. In the center of the room was a massive island where Uncle Owen sliced, diced and chopped with practiced skill. Luke was... impressed.

At one point, Uncle Owen broke the silence to tell Luke about his plans for the day.

"You and your sister can relax this morning, or do whatever it is that you do," Uncle Owen told him. "But this afternoon we need to go back into town."

"We do?"

"You still need clothes, don't you?"

Luke looked down at the clothes he was wearing, but he didn't say anything. As far as he was concerned, he had clothes.

"And you both need phones."

At that statement, Luke looked up sharply. "We need phones?" he said incredulously. "We don't need phones." (He forgot that he'd argued the exact opposite to his parents a year ago.)

"You live in the middle of the woods with only one other neighboring cabin close by. You need a phone," Uncle Owen said matter-of-factly.

The reasoning was solid, but Luke was still resistant. He didn't know if he was feeling annoyed by the way his uncle kept telling him what he needed, or suspicious that he was offering to buy them everything under the sun. Truthfully, he was probably just being a brat. But Luke didn't care. Uncle Owen was pushing, and whenever Luke was pushed, he always pushed back. He had the bruises and the reputation to prove it.

"We don't need you to get us phones. You have one and that's good enough. Besides, how do you know we don't already both have phones?"

Uncle Owen didn't miss a beat. "You can't rely on access to my phone in an emergency. You need your own phone. And you obviously don't have one already because if you did you would've known what time it was."

With that Uncle Owen turned off the stove and began transferring the meal they'd just finished cooking to the dining room for breakfast. Luke reached to help him, but Uncle Owen swatted his hand away.

"I got this," he said. "You go and get your sister. Tell her to get dressed and come down to breakfast."

Whether it was arguing or simply the act of working in unison to prepare breakfast, something had emboldened Luke. Instead of silently obeying to remain on his uncle's good side, Luke gave him a military salute, turned around and marched out of the kitchen.

"Smart aleck," Owen mumbled.

Left alone to work, Owen managed to move the food to the dining room table quickly, even considering the massive amount of food he had cooked. Truthfully, he had overdone it. By a lot. And the strange thing was, that he never cooked this much anymore. In fact, most mornings he usually had a small bowl of oatmeal and a glass of milk for breakfast. But something had come over him this morning. When he'd woken at 6:00 (a habit he hadn't broken himself of since he'd stopped practicing medicine), his thoughts were only of cooking breakfast. A big breakfast. But he didn't have to think too hard to figure out where the impulse had risen from. One day of watching his niece and nephew walking about with less meat on their bones than he was comfortable with left him wanting to fill them both with food. And as someone who truly enjoyed being in the kitchen but who'd had no one to cook for in a long time, well, Owen had been itching to flex his culinary muscles. Yep, he'd have those two at a healthier weight in no time. He was confident of this.

It was everything else that he was worried about. For starters the girl. How was he supposed to get through to her when she would barely even look at him, much less speak to him. He decided that today he would find out definitively if she could speak or not. That would be a start. But the boy. If Owen still believed in prayer, he would send one up for help with Luke. The kid seemed to enjoy arguing just for the sake of it. Seriously, what teenager declined a cell phone? Well, at least he was speaking to him. That had to count for something.

As he pondered his two new problems, Owen could hear the certain footfalls on the stairs, signaling Luke's return. Moments later, the teenager Owen had just been thinking about appeared in the dining room.

"Mission complete sir," Luke said, saluting Owen once again.

Owen shook his head, and mentally added smart aleck to the list of issues that he would have to deal with. Aloud, he said, "Would you like milk or orange juice with your breakfast?"

"Um..." Luke stared at him like a deer in headlights.

"Never mind, I'll decide," Owen said, seeing the indecision on his face. "Why don't you grab the orange juice from the fridge while I set the table?"

This time Luke simply nodded and did as he was told.

Owen sighed. He didn't know what to think. One minute Luke felt comfortable enough to argue back and deliver a heavy dose of sarcasm, then the next he shut down completely and couldn't answer a simple question. It was like he was afraid of something, and Owen honestly didn't know what to do. While he hadn't enjoyed the backtalk, at least the boy was expressing himself. That was all Owen really wanted – for his niece and nephew to feel comfortable enough to be themselves, instead of hiding away in the shells they were currently trapped inside of. Owen just had no clue how to make that happen.

⚜ 6 ⚜

Lacey was awakened by the tantalizing aroma of bacon. The wonderful smell entered her dreams, pulled her out of sleep, and drew her into complete consciousness. Then it caused her stomach to grumble in a definitive announcement of breakfast time. She stretched and yawned the sleep away before reaching over to wake up her brother.

"Luke," she called, before noticing the vacant pillow next to her. It appeared he was already up and about. She wondered what could have happened to him. He wasn't in the bathroom. The door was ajar, and she could see from her perch on the bed that it was empty.

She might've begun to worry if at that moment Luke hadn't opened the bedroom door and stuck his head inside. He was fully dressed for the day and appeared to have been awake for some time.

"Hey," he said to her. "You're awake. Good. Uncle Owen said for you to hurry up and get dressed. It's time for breakfast." And then he was gone again.

Lacey obeyed, heading into the bathroom for a quick shower. She brushed her teeth, combed her hair, and dressed in a fresh t-shirt and her old shorts. The process took no more than 10 minutes, and the entire time she could think of only one thing. Luke had left her there.

She knew it was silly to think that he would wake her up just because he himself was awake, but the thing was, she would have done that for him. She wouldn't have left him alone in bed in a strange new environment, and up until this morning, she would have sworn that he wouldn't have done it to her either. Except that's exactly what he had done. She didn't know what to think about that.

Once Lacey was downstairs, her nose led her to a formal dining room with a swinging door at one end and the back door at the other. There was a window taking up the wall in front of her, the blinds raised to reveal a deck and the expansive yard beyond it. The center of the room held a table large enough to seat six. This was where she found Uncle Owen and Luke. They were serving themselves from the handsome spread laid across the table. Lacey joined them and began loading her own plate.

"Good morning sleepyhead," Uncle Owen greeted her.

She gave him a shy smile in response and grabbed a slice of the perfectly cooked bacon. After a bite, she was pleased to find that it tasted just as good as it looked.

"Just out of curiosity," Uncle Owen began. He took a bite of his own bacon and washed it down with a sip of the orange juice before him. "You don't have to answer if you don't want to," he said.

Luke braced himself for what would come next, but Uncle Owen was looking at Lacey, apparently addressing her alone.

"I just want to know," Uncle Owen said, and Lacey looked at him expectantly. "Are you mute?" he asked.

Lacey stared at him, and Uncle Owen elaborated. "I'm not trying to be rude. I was just wondering. I mean, I know nothing about your medical histories."

Lacey continued to stare at him while Luke started to

chuckle. Uncle Owen looked from one twin to the other, as if he were unsure of what the joke was.

"I was just wondering because I haven't heard you speak since you arrived."

Lacey put her fork down and tried to cover her embarrassment. It didn't help matters that Luke was chortling next to her. She could feel her ears burning and just hoped she didn't turn red from the humiliation. Why did everyone give her a hard time for being quiet? What was the big deal about being shy? Quite frankly, this world could probably use more shy people and less bold people. But that was just her opinion.

She mustered her courage and opened her mouth to answer her uncle. "No, I'm not mute," she said.

"Oh, okay," Uncle Owen responded and went back to his breakfast.

Lacey didn't feel so hungry anymore. In fact, she felt as though she'd rather be almost anywhere than at that table. She stood up abruptly, surprising both Uncle Owen and Luke.

"I'd like to go outside for a while. Is it alright if Luke and I go for a walk?"

"Of course," Uncle Owen answered without hesitation. "I don't have anything planned for us until this afternoon."

"Thank you."

"Actually," Luke said, "I don't really feel like walking right now. Especially not after that big breakfast. I'm really full." He patted his gut for emphasis. "Yeah, I'm just gonna stay here."

Lacey stared at him, taken aback. She hesitated for a moment, unsure if she should go without Luke. But she desperately wanted to get out of the house, so she did something she had never done before – she chose to go on her own.

"I'll go by myself then," she said, half expecting Luke to insist on her staying with him or maybe even taking back his earlier statement and deciding to go with her after all. But Luke did neither of these things.

"Have a good walk," he said without even looking at her. He

was too busy grabbing another piece of bacon despite his claims of being full.

Instead, it was her uncle who expressed concern for her going alone. "Well, if you're going by yourself then take Nosey with you."

The dog in question, who had been hanging around the table, hoping for a bite of human food to go with the breakfast he'd had earlier, perked up when he heard his name.

"He'll make sure you stay safe. And you won't get lost if you let him guide you. He knows this land better than I ever will."

Nosey seemed to understand Uncle Owen perfectly because he hopped over to the back door and began to whine for it to open. Lacey followed the dog who was waiting impatiently for the adventure ahead of him. His wagging tail and excitement elicited a small smile from Lacey. At least someone wanted her company.

.....

LUKE WASN'T LYING. HE REALLY WAS STUFFED. HE ALSO HAD no desire to go on another long and boring walk. It seemed like that was all Lacey ever wanted to do, and Luke always went with her. Not because he loved to exercise, but because he was terrified of something happening to her. But that was in the city. They were out in the middle of nowhere now. She should be perfectly safe to take a walk on her own. Plus, she would have the dog with her. Surely, the dog wouldn't let her get kidnapped, he reasoned.

Thus, after breakfast, Luke was free to engage in his own pursuits, such as completing his investigation. He'd limited his search to the first floor earlier, because he'd been worried that he might wake the others if he went snooping about upstairs. But now there was no one to wake, which meant he was free to turn over the bedrooms and see what he could uncover. He gave a pat to his pocket to make sure that his trusty flashlight was still there (you never knew when you'd run into a dark space and needed a light) and headed off to work.

Once he was on the second floor, he skipped over the bedroom that he and Lacey had shared. He doubted he'd missed anything during the cursory sweep he'd given the room when they'd first arrived. Besides, they were staying in that room, so he'd have easy access to search it more thoroughly at any time. He continued along the hallway and debated which room to start with. Without a doubt, the good stuff would all be found in the main bedroom at the end of the hall, but no way was Luke brave enough to search his uncle's room while the man was in the house. He could burst through the door at any moment and catch Luke combing through his personal possessions and then what? That was just it. Luke didn't even know him well enough to know how he'd react.

"Probably kick us to the curb," Luke said to himself only half joking, and then he sobered as he remembered his promise that he'd made just the night before. No. He couldn't do anything that might risk them getting removed from this placement.

This left him with two rooms to choose from. One was directly across the hall from the room he and Lacey shared – the one that his uncle had intended for one of them to occupy. The other one was right next to it. The choice was clear. If his uncle were going to hide secrets, he wouldn't put them in the room that he'd assigned to them where they could just stumble upon all his gory deeds. No, he would stash them away in the secret spare room and then tell them to stay away.

Luke decided to ignore the small fact that Uncle Owen had never told him to stay away from the spare room and made his way down the hall to his target. He was sure the door would be locked, because who hides their secrets in an unlocked room?

Therefore, he was surprised when he turned the handle and the door opened.

"Rookie mistake," Luke whispered, shaking his head. Apparently, Uncle Owen wasn't as smart as he looked. He must've been trusting that no one would go prying into his misdeeds. Well, he'd been sadly mistaken.

Luke peeked his head into the room and looked about for booby traps. Not seeing any obvious ones, he slid quietly into the room and shut the door behind himself. Once inside the room, he had a good look and was surprised to see that it was not a spare bedroom after all. Instead, the room was being used for storage. Cardboard boxes and plastic storage bins were piled high on top of one another, and they filled the entirety of the floor. So cluttered was the room, that there was very little space in which to walk, and Luke found it difficult to maneuver about. He managed by weaving in and out and around the boxes on the floor, and at times had to turn sideways just to squeeze by.

Why were there so many boxes? And what was inside them? Only one way to find out. Luke rubbed his hands together and got to work. He chose one stack at random. There were two boxes stacked on each other with a bin balancing precariously on top of them. The bin reached his abdomen, so he had no problem unlatching and pulling the top off.

If Luke had been surprised to find that the room was filled with boxes, he was completely stunned by what was inside of the boxes.

"Clothes?"

He rifled through the bin he had opened and then moved it aside with only a moderate amount of difficulty. He searched the box underneath, and then the box underneath it. Clothes, clothes, and more clothes.

Luke could feel the bitter taste of disappointment in his mouth. Where were the newspaper clippings? The police reports? The handwritten confessions? All of them detailing his uncle's wicked past. He'd seen enough crime shows to know that one of these boxes were supposed to hold all the evidence.

He moved onto another stack. There had to be something here. Luke opened the first box. Fake jewelry and knickknacks? Disgusted, Luke shoved the box aside. He opened the box underneath – more junk. And the box underneath that appeared to be more of the same, except partially concealed underneath a couple of necklaces was a framed photograph. He retrieved the picture, expecting it to be a boring old photo of boring old people. Or a landscape. Adults liked pictures of beaches and stuff.

It was a wedding picture. That much was obvious because there was a couple in the photo, and they were dressed up in a wedding dress and tuxedo. The woman even wore a flowery headband and held a bouquet in one hand. The couple was holding hands and smiling at each other. They looked happy. Very happy.

None of this would've meant anything to Luke if it weren't for the fact that he knew the man. He'd recognized him immediately. Even though he'd only just met him, and he was clearly older now, Luke could identify the man in the photo as his uncle without hesitation. Which meant...

"He's married?"

Luke looked closer at the picture in his hands. The woman in the photo was very pretty. She was Native-American as well with long black hair, a sharp nose, and a petite figure. He looked up at her neckline and to his surprise, Luke recognized the necklace that she was wearing. He looked back into the box where he had found the photo and sure enough, one of the necklaces lying in the box was the same necklace the woman had worn on her wedding day. This realization made Luke aware of something that he had overlooked during his first pass through. He immediately began going back through the boxes he had already searched and confirmed it.

All the clothes were women's clothes. All the jewelry, the

knickknacks, everything that he had found so far had belonged to a woman. Luke picked the photo up again and stared at the beautiful woman, his uncle's wife.

"What happened to you?" he asked, and for reasons he couldn't understand, Luke wished desperately that she could answer him back.

❧ 7 ❧

A short while later, Lacey was wondering if Nosey was as good as her uncle had claimed. He'd led her out of the backyard and directly into the woods. Trusting what she'd been told and not knowing what else to do, Lacey had followed him blindly and now was in the middle of the woods with no idea where she was. She would've gone back the way she came, except that there was no clear path that she could make out and she'd gotten turned around. As far as Lacey could tell, the dog had gotten lost, and he'd taken her with him.

She may have been able to keep her bearings if she had been paying closer attention to her surroundings, but she'd found it impossible to keep her mind off Luke. She was still trying to process the fact that he'd chosen to stay behind. Luke, who always went on walks with her. He loved being outdoors, even more than Lacey. Also, he would never leave her to go off on her own in a new place. At least he never would've in the past.

Nosey barked, pulling her from her thoughts and into the present. She looked up and saw that he was standing a short distance ahead of her, and he'd turned back to wait for her. Another bark told her that he was growing tired of her slow pace and urged her to put a little pep in her step. Lacey complied and followed the dog even further into the woods. She consoled herself with the thought that when they eventually had to send search parties out to find her, they might at least be able to follow the sound of the dog's barks.

However, it wasn't long before the woods abruptly ended and opened into another backyard. At first, Lacey thought that she'd gotten turned around and had ended up back at Uncle Owen's where she'd started. For this place had an expansive yard just as her uncle's and held a cabin as well. At second glance though, she noted that this cabin was bigger than the one she had left, if that was even possible. This place was at least three stories and maybe even twice as wide. Instead of the deck leading into the backyard behind Uncle Owen's cabin, this cabin had a patio with brightly colored furniture. From her viewpoint emerging from the woods, Lacey could see that the backyard was larger than Uncle Owen's as well, but the grass extended all the way to the lake. It was an impressive sight to Lacey.

"These people must be really loaded," she said to no one in particular, as she tried to take in the sheer size of the structure in front of her. "Wait 'til Luke sees this place."

Nosey, who had inexplicably led her there, was now shooing her forward with his nose to her leg. He gently pushed her onward and then not so gently pushed her.

"I can't go over there," she said to him. "That's trespassing. They'll have me arrested. We shouldn't even be in their yard."

Nosey not only didn't believe a word she said, but he gave up on trying to include her in his adventure. He gave a bark and then ran onward, going further into the yard.

"Wait," she called, then after hesitating for a moment, she ran after the stubborn dog. She needed to grab him and get out of dodge before the owners noticed they were ever there.

Lacey followed the dog's path right up to the cabin, where there was a small garden in the making. The area had been cordoned off to indicate where the garden would begin and end. Inside the sectioned off area, the land had been halfway dug up, but that was as far as the landscaper had gotten. Stacked to the side of the would-be garden were bags of soil, and several colorful potted plants, as well as a few gardening tools. It looked like whoever was creating this garden had a long way to go. They probably needed a hand in digging up the earth to get a jump start on the project.

No sooner had she thought this, then Lacey spotted Nosey. He clearly had come to the same conclusion that she had, because he'd entered the sectioned off area and was hard at work digging up a hole. As Lacey watched with horror, he moved on and began another hole.

"Nosey!" she cried. "Nosey, stop that! Cut it out!"

Nosey paused just for a moment to see who was calling his name. Then he chose to ignore her and resumed his gardening.

Lacey was beside herself. Her uncle hadn't warned her that his dog was a menace. That seemed like pertinent information she should've been given.

As Nosey moved onto his third hole and Lacey was at her wit's end, she heard a voice from behind her.

"Excuse me. Can I help you?"

Lacey whipped around to find an African-American woman with curly brown hair piled on top of her head in a bun, and a bright smile. She was dressed in overalls and held a pair of gardening gloves in her hands. The owner had come outside, and she looked like she was about to do some gardening. Little did she know that it had already been done for her.

Lacey couldn't find her voice. All she could manage was to wring her hands.

"What are you doing here?" the woman asked as she came closer. Soon she would be upon them, and she would see the fine work that Nosey had done. Lacey felt sick to her stomach.

The woman cleared her throat. She was waiting for Lacey to answer her question, but Lacey couldn't make her voice work for the life of her. This always happened to her whenever she became frightened or nervous or even slightly intimidated. Her mouth would clamp shut and nothing would come out. And unfortunately, this time Luke wasn't there to speak for her.

At that moment, the troublemaking dog appeared by Lacey's side and nudged her fondly.

The woman frowned at Lacey expectantly and Lacey willed her mouth to make some sound - a noise, a word, something - but to no avail. To Lacey's surprise though, as her voice was failing her yet again, the woman looked away from Lacey's frightened face, down to the dog by her side, and began smiling again.

"Oh," she said, noticing the affectionate way that the dog stood next to Lacey. "You're here with Nosey?"

All Lacey could manage was a nod.

"Well, why didn't you say so?" The woman walked over to Nosey and pet him with familiarity, and the dog licked her hand in return. "Welcome to my home," she said to Lacey, but with her attention still on the dog.

Lacey didn't mind the woman's divided attention. She was just relieved that she wasn't being arrested for trespassing. Apparently, association with Nosey was all the clearance she needed here.

"Come on boy," the woman said to Nosey. "Let's get our gardening done." Then she turned around and began walking towards the garden.

A strangled sound came from Lacey's throat as the woman neared the scene of the crime, and the woman turned back around to face her. Lacey, certain that she was in big trouble now, somehow forced the words out.

"He...um...he...well...he got into your garden and started digging holes. I'm so sorry. I tried to stop him."

"Well, of course he did," the woman said with a laugh. "He's a dog. That's what dogs do. They like to dig in dirt. So, I let him dig holes while I garden. It saves me from having to dig up all this dirt myself."

She pulled her gloves on and knelt into the dirt. "I usually garden around this time every Saturday," she told Lacey. "Nosey always finds some way to slip away from Owen and come over. But what brings you to my garden? And how do you know Nosey?"

Lacey, who was thrown off by this turn of events, found herself once again unable to speak. As it turned out though, she didn't have to because the woman looked back at her with a giant smile on her face and her brown eyes lit up as big as saucers.

"Wait a minute," she said. "Are you Owen's niece? The one that's come to live with him?" Then, without giving Lacey a chance to respond she said, "You are, aren't you? Of course you are. I can see the family resemblance now."

This caused Lacey to subconsciously touch her face, wondering if she really did look like her uncle. She had always been told that she looked like her mother.

The woman continued with her revelation, seemingly needing no encouragement from Lacey. "You're one of the twins. That's why you were with Nosey. That clever dog tricked you into coming over here, didn't he?"

At this, Lacey couldn't help but smile. "I guess he did," she said quietly.

"Well, I'm your neighbor, Olivia, but you can call me Miss Olivia. That's what all the other girls call me. I live here with my sister, Annika. And I guess since you're here you may as well help me garden. There should be an extra set of gloves over there by the tools." She nodded toward the gardening accoutrements piled up on the side of the cordoned off area.

"Wait a minute," Miss Olivia said, as if she'd just thought of it. "You're not allergic to anything like the sun or, I don't know, the garden or dirt or hard labor, are you? I mean, I'm not going to get in trouble with your uncle for putting you to work, am I?"

Lacey giggled. "No," she said. "I'm not allergic to working."

She went to collect the extra pair of gloves and then joined Miss Olivia and Nosey, who was working on a fresh hole.

Miss Olivia noticed her looking over at Nosey and said, "Don't tell Owen that I let him dig holes. I don't think he would approve. He'd probably say something like, 'you're encouraging him to be naughty' or something boring like that. He might even get paranoid that Nosey might start digging holes in his own yard." She thought for a moment, and then said, "I wonder if he has begun digging holes in Owen's yard."

"Well," Lacey responded, "I haven't noticed any holes, but I've only been there one day."

Miss Olivia nodded. She seemed satisfied with that answer. Then, as if to cover her bases, she said, "If he does start digging up Owen's yard, don't tell him I was the one behind it all."

"I won't," Lacey promised. Then the two of them got to work.

An hour later, they were both tired of gardening and called it a day. The Florida sun was scorching everything in its path, including the two of them. Nosey had long since quit on his endeavors and was now alternating his time between rolling around in the grass and chasing any daring squirrels that came his way.

"That's enough for today," Miss Olivia removed her dirty gloves and wiped at the sweat gathering on her forehead.

Lacey didn't argue. She removed her own gloves and returned them where she'd found them.

"Let's go inside and get something cool to drink," Miss Olivia suggested and turned around and walked away, presumably to do just that.

After a hesitant look to Nosey, who was now sunbathing, Lacey shrugged her shoulders and followed Miss Olivia. She'd thought that was an invitation. It had certainly sounded like one. Nosey, seeing the two of them headed toward the house, jumped up and went along. He seemed to be in need of a cold drink as well.

At the back door, Miss Olivia removed her dirty shoes before stepping inside her home. Lacey mimicked her actions. Nosey, having no shoes to remove, tapped his paws on the doormat. Lacey wasn't sure how much dirt this removed, but it was cute to watch.

"I taught him to do that," Miss Olivia said, grinning with pride.

They entered the cabin and Miss Olivia led her visitors through the sunroom and into the dining room.

"Have a seat," she threw over her shoulder, as she headed to the adjoining kitchen.

Lacey did as instructed and settled into one of the comfortable looking chairs at the dining table. It was an enormous table made of wood, large enough for at least 12 people to sit. A vase of fresh picked flowers had been placed in the center of the table, filling the room with the smell of spring. Lacey leaned over and took an obligatory sniff of the floral bouquet before marveling again at the size of the house she had unexpectedly found herself in.

"These people really must be loaded," she whispered to Nosey, who had taken a seat as well. He was resting at Lacey's feet, waiting patiently for his promised cold beverage. At the sound of her voice, he looked up to give Lacey a listening ear.

"Why do rich people always have to show off?" she asked Nosey.

Nosey didn't answer.

"I mean look at this place. Why's it so big? Do they really need this much space?"

Lacey recalled Miss Olivia telling her that she and her sister lived in the cabin. She shook her head. What did two women need with a house this size?

She was pulled from these thoughts by the return of Miss Olivia carrying a tray filled with refreshments. Miss Olivia set the tray on the dining table and Lacey got a full view of what her host had brought with her. She also saw why the woman had taken a little longer than expected to return from the kitchen. When Miss Olivia had offered a cool drink, Lacey had assumed that she would grab a couple of bottles of water from the fridge. She hadn't realized just how over-the-top Miss Olivia was, but she was beginning to understand.

Miss Olivia had brought a glass pitcher of what appeared to be ice water with cucumber slices floating about inside of it. There were two glasses on the tray and two small plates. The plates were meant to hold what had to be all the food from the kitchen. Lacey was certain that Miss Olivia had emptied out her entire pantry and fridge. She could make out chips, crackers, snack cakes, fruit slices, vegetable slices, dips, and...

"Are those peanut butter sandwiches?" Lacey pointed to the crustless creations at the edge of the tray.

"Oh no!" Miss Olivia said alarmed. "Do you have a peanut allergy? I didn't even think before I made them. They're the girls' favorite, so I thought that you might like them too."

"No, I love peanut butter," Lacey assured her.

"Oh, thank heavens," Miss Olivia blew out a breath in relief. She then grabbed the pitcher. "You like cucumber water?"

Lacey shrugged. It was an honest answer as she had never tasted it before.

Miss Olivia must have taken this as affirmation that she did like it, as she poured her a large glass before pouring a glass for herself. "You'll love it," she assured her. "The girls and I made it for the first time over the winter. It was so good that I've been making it ever since."

She left the table with the pitcher and began to kneel. It was then that Lacey noticed a water dish in the corner, which Miss Olivia slowly filled with iced cucumber water. Lacey watched as Nosey padded over to his water dish and began zealously lapping up his drink. Clearly, he was a fan of cucumber water.

Lacey decided she may as well trust Nosey's judgment. She picked up her own glass and gingerly brought it to her mouth for a sip.

"What do you think?" Miss Olivia asked as she returned to the table and took the chair across from Lacey.

Lacey swallowed and delivered a smile. "It's good," she admitted. "I really like it."

"Another convert," Miss Olivia cheered and began filling a plate, which she then passed to her guest. Lacey accepted the plate graciously while quietly thinking that there was no way she would be able to eat even half of the items on it. Perhaps she would be able to take her leftovers back with her to give to Luke.

Miss Olivia grabbed her own plate and began to pile it just as high. "Tell me about yourself," she said.

Lacey gulped. She hated when people said that. Correction. She loathed it entirely when people said that. Lacey couldn't think of anything worse than talking about herself. And now here she was being put on the spot. She didn't know what to say. She didn't know what Miss Olivia wanted to hear. She took a bite of her peanut butter sandwich to stall for time, but the peanut butter got stuck to the roof of her mouth and she had to gulp down water to dislodge it. It was at least two or three minutes before her mouth was empty, but she found that the wait had not changed Miss Olivia's curiosity. She chewed her own food while waiting patiently for Lacey to talk.

"Uh, what do you want to know?"

"Everything," Miss Olivia answered with enough enthusiasm to make Lacey uncomfortable.

She fidgeted in her seat as the peanut butter she'd ingested turned into a rock inside her stomach. What was she supposed to tell this woman who was essentially a stranger to her? She was nice enough, and she clearly knew her uncle and his dog, but Lacey didn't know her at all.

Suddenly, Lacey felt foolish. She was sitting in a stranger's house and eating her food all because a dog had led her there. No one even knew where she was. If something happened to her, no one would know. Lacey looked suspiciously at the half-eaten sandwich in her hands and the cucumber water that Miss Olivia had been so adamant that she try. If Miss Olivia was even her real name.

She needed to get out of there. Now. She was just about to bolt to the door (dog or no dog) when another woman walked into the kitchen. This woman she recognized, and that calmed her down enough to stay.

8

"**D**id I miss gardening time?" Annika Jones asked as she walked into the dining room. There was a note of disappointment in her voice that she had perfected before coming downstairs. In truth, she had carefully timed her arrival for just this moment – when all the work was done. "Awww! I was really looking forward to it." She laid it on thick.

Her sister, Olivia, rolled her eyes at the girl sitting across from her at the table.

"It would be more believable if she didn't say the same thing every Saturday," Olivia said to the girl, who covered her face with her hand to hide her laugh.

"Who's this?" Annika asked. She was only somewhat surprised to see a young girl sitting at their dining room table. After all, she and Olivia did run a camp for girls out of their home, so she was accustomed to seeing girls hanging around. But as far as she knew, Spring Break had yet to start, so there shouldn't be any campers about yet. Or had she gotten the dates wrong on her calendar? No, she was certain. Sort of.

"This is our new neighbor, Lacey!" Olivia announced a little too loudly and with far more enthusiasm than the moment truly called for.

Annika, well accustomed to her over-exuberance, ignored Olivia and narrowed her focus on the girl.

"I know you," she said after a moment. She squinted her eyes at the girl, as if that could somehow help her see better. Then she announced, "Oh, I know! You're the girl. You're Ebeneezer Scrooge's niece."

What were hidden laughs before became full out snickers.

"Annika!" Olivia shouted. "You can't call him that in front of her."

"Why not?" Annika shrugged, "It's true." She made her way over to the table and began helping herself to the ample leftovers still on the serving tray.

"You're going to give her the wrong impression of him," Olivia said. "She just met the man. Saying things like that are going to make her think the worst things about him." She turned to Lacey, "He's really a nice guy. It's just that he and Annika can't seem to get along. But he's not as bad as she's making him out to be." She threw a huge smile at Lacey, unaware that next to her Annika was making a face at her.

This was too much for Lacey, who was downright cackling now.

"Well," Olivia said. "I have to get ready for work, but I enjoyed meeting you Lacey and you're welcome to come and garden with me anytime." She stood up and Annika claimed her empty chair and her leftover food. "At least then I would have someone to help me." She glared at Annika, who either didn't hear her or didn't care that she was annoyed.

"Yes," Olivia said, as if she was deciding the matter. "You should definitely come by often and help." With that assertion she turned and left the room.

"Do you want some more cucumber water?" Annika asked. She had already refilled the glass that Olivia had been using and now had the pitcher hovering over Lacey's, waiting for her reply.

Lacey nodded her head and Annika poured.

"Look at all this food," Annika commented on the over-filled tray that Lacey and Olivia had barely made a dent in. "Olivia really does know how to overdo it, especially when she has someone to feed other than me. Still, I can't complain because everything is delicious." She helped herself to a puffed pastry.

"This is the second big meal I've had today," Lacey said quietly.

"Really?"

"Yeah," she nodded. "Uncle Owen made a huge breakfast for us. It tasted really good too."

Annika involuntarily scrunched her nose up at the mention of her neighbor. Then, catching herself, she corrected her face and thought of something halfway polite to say.

"He does like to cook," she acknowledged. "I'd forgotten that about him. At least now he has someone to cook for. Besides himself."

"My brother likes to cook too," Lacey volunteered. She appeared to be warming to the subject and to Annika. "He's really good at it too. I think he gets it from my mom." Then she lowered her head and said in an even softer voice, "I'm the only one in our family that can't cook at all."

"Oh, thank goodness," Annika said.

Lacey looked up sharply, surprise on her face.

"I thought I was the only terrible cook in a family of amazing cooks. Now I know I'm not alone. There is strength in unity Lacey. We will be strong. We will persevere. And we will eat all the delicious meals that they make for us."

This brought the smile back to Lacey's face and even elicited a small laugh.

"Agreed?"

"Agreed."

"How do I look?"

Olivia reappeared in a pink sundress that hugged her curves. Her hair was coiled and teased to perfection, and she wore a fresh coat of makeup.

"You look beautiful," Lacey answered.

"Thank you," Olivia beamed at the compliment.

"Um, you are just going to work, aren't you?" Annika asked in confusion.

"Yep."

"Then why are you so dressed up with the makeup and all? And are you wearing heels?"

Olivia cleared her throat. "I just, you know, um... well, we should always try and look our best no matter where we're going. Something you might consider yourself." She looked distastefully at Annika's cut-off shorts and tank top.

"I'm not going anywhere. I work the dinner shift again today, and nice try at deflecting."

Olivia huffed.

"Tell me," Annika said, refusing to give up on her quarry, "does this look have anything to do with your boss? Are you trying to look good for him?"

"No!" Olivia vehemently denied. "Absolutely not. I just want to dress appropriately for work."

"But you work in a hardware store. Jeans and sneakers would be appropriate."

"Since when did you become a fashion critic? You can't even tell the different designers apart."

"Wait a minute," Annika said, the teasing leaving her voice to be replaced by a note of concern. "Is there trouble in paradise?"

"No!"

"What happened?" Annika asked.

"I'm not going to discuss it right now. Besides I'm going to be late for work if I don't leave soon." She smoothed the non-existent wrinkles from her dress and left the way she came.

It was then that Annika turned around and saw that she had Lacey's full attention. Annika had been so focused on her conversation with Olivia that she'd forgotten the girl even existed. She never would've gone into Olivia's personal life if she'd remembered the teenager was there. Annika could only hope that Lacey hadn't been paying too close attention, or at least hadn't understood the entire conversation.

"So," Lacey said, once Olivia had left and Annika's attention was back on her. "Your sister is dating her boss where she works at that big hardware store in town. Only things aren't going so great right now so she's going to walk all around the hardware store looking hot to try and get his attention or make him jealous, whichever one will work."

Annika sighed. "You caught all that?"

Lacey shrugged. "It's not the worst idea. It's not the best either."

"It's ridiculous."

"Who knows? It might work."

Annika laughed because she had to admit, Olivia's plan was so absurd that it probably would work.

"My sister always comes up with outrageous plans," she told Lacey, "but every once in a while, she hits upon a really good one."

A noise came from the corner of the room and they both looked to find the source of the sound. It was Nosey, who having been neglected, had succumb to boredom and then sleep. This was Lacey's cue that it was time to end her visit.

"I think I should go back now," she said, but she made no move to stand. Instead, she looked down at her hands folded in her lap.

Annika watched her for a moment before speaking.

"You know, Olivia meant what she said. About you coming back. She really could use help in the garden, and I always find an excuse to get out of it. But the thing is, she's trying to get the project done before Spring Break starts and the camp reopens."

Lacey looked up at her and Annika answered the question on her face.

"We run a camp for girls - Olivia and me - right here out of our home for one week every season. And well anyway, there's a million things to do around here to prepare. So, if you wanted to come back some time, we would really love the help."

Annika watched as the frown that had come over the girl's face transformed into a shy smile.

"Okay," she agreed. Then she asked, "'Can I come over tomorrow?"

"Nope," Annika answered, and then laughed at the shocked look on Lacey's face. "I'm just messing with you. I'm sorry, but I couldn't resist. The truth is we won't be here tomorrow. First, we have church and then we're supposed to go over to the MacPhearson's and spend the day there." Then she muttered to herself, "Now that should be an interesting situation considering the current status of Olivia's love life."

She saw Lacey watching her curiously and waved the comment away. Hadn't she just decided not to discuss Olivia's private business? "Never mind that. Forget I even said it."

"Who are the MacPhearson's?" Lacey asked curiously.

"Oh, that's just Phillip's family. It doesn't matter. The point is that we won't be home."

Lacey studied Annika's face, as if she were trying to solve a riddle. The girl was astute. Annika would have to be more careful about what she said in front of her going forward.

"Um," Annika cleared her throat. "Would you like to come to church with us?"

Lacey hesitated. "Church?"

"Just think about it," Annika told her. "Hang on." She left the room for just a moment and returned with a small slip of paper with writing on it. "Here's my number. If you decide to go and you need a ride, then just give me a call. You can bring your brother too."

Lacey took the scrap of paper and folded it into her pocket.

"Okay. I guess you can bring Scrooge too."

Lacey laughed and stood up. "I think I really have to go now."

Nosey woke up at the sound of her chair scraping across the

hardwood floor. Seeing her standing, he stood too, somehow understanding that their visit was over. He gave a good stretch, wagged his tail, and went to stand by the door and wait for Lacey to say her good-byes.

"Do you want me to walk you back?" Annika offered.

"No," Lacey brushed off her offer. "Nosey knows the way."

Nosey gave a bark at this statement. This could have been his way of confirming her belief in his navigational skills, or it could have been a hurry up I want to go home bark. It was kind of hard to tell.

"Thank you," Lacey said to Annika, as she walked towards Nosey and the door. Once she reached the door, she turned around to face Annika and said, "I had fun." Then she gave a little wave good-bye and left out of the door that she'd entered through.

Several moments passed before Annika replied to no one, "I had fun too."

❧ 9 ❧

"Alright," Owen said. "Let's go over this one more time. I'm giving you money. You are going to use that money to buy clothes. Not a t-shirt. Not flip flops. Real clothes. Clothes you can wear. Got it?"

The two teenagers bobbed their heads in unison, but Owen had no false hopes that they would do as he intended. Not after the previous day's debacle. But he had to keep trying, no matter how many times it took.

The three of them were standing next to his truck in the exact same spot as the day before, aiming for a different outcome this time.

"Okay," Owen continued. "I'm going to the hardware store. It's on this side of the street just a couple of stores down from where you'll be. You both have phones now." Owen pointed to the newly purchased device in Luke's hand. His face had been planted to the screen since the moment the salesperson had given it to him. Owen found this to be an interesting reaction considering how hard Luke had fought against getting the phone. Now it looked like Owen might have to place a time limit on his screen time.

"You have my number," Owen continued, "so you can call me

if you have questions. If not, we'll meet back here in an hour. Okay then. Go on." He shooed them off, waited to see them cross the street and enter the clothing store, then he headed in the direction of the hardware store.

The Hardware House was one of the largest stores on the main thoroughfare. It sat on a corner lot and had elegant store-front windows under a wide blue awning. The owner was a tall African-American man in his early thirties who was eccentric but friendly, and who made sure that all his customers felt welcome in his store. Like the diner that Owen frequented, The Hardware House was a social hub of Port St. Annabelle. All the locals congregated there, and the place seemed to have a steady stream of customers regardless of the time of day.

Also, like the diner, one of Owen's neighbors was employed there. He saw her as he passed by the paint aisle. She was all dressed up like she was going somewhere special. She even had on heels. It was a bit impractical for a hardware store, but her attire could explain why she was surrounded by customers, mostly of the male persuasion.

Owen shook his head at the spectacle and continued on through the store. While both his neighbors tried his patience, he could at least deal with this one. It was the other one that really grated on his nerves.

As expected, the store was busy, but this didn't bother Owen as much as it might have in the past. He had been known to shy away from conversations and crowds, but he'd recently started venturing out a bit more. And now, he realized, he would have to spend even more time around people. With two kids, he no longer had the luxury of hiding away in his cave. It wasn't as though he could lock the two of them away. They needed to spend time among other people. He begrudgingly surmised that he might even have to start conversing with people. Owen brushed the thought aside. There was no reason to go overboard with this socializing thing.

Knowing exactly what he was looking for and the general

vicinity in which it was located, allowed Owen to quickly find what he'd come for. He then spent some time browsing the shelves to see what new items were in stock. Owen wasn't exactly a master carpenter, but he could handle a few basic home repairs. He'd had to get handy to keep his cabin in such great shape. He certainly wasn't going to hire the local carpenter to do any of the work. Everyone knew that the man was basically a criminal because the prices he charged had to be illegal.

Satisfied that he had everything he needed, Owen went to the front of the store to checkout. Thankfully, there was no line at the moment. He seized this rare opportunity and quickly stepped up to the checkout counter.

There was no one behind the register but he could see the store owner standing off to the side restocking flashlights onto the shelves. Actually, he was really just holding the flashlights while staring back at the paint section with a pained look on his face. Owen looked back to where his eyes were fixed and saw that his neighbor was still holding court with an even larger group of customers around her. Owen saw her tossing her hair and heard her giggling loudly from where he was. Owen shook his head again and turned back to the man who was still staring off in that direction. He cleared his throat and the man looked over, acknowledged Owen with a nod, and then made his way to the register.

Once he was standing in front of him, Owen could see that the store owner did not look like his usual cheerful self. His eyes were downcast, his face was haggard, and his clothes (normally a point of pride for him) were wrinkled and disheveled. Owen didn't know the man well, but he had encountered him multiple times and had even become somewhat acquainted with him after treating him for a head wound he'd sustained the previous year. So, Owen felt that he knew him well enough to know that something was wrong.

"Did you find everything okay?" Even his voice sounded ragged.

"Sure," Owen answered. "I think I know my way around here pretty well."

The man, usually a virtual chatterbox, said nothing more. He sat his unshelved flashlights down and began ringing up Owen's selections.

Owen was so distracted by the uncharacteristic behavior of the man in front of him, that he didn't notice the girl that walked up next to him until she spoke, causing him to jump.

"You're done already?"

Owen did a double take. He knew Lacey was quiet, but this was ridiculous. The girl was practically a ninja.

"What are you doing here?" he asked. "I thought you understood the plan. You were supposed to buy something to wear."

"I did." She held up the bag she'd been holding for Owen to see.

It was only one bag, but it was significantly larger than the previous day's bag, so Owen reassured himself that she must have bought more than a pair of flip-flops this time. He decided to consider this a win and let the matter go.

"What are you doing here?" he repeated. "And where's your brother?"

"He's still shopping. I finished and I wanted to see the hardware store, so I came to find you." She hesitated and then asked, "Is that okay?" Her brow furrowed and she bit her lower lip.

"Yes," Owen waved away her concern. "There's nothing wrong with you coming to the store with me. I just wanted to make sure that you got something to wear."

"I did."

"Okay."

The matter settled, they both turned their attention to the store owner who had finished scanning Owen's items and was now in the process of bagging them.

"Your name's Phillip?" Lacey asked, even though the man was wearing a name tag with the name Phillip prominently displayed.

"Yeah," Phillip answered.

"Is your last name MacPhearson?"

That was a random question if Owen had ever heard one. Why would Lacey care about the man's last name?

Phillip paused briefly to answer Lacey's question with a nod, and then resumed bagging the items. He told Owen the total, who handed over his credit card for Phillip to swipe.

"And you're the boss around here, right?"

This time Owen gave Lacey a look of bewilderment. The girl barely spoke and here she was interrogating a complete stranger.

Lacey gave him an innocent shrug and looked away from his questioning gaze.

If Phillip found her line of questioning to be either intrusive or bizarre, he gave no indication of it. He simply answered her questions and went about his work.

"I own this store," he said in that slightly raspy voice he'd been speaking in, "so yeah, I'm the boss."

"That's interesting," Lacey said.

Phillip handed Owen's card back and passed him the bag filled with his purchases, all without speaking another word. Owen, who at this point was eager to leave, took the bag and left the store with Lacey following behind, shooting curious looks to Phillip on her way out the door.

Back at the truck, Luke was waiting for them.

"At least someone can follow instructions," Owen muttered to himself. To the twins he said, "Alright, mission accomplished. Time to head home."

"We're not eating at the diner?" Lacey sounded disappointed.

Owen shook his head. "I know the food's good but we can't eat there too often. It's just not healthy."

He looked back at the diner where Annika was visible through the windows. She was walking from table to table, busy at work. Owen narrowed his eyes at her, although she appeared far too occupied to even notice him standing outside.

"Also," he added, "I don't much care for the waitress that's working today. She may be cute, but she has a terrible attitude."

He turned his attention back to his niece and nephew just in time to see them exchange another one of their looks. This one had them both grinning.

"What?" Owen asked, wanting to know what they had just communicated to each other, but at the same time, not really wanting to know. They looked at him with matching smiles that told Owen he wouldn't like whatever they were thinking.

"Oh nothing," Luke said, attempting to sound casual, but he was given away by the smile still on his face. Then he threw out, "So, you think the waitress is cute?"

"What?!"

"That's what you said." This came from the girl. When did she learn to talk?

"No!"

"You did," the boy picked up. "You looked right at her, and you said she's cute."

"I-"

Flustered, Owen looked back and forth between the little monsters in front of him. They had him cornered and they knew it. Is this what having kids was like? Well, it was a good thing he and Natasha had never had any.

Owen gathered his wits. "We are going home and I'm going to cook for us," he announced. He thought about it and revised his statement. "Actually, *we're* going to cook for us. I'm going to cook and you two will help."

Their separate reactions could be seen from a mile away. Luke lit up with excitement. Lacey shriveled in on herself. Owen ignored them both. His decision had been made.

"Let's go!" Owen said, and they all climbed into the truck to head home.

D inner turned out better than Lacey had expected, considering she'd been in the kitchen when it was being cooked. In fact, she'd go so far as to say that it was delicious. They were having pasta primavera, another first for Lacey. (Her father had been an avid meat lover and never would've allowed anything vegetarian to be served at the dinner table.) She was starting to think that she might need to make a list of the yummy new things that she was getting to try. So far, the list consisted of cucumber water and now pasta primavera.

Truthfully, it had been a while since she'd eaten so well. Not since her mother had cooked for them. Thinking about her parents put a lump in her throat and brought that all too familiar tightening to her stomach. The food that had tasted so delicious a moment before, now held the same appeal as dirt and became difficult to swallow. Lacey set her fork down. She doubted she'd be able to eat any more food.

Across from her, Luke didn't seem to have any problem eating his meal. He was devouring the food at a breakneck pace. At least someone was enjoying it, Lacey thought to herself.

"Well," Uncle Owen said, "I don't have anywhere planned for

us to go tomorrow, so you two are free to do whatever you want. Unless there was somewhere either of you wanted to go."

Lacey perked up. She had been looking for the right moment and here it had finally presented itself. She cleared her throat to speak.

"Nope. We don't want to go anywhere."

Luke made this declaration and then shoveled another forkful of pasta into his mouth. He seemed oblivious to his sister shooting daggers with her eyes at him from across the table. He hadn't even asked her. He'd just assumed and then spoken for both of them. Why didn't he at least ask her first?

It was at that moment that Lacey came to a surprising revelation. Luke had become so used to speaking for her, that he now did it automatically, and without asking for her opinion. For reasons she couldn't explain, this unsettled her. Well maybe, just maybe, she would have to stop letting him speak for her. Maybe she had to start speaking for herself.

"Um," Lacey said. She kept her eyes trained on her barely touched meal. "I know where we could go tomorrow." She twisted her hands in her lap while still looking at her plate. The pasta was getting cold now and the shredded cheese on top was starting to look like something out of an alien movie.

"Where," Uncle Owen asked, setting his fork down, his plate cleared of food. He turned his full attention to Lacey, although she didn't look at him.

Lacey hesitated and then decided to just say it. It's not like she was asking for anything bad. And who knew, maybe they would even like her suggestion. Lacey took a deep breath and blurted out the word, "Church."

She meant to blurt it out, but it came out as more of a whisper. In the quiet of the room however, both of the other occupants heard her clearly. And they both had equally strong reactions. Luke dropped his fork (which was just as well because his plate was empty at this point) and stared at Lacey, mouth hanging open. Uncle Owen shook his head vigorously.

"Nope," he said. "No. No way. I'll take you to the moon before I take you to church."

Lacey was shocked at his strong reaction. Apparently, this was a touchy subject for him. His tone was definitive and left no room for arguments. Not that Lacey would have argued with him anyway. She'd barely found the courage just to ask him. Still, she made a mental note not to bring it up with him in the future.

"I'm sorry," Uncle Owen continued, "but that's out of the question."

His verdict delivered, Uncle Owen stood from the table. "I'll do cleanup tonight," he said, and began gathering the dishes from the table. "Tomorrow will be your turn. We can rotate after that." He spared one last look at Lacey before he headed to the kitchen to wash the dishes.

Lacey didn't look at Luke, whose stare she could feel on her from across the table. She'd be lying if she said she wasn't disappointed in her uncle's reaction. But she didn't know him at all. Therefore, she'd had no way of knowing how he felt toward religion. It had been a gamble, asking him to take her to church. A gamble that hadn't paid off. However, she wasn't too upset because she had a backup plan. Although not her ideal scenario, it was a plan, nevertheless.

.....

BACK IN THE BEDROOM THEY SHARED, LUKE DUMPED HIS shopping bags onto the bed, while Lacey clutched her own bag in her arms. He went through each item until he found what he was looking for, a brand-new set of pajamas. Although reluctant to spend his uncle's money at first, Luke had overcome his fear of overspending on their second shopping trip. His uncle's reaction when they hadn't spent the money coupled with the way he'd laid down a ton of money to get them both a nice set of phones, had convinced Luke that he really meant for them to have new clothes. And though he'd felt wary and somewhat suspicious of this generosity, Luke had purchased several pieces of clothing for himself anyway. He just hoped he didn't regret it. After all, he'd been burned by fake generosity from a guardian before. Luke gave an involuntary shiver at the memory he'd just conjured. Then he did his best to push that nightmare to the back of his mind.

He looked up and saw Lacey sitting on the edge of the bed and holding onto her bag for dear life.

"What did you buy?" he asked.

He didn't bother to ask her why she hadn't bought more than just one bag of clothes. He knew what her answer would be. She didn't trust free gifts any more than he did, and for the same reason. Luke looked over his haul spread across the comforter covering the bed. Again, he wondered if he'd made a mistake.

"A dress," Lacey answered his question and brought his attention back to her.

It took him a moment to realize that she was answering his question, because her answer didn't make any sense.

"A dress?"

She nodded.

"You bought a dress?"

Lacey nodded, and squeezed the bag closer, as if afraid that he might try and take it from her.

"Why?"

Luke was genuinely confused. Lacey never wore skirts or dresses anymore. They were impractical and a hazard. They found that out the hard way as well. Ever since that one foster father - Luke slammed the breaks on that memory immediately. He locked it away in a vault marked 'Never to Be Opened'.

"Why'd you buy a dress?" he repeated his question.

"For church," she replied, and Luke repeated his reaction he'd had at the dinner table.

"Church?"

She nodded.

"Wait, you were serious? I thought you were planning something, but you actually want to go to church?"

"Yes."

"But why?"

"Why not?"

Luke scoffed. "Because we're not religious. Because we've never gone."

"That's right, we've never gone. So, we should try it. It might be fun," Lacey reasoned.

Luke stared at his sister for a long moment. She stared back at him. She didn't blink or turn away. She just looked at him while holding that bag. He tried to figure out what was different about her, what had changed. But her face, so similar to his own, looked the same as always. So why, all of a sudden, was she talking nonsense?

"What's with you?" he finally asked when he could see no visible change in her.

"Nothing," she said, her tone defensive. "What's with you?"

"I'm not the one exhibiting signs of craziness." He squinted at her, and she shifted under his scrutiny. "Nope," he deduced, "something's up with you."

"What do you mean?"

"First," Luke ticked off on his hand, "you buy a dress."

"I like dresses," Lacey argued.

"Yeah, well there's a reason you stopped wearing them," Luke reminded her.

Lacey lowered her head. She didn't need to be reminded of that – not now or ever.

"Then," Luke continued, as if he hadn't just brought up one of their collective worst memories, "you took off on your own today instead of staying at the store with me."

"I was done shopping and I wanted to see something in the hardware store," Lacey explained.

PAMELA BROWN

"You know how dangerous that is? Walking around a strange town all by yourself? Anything could've happened to you."

"It was just down the street. I was totally safe."

Luke shook his head. Sometimes it seemed like his sister had no self-preservation instincts whatsoever.

"Now," he finished off his list, "you're talking about going to church? Talk about random. Where did this even come from? What made you even think of it?"

"I was invited."

"You were invited?!" Luke asked, completely thrown off. Of all the things he thought she might say, that wasn't one of them.

Lacey simply nodded and offered no further explanation.

"By who?" he asked her, and then looked around as if this mysterious person might be there in the room with them. "You don't know anyone. We just got here yesterday. Who could've possibly invited you?"

So, Lacey told him how she'd spent her morning, about meeting their neighbors and the invitation to join them at church.

"Let me get this straight," Luke said, once she'd finished sharing. "The waitress at the diner, the one that was all weird with us, is our neighbor? And she and Uncle Owen hate each other?"

"That's right."

"But she just invited you to go to church with her out of the blue?"

Lacey could hear the skepticism in Luke's voice. "She was really nice," she tried to explain.

Luke snorted. "I'm sure she was. That's how stalkers are at first. Next thing you know, they're tossing your body in a lake or something."

"I don't think so," she began, and Luke rolled his eyes. It was remarkable how naïve she could be after all that they'd been through in the past several months.

84

However, Lacey seemed unfazed by his reaction. "You'll see for yourself when we go to church with-"

"We're not going to church." Luke put an end to the discussion. "You heard Uncle Owen. He doesn't want to go. I sure don't want to go. We're not going. So just drop it." He shook his head as he walked to the bathroom to change, brand new pajamas in hand.

Something was definitely going on with Lacey. Luke was just glad that he'd put an end to the ridiculousness before it had gone any further.

.....

LEFT ALONE WITH HER THOUGHTS, LACEY BIT HER LIP AND worried. Although she hadn't let on, Luke's comments had bothered her. The neighbors had been nice to her, but had she been naïve in accepting their kindness at face value? Were they only being kind to her so she would lower her guard around them, and then perhaps they would do something terrible to her later. She'd thought that she could trust them, but now Luke was planting seeds of doubt in her mind. Lacey carefully thought over her day and her interaction with the two women. No, she decided resolutely. They had been genuine. She was sure of it. She was also sure that Luke would like them too, once he'd spent time with them as she had.

Unbeknownst to Luke, his sentiments had not deterred Lacey. Well, maybe slightly. She had been nervous about what was essentially going behind her uncle's back, but she'd been prepared to do it because she had assumed that she wouldn't be alone. Luke would be with her, as he always was. His refusal to join her had left her somewhat blindsided. That was until Lacey reminded herself that she'd spent the entire day independent of her brother. She'd done what she wanted without Luke's input, and she'd even spoken for herself, something she couldn't ever remember doing. Certainly not since everything had changed.

Lacey stared at the dress, still in the shopping bag, that she'd carefully chosen from the store. It had been important to her that she chose just the right one. From the brief time that she'd spent with her neighbors, she could tell that they dressed very nicely and she didn't want to embarrass them by showing up to their church in her shabby clothes. Or worse, have them regret inviting her at all. Because the thing was, she'd had fun today – meeting the neighbors and investigating Miss Olivia's love life. She'd had a lot of fun. And Lacey honestly didn't know the last time that had happened. What she did know was that she wanted it to happen again.

That was why, while Luke was out of earshot behind the bathroom door, Lacey pulled her new phone out of one pocket and the slip of paper with Miss Annika's phone number from the other pocket. She sent off a quick text message and had both items back in her pockets just as Luke re-emerged from the bathroom.

She hoped it wasn't too late at night for her to text. She also hoped that Miss Annika hadn't changed her mind about giving her a ride. She really hoped that she'd been serious about the offer in the first place and wasn't just being polite. Still, she felt a gnawing sense of guilt tugging at her for being deceitful and going behind her uncle and her brother's back. Although, she wasn't really deceiving them, she reasoned as she looked once more at her dress. (It really was a very pretty dress). The fact was that they had both said they weren't going. Yet, they'd said nothing about her going. And she slept well that night, resting her conscience on that technicality.

L acey set the alarm on her new phone to 5:30 to ensure that she would wake up early. She also set it to vibrate to ensure that Luke would not wake up early. She'd received a text message from Miss Annika the night before almost immediately after she'd contacted her, confirming that the woman would take Lacey to church with her and telling Lacey what time to expect her. Lacey wouldn't have to trek through the woods this time, as Miss Annika would stop by and collect her on the way to church.

When the alarm went off, Lacey was already wide awake. She was so excited that she'd woken early. She had no idea what to expect but it was something new. And something good. She hoped.

She slipped out of bed and felt a twinge of guilt at leaving her sleeping brother behind. Then, remembering that he had done the exact same thing to her the day before, she shrugged it off. Besides, she had invited him, and he had refused.

Lacey grabbed her things which she had strategically set out the night before, while making up half excuses to Luke's probing questions as to why she was setting her toiletries near the bedroom door. With her belongings stacked up in her arms, she slipped out of the bedroom and into the dark hallway. There was little to no visibility, but she was going directly across the hall, so she felt certain that she'd be able to find her way without tripping or falling.

When she made it to the bedroom adjacent to the one she shared with Luke, she went inside, turned on the light, and sighed. She'd made it through the first part of her plan. Now she had to get ready.

Even in her haste, Lacey still took the time to note the similarities between this room (which was technically her bedroom) and the room she'd just left. This room held the same mirrored dresser and four-poster bed with elaborate bedding as the other one. However, there was no window overlooking the backyard here, and the rug on the floor of this room had a colorful striped pattern.

Walking through to the bathroom, Lacey could see that the similarities continued here as well. Like the bathroom attached to the other room, this one had a marble countertop and stark white tiling along the shower wall which contrasted with the cheerful pattern of the shower curtain (stripes again, matching the rug on the floor, whereas a paisley curtain hung in the other bathroom).

Lacey dropped the few toiletry items she owned (a toothbrush, a hair comb and deodorant) onto the countertop and silently thanked Uncle Owen. As she and Luke had discovered when they'd first arrived, their uncle had already stocked the bathrooms with clean linen and an abundance of hygiene products.

Lacey picked up the brand-new bottle of shampoo, opened it and took a sniff, then did the same to its twin bottle of conditioner. They smelled like vanilla. They smelled expensive. Lacey, who would've been content with cheap and foul-smelling hair products, felt very thankful indeed.

As she showered and got ready for church, Lacey couldn't help but be grateful that her uncle's house was so large. She could see how it would be quite convenient for everyone to have their own bedroom and bathroom. For one, she wouldn't have had to go through the cloak and dagger routine just to get ready.

When she'd finished getting dressed, she examined herself in the bathroom mirror. The dress was a soft shade of yellow with thin shoulder straps and a full skirt that twirled about her legs when she walked. Lacey honestly didn't know if it was currently in style or not. She'd never kept up with the latest trends, not like her mother had. But she thought it looked nice, and it fit her, unlike all her other clothes.

Lacey puckered up her lips. She wished she had some lipstick. Her father had been adamant that Lacey could not wear makeup until she turned 16, but every now and then her mother would allow her to wear lipstick. She would let Lacey choose the color from her makeup bag and then apply it with care to Lacey's lips. Afterwards, she would always do the same thing. She'd step back, look Lacey over, and then say one word, "Beautiful."

Her reflection in the mirror became blurry and Lacey blinked away the tears. She immediately shoved the intrusive memories to the back of her mind where they belonged, squared her shoulders and left the bathroom behind to finish getting ready.

Time for shoes. Lacey examined her shoe collection. She'd set them on the floor when she'd entered the room, and now she looked them over with a dissatisfied frown. Which pair should she wear – her old sneakers (which were a size too large and dirty) or her flip flops? The flip flops were new, from her first shopping trip with Uncle Owen. They weren't very fancy, and they had no decorations on them. In fact, they'd been the cheapest pair that she could find. Still, Lacey was ecstatic when Uncle Owen had allowed her to keep them. It felt nice to have two pairs of shoes. It felt even better to have something that wasn't a hand-me-down or a charitable donation. Something that she had picked out for herself.

But the question remained. Which pair of shoes went best with the dress? After a few moments of deliberation, Lacey grabbed the flip flops and slipped them on. They were new and clean and pink – three very good reasons to wear them.

Satisfied that she was church ready, Lacey grabbed her phone and left the bedroom, easing the door shut behind her. She checked the time as she made her way to the stairs. She was cutting it close. Miss Annika should be arriving at any minute. Lacey had planned to be waiting outside when she arrived. Then she wouldn't have to deal with explaining to her uncle why the neighbor woman that he hated was standing in his living room, talking about taking his niece to church after he'd just said no the night before. Yeah, it'd be better if she could just avoid that whole scenario. She'd just leave a note somewhere where he could find it and slip out of the house.

It was a foolproof plan, which was why the sound of the doorbell ringing stopped Lacey in her tracks. She stood frozen on the stairs in shock as Nosey barked, the doorbell rang again, and the unmistakable sound of footsteps headed from the kitchen to the front door.

Uncle Owen was awake already? How early did he get up anyway? Then she heard another set of footsteps. These were lighter, but they were coming from the kitchen as well and headed in the same direction. Lacey recognized the sound of her brother's footfalls and didn't know whether to feel more horrified or confused. Hadn't she left him asleep in bed? What was he doing in the kitchen? And how was she supposed to slip out quietly with the three of them (brother, uncle and dog – Nosey sure wasn't helping the situation by barking loudly and announcing to the world that they had visitors) standing at the front door.

Lacey couldn't see the foyer or the front door from her position on the stairs, but she could hear what was taking place. One of them was unlocking the door – she could hear the deadbolt turn. And then there was the sound of the wooden door opening.

"Good morning. Is Lacey ready?"

The voice belonged to Miss Annika, and at the sound of it, Lacey's legs began working again. She rushed down the remaining stairs at a surprising speed and dashed into the foyer. Uncle Owen, Luke, and Nosey stood in a row. They had been looking at the woman who stood just inside the front door, but their attention turned to Lacey at her arrival to the scene. Her appearance startled everyone present. Even Nosey had stopped barking.

"I'm ready," she said, panting from her sprint.

Uncle Owen, Luke, and Nosey stared at her, stupefied. Lacey took advantage of their moment of shock.

"Miss Annika said that I could go to church with her," she said hurriedly as she made her way to the front door. "I should be back soon. I'll see you all later."

Miss Annika looked from Lacey to the others, clearly just as confused as everyone else. But Lacey gave her no time to ask questions, as she all but shoved the woman out the door.

"Bye," she threw over her shoulder before joining Miss Annika on the front porch, shutting the door behind her. "Okay, let's go," she said, and headed towards the driveway where a pink SUV was waiting behind Uncle Owen's truck with Miss Olivia in the driver's seat.

Miss Annika followed but at a slower pace. She looked to be trying to work out what had just occurred, and whether or not she was kidnapping her neighbor's niece.

.....

"UM, WHAT JUST HAPPENED?" LUKE ASKED.

Owen wasn't sure if his question was rhetorical or not, but either way he didn't answer it, mainly because he couldn't answer it. He wasn't quite sure what had just transpired himself. He stood in the foyer, turning over the events in his mind, trying to put the pieces together. Luke and Nosey stood silently watching, as if waiting to take their cue from him.

Owen thought it through, but when he'd drawn the lines together, he still didn't know what to do. At some point yesterday, Lacey had met and befriended the neighbor. (Had it only been yesterday? It seemed like weeks had passed since the twins had come into his life.) The woman must have invited Lacey to attend church with her and now she was out doing just that.

So, the question remained – should he be angry that she had basically defied him and was now out gallivanting about with a questionable adult, or should he be impressed that she'd outsmarted him. She had asked him the night before and he'd told her no. Yet, she'd gone anyway. Well, technically he'd told her that he wouldn't take her. He never told her she wasn't allowed to go. And she wasn't really gallivanting about – he knew exactly where she was. Also, if he was being fair, he didn't really consider the neighbors as bad influences. They were noisy, obnoxious, and discourteous, but he didn't think they were dangerous. Lacey should be fine with them for a couple of hours.

"Sooo, did Lacey just run away with the stalker woman next door?"

This came from Luke, who looked as though he was about to chase after the two of them and rescue his sister. Apparently, he was done waiting for Owen to decide what to do and was ready to act himself. Nosey sniffed the closed door and whimpered. It seemed that he sided with Luke on the matter.

Owen, who had momentarily forgotten about Luke and Nosey, was pulled from his thoughts just in time to see Luke opening the front door and Nosey barking beside him, urging him on.

"Nope," Owen shoved the door closed. "Whatever you're thinking, the answer is no."

Owen turned and headed towards the kitchen. "Come on," he called over his shoulder. He didn't bother to turn around to see if they would listen. He was pretty sure by the confused look on Luke's face that he would follow him out of curiosity or just because he didn't know what else to do. And Nosey would obey because that was what he'd been trained to do.

Sure enough, Owen could hear Luke's soft footsteps following behind him, along with the tapping of Nosey's toenails on the hardwood floor, alerting Owen that it was about time to take the dog back to the groomers.

However, even though Luke followed, Owen was in no way under the delusion that he would come along quietly. He had already had a preview of the boy's mouth the day before as they'd prepared breakfast together. So, Owen wasn't surprised when he heard him speak.

"But wait a minute. That lady-"

"Is our neighbor, not a stalker." Owen finished for Luke, although he was sure that wasn't the way Luke had intended for the sentence to end. A glance back affirmed that, and it also told Owen that he didn't believe what Owen had said.

"Look," Owen said, as he led his entourage through the house toward the back door, "you can calm yourself down. Lacey's perfectly safe. She's just going to church with the neighbor, who is completely harmless."

"That's not what you said about her yesterday," Luke muttered.

"And," Owen continued, ignoring the smart comment, "she won't be gone long, and I know exactly where she'll be the entire time."

They had reached the back door now and Owen opened it.

"Where are you going?" Luke demanded. He looked appalled that Owen would be taking off in the middle of a crisis.

"*We* are going fishing."

A t the edge of Owen's property, behind the cabin and beyond the backyard, stretched a lake, secluded by the woods that enclosed around the land which had been carved out for Owen's home. It was there that Owen took a dubious Luke and an excited Nosey to go fishing. Owen had only to begin pulling the fishing rods from the shed for Nosey to recognize the gear and begin jumping about and barking with anticipation.

But if Nosey was ecstatic to go fishing, Luke's feelings were the exact opposite. He was less than thrilled with Owen's choice in activities and made it very clear with his loud sighs and his slumped shoulders. Although his attitude about the matter was obvious, Owen couldn't help but feel grateful that at least he was complaining verbally.

"Why are we sitting here? This is boring. Are you sure there's even any fish in there?"

Owen sighed, but otherwise pretended he didn't hear the voice beside him. He also found himself wishing now that he'd been left with the nonverbal twin, although, she seemed to be more talkative by the day.

They were sitting on the side of the dock each with a fishing rod in their hands, although Luke's hung lazily, as though he would drop it at any moment. Nosey was squirreling about, pawing at the grass, chasing down insects, and tentatively investigating the water. At the end of the dock was Owen's small boat, moored to the posts. It was bobbing with the gentle motion of the water.

It was a typical spring day in Florida, which is to say that it was hot and humid. At just after 10:00 in the morning, the sun was out and shining in all its glory. But being native Floridians, they had both known what the weather would be like and had dressed accordingly in shorts and t-shirts.

"We're wasting our time here. We should be checking on Lacey. How do you know she's okay?"

"Let's talk about you." Owen changed the subject with the first thing he could think of.

He was met with silence. Then a soft, barely audible, "What? What do you mean?"

"I mean tell me about yourself. Tell me about your sister. Tell me about both of you."

"Why?" This came with a side look. Owen caught the suspicious glare from his peripheral view.

Owen sighed. "Look," he said, "I don't know anything about you two. The only information I have is what your caseworker gave me, and she wasn't exactly forthcoming with any details. So, I tell you what, you can ask me a question about anything, and I'll answer it honestly. Then I'll ask you a question and you have to answer it honestly. Deal?"

Silence. A look to the side of him, told Owen that Luke was biting his lower lip in contemplation. He must have been considering the offer, hesitant to disclose any information about himself. Either that, or he was wondering if he could trust Owen to hold up his part of the deal.

Owen had always considered himself to be a very private and guarded person, but this kid took it to a whole new level. Then again, Owen reasoned, if he'd been through half of what Owen was beginning to suspect Luke had been through, he'd probably find it hard to trust anyone too, especially adults.

"Alright," Luke finally agreed to Owen's terms.

"Okay, you first. What do you want to know?"

"Why don't you know anything about us?" Luke asked.

"What? I just told you that the caseworker–"

"Yeah? Well, the caseworker shouldn't have to tell you anything." Luke cut him off. He was facing Owen directly now, his voice getting louder, accusing. "You're our uncle, our mom's brother. Why didn't you know about us? Why didn't we know about you? Where've you been?"

Owen could feel Luke's stare, as if daring him to renege on their deal. Or worse, make up an excuse for being absent from their lives. He could almost hear Luke's thoughts and felt the expectation of disappointment radiating from the boy. He recognized this moment as the test that it was and somehow knew that no matter what, he must pass it.

Not sure what Luke wanted to hear, Owen decided that he would go with the truth, as painful as it would be to admit.

"Because I was a terrible brother."

He stated it matter-of-factly. Then Owen sighed and let go the burden of the truth he'd held in for so long.

"Anna, your mother, and I were close, really close. We were only a year apart, so we were each other's first friend. We were best friends. But then we grew up and we grew apart. I always had trouble making friends and so I was more reliant on her than she was on me. Anna was a social butterfly – everyone just gravitated towards her. She had no shortage of friends and as we grew older it seemed she had less time for me."

Owen paused for a moment to gather his thoughts. A glance to his side told him that he had Luke's undivided attention. Luke's rod was sitting next to him, tossed aside at some point during Owen's tale, which was just as well since he hadn't truly been using it anyway. Owen deduced that Luke would not become an avid fisherman anytime soon. Luke was watching Owen now, patiently waiting for him to continue talking.

Owen prepared himself for the next part, the part that he could barely admit to himself, let alone to someone else. But he knew that he had to say it. Luke needed to know this. He deserved to know this.

"After high school," Owen continued, "we both went away to college. Well, Anna went first, and I felt like she was abandoning me. We had words and if I'm being honest, the relationship was fractured from that point on. I was being ridiculous, trying to get her to stay. It was hypocritical of me too because I left for college the year after. But I didn't give any of that a thought at the time. I was so selfish. I wanted things my way, and I really didn't care about her feelings or what she wanted. Well, it all fell apart after college when I came back here."

"You came back here?" Luke interrupted.

"Yeah," was Owen's offhanded reply. Then, seeing the confusion on Luke's face, he explained. "I guess I didn't tell you, did I? This was our family home. Anna and I grew up here. Our parents built this place from the ground up, and they left it to me and Anna when they died. In fact, I used to sleep in the room you're in now. Anna was in the room right across the hall."

"Really?"

"Yep, but anyway," Owen continued his story, "after college I came home, and Anna didn't. Our parents were gone by then. They'd died while we were in college. Dad had a stroke and not too long after, mom had a heart attack. Anna used to say that she died of a broken heart.

"Regardless, she didn't want to come back here with mom and dad gone. She said it was too depressing, that it wouldn't feel like home anymore. I told her we could make it feel like home, but I couldn't persuade her. I could hear what she was saying, but I didn't care because in the end it just felt like she was rejecting me. Like by refusing to return to our home, she was refusing to return to me, refusing to be a family again. I know that doesn't make sense, but I was extremely insecure."

Owen stared out at the lake, unseeing. He could still see the pain on his sister's face as he hurled insults at her. It was a vision that haunted him to this day, all these years later. He doubted he would ever forget the tears in her eyes, tears that he'd put there.

A rare breeze blew across the lake but was quickly snuffed out by the humidity. Owen cleared his throat and hurried on, anxious to finish his story, so that he could shove the painful memories away again.

"I didn't handle her decision well. I decided that if she was rejecting me then I would reject her. So that's what I did. I said a lot of things, hurtful things. Don't ask me to repeat them because I won't. I'll just say that I didn't mean any of it and I regretted it the moment the words left my mouth. But some things you can't take back. You can apologize all you want, but the person can't unhear them."

Owen risked a look at Luke, attempting to gauge how he'd taken this information. Luke was staring out at the water flowing beneath them, his feet dangling off the side of the dock, so Owen continued.

"That was the last conversation I had with my sister - me screaming ugly hateful things that I didn't mean. I didn't even try to apologize at first, even though I missed her like crazy. My pride kept me from acknowledging what I'd done. Then, as time went by, I grew older and a little wiser, and I was finally ready to make amends. I tried reaching out, only to find that all her contact information had changed. I tried looking for her, but by then she had a different name. I guess she changed it when she got married. I didn't even know she was married. Didn't know she'd had kids."

Having already told him the details, Owen figured he may as well admit to Luke the ugly truth.

"That's why I haven't been in your life. My pride and selfish-ness caused me to be a terrible brother. And because I was a terrible brother, I wasn't around to do my job as an uncle. But I'm here now Luke. I know I'm late to the party but I'm here. And like I said, I'm older and wiser. Now I understand how important family is, and how it's not something you just throw away."

They sat in silence, the words spoken hanging loudly between them.

It was Owen that broke the quiet, posing a question he was afraid he already knew the answer to.

"Why do you two dress alike? You have the same haircut, the same clothes. With your small frame and Lacey in baggy clothes, if I hadn't been told otherwise, I would've thought that you were two young boys, around 12 or 13."

Silence.

"But something tells me that's intentional. Am I right?"

Luke gave a slight shrug but didn't speak, and Owen took it as confirmation that his suspicions were correct.

"It makes sense, I guess. After all, men who go after teenage girls aren't as likely to mess with a 12-year-old boy, are they?"

Luke still didn't speak. He didn't even look at Owen, his eyes remained fixed on the water below.

Owen felt the heat of anger rise up in his chest along with a surge of protectiveness. He may not have known with certainty what his niece and nephew had endured during their time in the foster care system (and he'd bet money that Luke wouldn't be divulging details anytime soon), but the boy's reaction was enough to confirm Owen's worst fears.

His first instinct was to demand information from Luke. Owen wanted names, and he wanted to personally see that every one of them paid dearly. But even more than that, he wanted to take care of Luke and Lacey. He wanted to make them feel safe again. So, he tampered down his rage and his own desire for vengeance, and addressed Luke.

"You know," Owen said gently, "you don't have to worry about that here. No one's going to mess with her. Or with you."

Owen pretended not to notice Luke wiping away a tear. Instead, he sat with him in silence and hoped his words would sink in. Owen didn't need him to talk. He needed him to listen.

The quiet was broken by the shrill sound of Owen's phone ringing. This was particularly startling for Owen because his phone almost never rang. But one look at the screen had him answering in a panic. Surely, she wouldn't be calling him unless it was an emergency.

But the voice on the other end wasn't a girl's voice at all. It was a woman's voice, one that he'd know anywhere.

"Hi neighbor," she said in a sing-song voice that instantly put Owen in a bad mood.

"Why are you calling me?" he demanded. "First you kidnap my niece and now you're using her phone. For what? To demand a ransom?"

"I didn't kidnap her," the cheerful voice turned indignant at his accusation. "I had no idea she didn't have your permission."

"You didn't ask."

"She's 14 Owen. What are you gonna lock her up in a cage and never let her out. That'll work out great!"

"Is that why you called me? To criticize my parenting skills? Or did you just need someone to yell at, and I'm the nearest target?"

"Oh, right," Annika said, as if she had forgotten the original purpose of her phone call.

Owen shook his head. Some people were impossible to deal with, and she ranked at the top of the list.

"The reason I called," she said, "was to tell you about Lacey."

"Yeah, I figured that part out myself."

"Are you going to let me talk?" Annika snapped.

Owen grumbled something along the lines of "You've been talking this whole time," which she ignored.

"Lacey's sick," Annika blurted out.

"What?!" Owen jumped to his feet, his forgotten fishing pole rolling onto the dock.

"Well, she's not really sick. She's just not feeling well."

"And it took you 20 minutes to tell me this?" Owen bellowed.

"It's not a big deal," Annika said calmly.

"Not a big-" Owen tried to control his fury that this intolerable woman was being so cavalier about the health of his niece. "I'm on my way," he managed to get out through gritted teeth.

"Oh, you don't have to come. We've made her comfortable and she'll feel better soon. I'll drive her back home then."

"I'm on my way," Owen repeated, then hung up the phone before he had to hear another useless word out of that woman's mouth. To think he'd entrusted her with his niece's well-being. What was he thinking?

Owen wasn't surprised to turn around and find Luke standing at attention. He'd evidently heard enough of Owen's phone call to know that Lacey was in trouble, and he was now ready to go. Indeed, he had repacked their fishing gear into the utility bag that Owen kept everything in. Now he was holding the bag and their two rods in his arms. He had even called Nosey back from his explorations and had him standing at his side.

"Are we going to get Lacey?" Luke asked.

Owen nodded. "She's sick," he explained. "I don't know what it is, but apparently, she's not feeling well enough to come home. I'm going next door to check on her. You can come along if you want."

"Sick?" Luke asked, sounding panicked. Then, astonishingly, his whole demeanor changed. "Ohhh," he said and waved off Owen's concern. "She'll be fine." Then he actually sat back down.

Owen almost fell over. Who was this kid and what had he done with Luke? Just that morning, he'd been ready to launch an all-out attack because his sister would be away from him for a couple of hours. Now that she was gravely ill, he couldn't be bothered to care? Owen decided that he didn't have time to deal with the mood swings of a teenage boy right now. His niece needed him and that was what mattered.

"I'm going next door to get her," he announced. Then he

headed back towards the house, not really caring if Luke followed or not.

After a moment of hesitation, Luke called out. "Wait, I want to go with you. This could get interesting." And he rushed to catch up with Owen, Nosey close behind.

⁂ 13 ⁂

When Annika Jones had invited Owen Stillwater's niece to church, she had done so out of courtesy. She had no expectations that the girl would want to go. Plus, Annika wasn't so sure that Owen would even allow his niece to go with her, considering his unfounded animosity toward her. Thus, she was surprised when she'd gotten a text message late at night from Lacey, asking for a ride. Of course, Annika agreed to pick her up and was knocking on Owen's front door at the agreed upon time.

When Owen answered, Annika was pleased. She'd wanted to thank him for looking beyond his prejudices towards her and allowing her to take Lacey to church. However, she never got the chance because Lacey appeared in a whirlwind and took charge of the situation. She maneuvered herself in between Annika and Owen, and in a matter of moments, she was saying good-bye to her uncle and her brother (who had appeared at the door right behind Owen) and was whisking Annika out the front door. They were in Olivia's pink Range Rover (which Olivia herself was driving) and headed back down the long driveway in record timing, leaving Annika's head spinning.

Annika turned and looked back at Lacey who was sitting

behind Olivia in the passenger seat. She looked the picture of perfect innocence with a bright smile, a cute dress that looked to be new (yep, the tag was still attached to the side), and a pair of pink flip-flops. Lacey noticed Annika looking at her and gave her a dazzling smile.

Annika narrowed her eyes at her. She wasn't taken in by this cute act. After running a camp, Annika had spent enough time around young girls to know that the cuter they looked, the more devious they were, which was why she'd definitely be keeping an eye on this one.

Yep, Annika had seen things in her life. She was older. Wiser. Nothing could surprise her anymore.

"I don't think we should sit with the MacPhearsons at church today."

"What?"

Annika tried to turn around in her seat at Olivia's shocking statement, but unfortunately for her, Olivia hit a bump in the dirt road at that very moment, sending Annika (who had yet to put on her seatbelt) rocking about in her seat. She hit the roof, she hit the door, and then she hit Olivia in the arm in retribution.

"Oww!" Olivia rubbed the spot on her upper arm that had just received the angry punch. "What was that for?"

"That was for trying to kill me," Annika said, as she grabbed desperately for the seatbelt before Olivia could finish the job.

"It's not my fault you didn't put on your seatbelt."

Annika didn't have a response for that logic, so she just buckled the seatbelt and quietly fumed. Then she remembered Olivia's initial statement.

"You don't want to sit with the MacPhearsons? Why not?"

To Annika, the MacPhearsons were practically family. When she and Olivia had moved to Florida the previous year, they had left behind their mother and father in Washington, DC. Prior to that, their family unit had been very close and spent a lot of time together. It had been difficult for Annika to make the decision to move away. Difficult but necessary, and she didn't regret it one bit. She knew that they'd made the right choice. But although their parents had visited the sisters in Florida twice already and had faithfully kept in contact, she still missed them, especially her father with whom Annika shared a special bond.

That was where the MacPhearsons had come into the picture. Don and Meredith had all but adopted Annika and Olivia into their family almost immediately upon their arrival to Port St. Annabelle. They'd played somewhat of a surrogate parental role in the sisters' lives. When their real parents had met the MacPhearsons for the first time, the four older adults had embraced as good friends, even though they'd never met before. Annika's father had even pulled her aside and told her how pleased he was that she'd found such good friends.

Thus, Olivia's announcement that she'd rather not sit with the MacPhearsons (whom they sat with every Sunday morning) was shocking and bewildering to Annika, to say the least.

"Why don't you want to sit with them?" Annika pressed.

Olivia shot her a side look but wouldn't answer.

"Spill it," Annika ordered.

"Well," Olivia began, which was the tell-tale sign alerting Annika that nothing her sister was about to say would be true. "I just don't think it would be prudent. I mean, we shouldn't be sitting in the same seat with the same people every week. We should move about, socialize more, get to know our fellow citizens in the community. You know, it wouldn't hurt you to expand your friend circle."

Annika just stared at Olivia, amazed at the heaping pile of crap that had just come out of her sister's mouth.

Then a small voice piped in from the backseat, surprising Annika who had forgotten that the girl was there. She'd been so quiet, and Annika had been distracted by the bruise that was forming on her elbow from her crash into the door.

"Is it that you just don't want to sit next to the hardware store guy? Phillip MacPhearson? That's his name, right?"

Olivia gasped, giving herself away.

Annika pounced on her reaction. "That's it, isn't it? What is going on with you two?"

"Nothing. I mean, I don't know what you mean," was Olivia's unconvincing answer.

"Really? Cause two weeks ago you were gazing lovingly into each other's eyes every chance you could, and now you're trying to avoid him."

"Not true," Olivia lied.

"He calls - you won't answer the phone. He comes by - you won't go to the door. I think that's called avoiding. Let me look it up to be sure though." Annika pulled her phone from her purse and began typing the word avoiding into the search bar.

"I'm mad at him, okay," Olivia finally admitted.

"Why?" Annika asked, putting her phone down as it had served its purpose of dragging the truth out of Olivia. "What happened?"

"We broke up," Olivia announced.

"Well did you tell him? Cause I don't think he knows."

Olivia didn't answer but shot a guilty look Annika's way.

"Okay, so then you didn't break up."

Olivia shrugged.

Annika shook her head. "Okay, we'll deal with that part later. First let's deal with why you felt the need to break-up but not break-up with him."

Olivia shrugged again.

"Did he do something?" Annika probed.

Olivia shook her head.

"He didn't do anything?"

"That's just it," Olivia exploded. "He hasn't done anything. We've been on just a handful of dates and that's it. He's dragging his feet like he's afraid of commitment or something and I've had enough. So, I'm moving on. Leaving him in the dust. I'm over that guy. He's in the past and I'm looking to the future. Totally over him."

"Okay then."

"So, we'll sit somewhere else today."

"Oh no. I'm sitting in my normal spot next to my friends. You can sit wherever you want though. Once you talk to him and actually end things, we can revisit the seating arrangement, if you'd like."

Olivia shot her a scathing look. "So much for solidarity."

A shrug was all Annika offered. By this point they had made it to the church and Olivia was maneuvering the SUV into a vacant spot on the lawn. While Olivia was focusing on her parking task, Annika glanced back at Lacey.

"What do you think?" Annika asked the teenager. "Should we sit with the MacPhearsons?"

"You're asking her?" Olivia said incredulously. "You're allowing a teenager to determine my love life?"

Annika snickered. "Olivia, at this point she knows more about your relationship than you do." Then she turned back to Lacey, "So, where should we sit?"

Lacey pondered the question for a moment before answering. "Hmmm," she said. "I think we should sit with the MacPhearsons."

Olivia scowled.

"But," Lacey continued, "Miss Olivia should sit all the way on the end. That way you get to sit with your friends and she won't feel so uncomfortable."

Annika and Olivia looked at each other and both shrugged, neither of them finding a problem with Lacey's arrangement.

"Okay then. It's settled," Annika announced, and they all exited the vehicle.

The community church that the sisters patroned was a humble establishment. In contrast to the elegant chapel just down the street, their church was rundown and although not in shambles, one could be forgiven for assuming that it was. There was no space for parking, leaving the congregants to make do haphazardly on the front lawn. Indeed, the three of them were now carefully making their way through the dew-drenched grass where Olivia and everyone else had parked, trying not to get their shoes too wet or muddy. Annika looked down at the pink flip-flops that Lacey was wearing and instinctively knew that the girl's shoes would need to be cleaned later.

The building itself was less than impressive. It looked like whoever had built it had been in a hurry, or maybe just wasn't very good at building things. It looked lopsided, or perhaps it was just leaning. And it was halfway through a fresh paint job, leaving the building two different colors – neon peach and deep purple - neither of which was very appealing to the eye.

Phillip MacPhearson, Olivia's not-boyfriend boyfriend, was the church's unofficial handyman and painter, and he was known for his interesting color choices. But while he may possibly be color blind, he was a highly skilled and competent carpenter. Annika knew this from experience, as Phillip along with several of his friends, had restored her home just last year. It had been in shambles, but Phillip and his friends had practically rebuilt the cabin from the ground up. Thus, even though the church building looked like it was breaking at least 50 safety violations, she knew that if Phillip had declared the building safe, then it was.

As they entered the church with the other parishioners, Annika couldn't help but travel down memory lane to the first time she'd attended services there. It was nothing like she had ever experienced before. Coming from Washington, D.C., Annika had been accustomed to elegant churches with extravagant details and well-structured services. Her experience here had been the complete opposite.

Looking over at Lacey, Annika realized that this would be her first time attending service here. This led Annika to wonder what type of church Lacey had attended before. Was she used to perfectly scheduled services, white-gloved ushers, and robed mass choirs the way Annika had been? Would this experience be as much of a culture shock to Lacey as it had been for Annika when she'd first arrived? Regardless, Annika knew that if Lacey gave it a chance, just as Annika had learned to, then she would grow to love the church as well.

The three of them walked through the foyer, past the greeters all wearing oversized hats decorated with flowers and into the main part of the church. As usual, the building was alive with people. Two rows of wooden pews were filling quickly and as they walked down the center aisle towards the front of the sanctuary, Annika could see that the building would be at maximum capacity soon. Still, the Jones sisters were regulars, and had no trouble finding their usual spot in the quickly crowding room.

They headed to the front of the church to a pew that was nearly full, but had just enough space left for the three of them to sit comfortably. They sat next to an African-American family of three, consisting of an older couple and a younger gentleman dressed in a turquoise shirt covered in rhinestones.

"I gave him that shirt," Olivia hissed to Annika. "How dare he wear it today?"

Annika just shrugged, choosing not to debate Phillip's clothing choices with Olivia. Instead, she made her way into the pew with the other two following her lead. Annika sat closest to the MacPhearson family, which put her right next to Phillip. Normally, she wouldn't have minded, but today he kept looking in their direction with sad doleful eyes. Lacey sat in the middle of the two sisters, and as previously discussed, Olivia sat on the end in the aisle seat, her gaze strictly focused on everything but the gentleman constantly staring in her direction.

The worship service was in full swing. On the stage directly in front of them, the worship singers, dressed casually in street attire, were belting out a powerful tune to the booming music played by the band. Almost everyone was on their feet, clapping and singing along. Even those who couldn't stand - the elderly, mothers holding infants, etc. - could be found tapping their feet or bobbing their head to the tune. Annika set her purse down on the pew before clapping and singing along as well. This was one of her favorites and though she'd only learned the chorus thus far, she sang that part with gusto.

When the song ended, everyone took their seats, and the sermon began. Although normally inspired by the pastor, this time Annika found it difficult to focus on the message. Her attention constantly diverting to Lacey. Annika kept watching her, wondering if she was enjoying the service and hoping that she would want to return. Lacey's demeanor gave Annika no clues as to what she was thinking. She watched the pastor attentively, but her face held no expression. Annika couldn't decipher what it meant. And when Annika wasn't preoccupied with Lacey, she was distracted by Phillip looking over with those pathetic lovesick eyes and Olivia resolutely ignoring Phillip's lovesick eyes.

Once service had ended, Olivia jumped to her feet and grabbed her purse with impressive speed. She was out the pew and nearly to safety when the older woman, Meredith MacP-hearson, called out to her.

"Oh Olivia! Olivia, just a moment!"

Olivia hung her head in an acceptance of defeat and returned to the pew to speak to her ex-boyfriend's mother. To her credit, by the time she'd reached the woman, Olivia had managed to plaster a smile onto her face.

"Hi Meredith," Olivia said, sounding cheerful enough. "How are you today."

By this point they'd all managed to exit the pew and were standing as a group in the aisle. Thankfully, most of the parishioners were either engaged in conversations themselves or had already headed toward the exits, as they would have blocked anyone attempting to get by them.

"Well, I can't complain. Don here's been having some back trouble lately." Meredith gestured to her husband next to her. "But he's feeling much better today, so all in all we're doing well.

Except that... well, we haven't seen you in a while. You stopped coming over to visit."

Phillip released an audible groan, and his dark skin began to turn purple from blushing. Olivia stared at the floor, clearly not wanting to discuss her break-up with her ex-boyfriend's mother. Annika cringed inwardly from the awkwardness of the situation, and wished she was anywhere else right now. Next to her, Lacey seemed just as uncomfortable as the adults around her as she wouldn't even look anyone in the face. She kept her head down, staring at her shoes, probably wishing she were somewhere else just as much as Annika did.

Meredith must have realized just how uncomfortable she had made everyone because she hurriedly added, "It's okay. I'm sure you have your reasons." At this she gave a very pointed look to her son before continuing. "In any case, that's not what I wanted to speak to you about. Well, not really. That is to say, I did want to invite you over for dinner."

Olivia began shaking her head and opened her mouth to offer what most definitely was going to be a decline, but Meredith continued speaking before she could utter a word.

"It's a special occasion," Meredith said. "My daughter, April, you remember I told you about her, well she's coming back home from college. It's Spring Break and she'll only be here for the week, so we're going to be having a special dinner for her Tuesday night and it would just mean so much to me and Don if you could come."

Don nodded enthusiastically at his wife's statement, and then added to the invitation. "Annika, we'd love for you to come too. And bring your young friend there." He pointed to Lacey, who not only didn't acknowledge him, but she didn't even look up. She simply sat back down in the pew that they'd all just left and continued to stare at the floor.

Annika might have found her behavior peculiar if she weren't distracted by Olivia's attempts to avoid Meredith's dinner party.

"Umm," Olivia said, pretending to think it over, "I'm just not sure that's a good idea."

"Well, of course it is," Meredith insisted. "We really want you to come."

"We sure do," Don seconded.

"I just don't know if I'll be able to. I have so much going on. I'm busy every night this week."

"Oh but, April will be so disappointed if you're not there," Meredith said. "She's really been looking forward to meeting you. She told me that just yesterday."

"Umm," Olivia squeaked.

"Also," Don said, "I have some information to share with you. Official council business."

"Don's on the city council," Meredith said.

This actually wasn't true. Over the past couple of months, Don had begun attending every city council meeting and he had become friends with several council members. Technically, this made him more of a council fan than a council member. No one bothered to correct Meredith though. They simply nodded in agreement with her.

"We can discuss what's been going on at dinner," Don said.

Annika shriveled inside at the thought of sitting through dinner while Don carried on about official council business. She loved the man like a father, but ever since this new interest in city politics had taken hold, Don had developed the tendency to drone on about mundane council affairs every time he got the chance. She couldn't imagine being held hostage through an entire dinner while he updated them on new sewer lines or updated zoning codes. Annika would hate to be in Olivia's shoes right now.

"I'm sure you can spare one night," Annika said unhelpfully.

Olivia glared at her sister, and then turned to Meredith and said, "I'll try to make it. I'll really try."

"That's all we want," Don said. "We can't ask for any more than that." Then he took his wife's arm. "Come on honey. Let's get on home." Then the two of them waved good-bye to the group and left the church arm-in-arm.

"I'm really sorry about that," Phillip said after his parents had left. "If you–"

"Hmmph." Before he could complete his sentence, Olivia turned a cold shoulder to him, marched down the aisle and out the church.

Phillip trudged slowly after her, head hung low.

Annika shook her head at the spectacle she'd just witnessed. "Leave it to Olivia to turn a day at church into her own personal soap opera." She turned around to find Lacey still sitting in the pew.

"What are you doing still sitting there? It's time to go."

She walked closer to Lacey who was leaning back against the pew with her eyes closed. For the first time, Annika noticed she was trembling and her brown skin looked washed out and pale.

"Are you okay?" she asked, although it was clear to anyone with eyes that the girl was not okay.

Lacey didn't even open her eyes. She just slowly shook her head in answer to Annika's question.

"Okay," Annika said, "let's get you out of here. And I think it's time to call your uncle."

14

L uke hopped into the passenger seat of his uncle's truck with unbridled enthusiasm. A glance over at his uncle who was already settled behind the wheel, confirmed that he was riled up. In the short time that Luke had known the man, it had become apparent that his uncle was a calm person. So far, it seemed that nothing really rattled him. Nothing except the waitress neighbor woman, who for reasons unknown to Luke, really got under Uncle Owen's skin. Just the thought of the woman seemed to make his uncle's blood boil. Luke was certain that when Uncle Owen got to her house, they would squabble again. And in a town, which he was beginning to realize was exceptionally dull, Luke was willing to take any form of excitement that came his way.

Initially, he had been uncertain about whether to tag along on this rescue mission. This was a rare opportunity that his uncle was guaranteed to be away from the cabin. Luke would have free reign to continue his investigation. He could dig further into that secret room with the boxes, which Luke guessed were filled with the mysterious woman in the photograph's belongings. He could possibly even search through the main bedroom, although Luke doubted his uncle would be gone long enough for a thorough examination of that space. The temptation to stay behind and ferret out his uncle's secrets was great, but in the end, the promise of entertainment won out.

The drive was short, and they were walking up the gravel path to the front door in minutes. Luke got a full view of the neighbor's lodgings for the first time and his eyes nearly bulged from their sockets. The neighbor lived in a log cabin as well, but it was nearly twice the size as Uncle Owen's. Were all the people in this town rich? It was certainly looking that way.

The front porch held a table and chairs for gathering on one side, and a chair swing for relaxing on the other, along with colorful potted plants for decoration.

Uncle Owen didn't marvel at the surroundings, or appreciate the decorative furnishings, or hesitate at all. He marched right to the door and banged with his fist.

The jarring sound of hand meeting a solid wooden door made Luke jump. He looked at his uncle quizzically.

"Why didn't you just ring the doorbell?" he asked.

Uncle Owen looked at Luke, who pointed to the small round button installed next to the door. With a sheepish look, Uncle Owen pressed the little button and stood back.

Once the chime of the doorbell ended, the front door swung open and an African-American woman with curly hair, wearing a ton of make-up and a stylish looking dress stood in the doorway, scrutinizing the two gentlemen standing on the front porch. Luke wasn't sure who she was. She wasn't the waitress that he'd met days ago, but she certainly seemed comfortable in the waitress' house as she stood with her hand on her hips. She was looking the two of them over and by the look on her face, she didn't care for what she saw.

If Luke was uncomfortable, Uncle Owen was impatient. "Where is she?" he demanded.

At his question, the woman turned and yelled over her shoulder, "Annika, you have company!" Then she walked back into the house, leaving the door open.

Uncle Owen must have taken this as an invitation to enter, because he walked right into the house. Luke thought it over, shrugged and followed behind him.

"I wasn't asking about *her*," Uncle Owen said, as if it pained him to say the woman's name. "I was asking about my niece."

The woman turned around and glowered at both Luke and Uncle Owen. If looks could kill, the two of them would be dead. Luke gulped audibly and Uncle Owen shifted from one foot to the other, looking much less confident than he had a moment ago. So, the two of them stood in the foyer, (she hadn't invited them any further into the home) and tried to look anywhere but at the woman who looked like she was plotting their deaths in her mind.

Luke looked up at the wooden beams stretched across the tall ceiling. He admired the towering green plant beside the door that grew taller than him. He noted the pair of hot pink heels lying next to the umbrella stand as though they'd been stripped off and tossed there the moment the owner had stepped inside the door. He studied the wooden floor beneath his grubby old sneakers. And he counted the seconds as they ticked by slowly.

They only had a short while to endure this awkwardness before the woman being summoned arrived. Luke recognized her as the waitress that he'd recently met. But by the look on her face, she was even less pleased to see the two of them than the woman who'd answered the door.

At this point, Luke didn't really care about the feud between his uncle and this woman. He just wanted to collect his sister and get out of there. However, this proved to be more challenging than one would've expected because, as Luke had initially anticipated, sparks flew and drama ensued.

It started the moment the second woman (Annika was what the first woman had called her) arrived. The other woman threw one final withering look at the two visitors and stomped away.

"You'll have to forgive Olivia," the waitress said. "She's not feeling very friendly toward the male population at the moment thanks to a bit of drama with her boyfriend." Then she crossed her arms and nailed Uncle Owen with a menacing scowl. "But then again, you aren't supposed to be here," she accused.

Uncle Owen squared his shoulders and stared her back down. "I'm here for my niece. Hand her over and I'll be on my way," he commanded.

"I told you she'd be fine and that we'd bring her home when she's feeling better," Annika responded through gritted teeth, making Luke forget about how anxious he was to leave just moments before. This was the show he'd come to see.

"Oh," Uncle Owen responded, "well, excuse me if I don't take your word for it. I think I'll just see for myself."

"You don't need to see," Annika said, her voice now rising.

"Really?" Uncle Owen's voice rose to match hers. "Tell me what's wrong with her then? Does she have a cold? The flu? What is it? You don't know, do you? So clearly, I do need to see her to find out what's wrong with her."

"I know what's wrong with her!"

"No, you don't!"

"Yes, I do!"

"Then what is it? Tell me what's wrong with her! What's wrong with her?!"

"She started her period and she's cramping!"

Luke, who had been watching this entire exchange with nothing short of glee, couldn't stop the snort of laughter that escaped when Annika shouted this information so loud that everyone within a ten-mile radius must have heard it. The subsequent look of horror that came across his uncle's face afterward only made him laugh that much harder.

To his credit though, Uncle Owen recovered quickly, or at least attempted to. "Well," he spluttered, "well, why didn't you just say so in the first place?"

"It's called discretion. Maybe you've heard of it."

They glowered at each other for a moment.

"Would you please go and get her so I can take her home?" Uncle Owen finally broke the stare down.

"Why can't she stay here for now? She's perfectly safe and we can keep her comfortable. We know how to take care of her."

"I know how to take care of her. I'm a doctor."

At this statement from his uncle, Luke, who had been following the volleying match closely and enjoying every minute of it, sobered quickly. A doctor? Uncle Owen was a doctor? Exactly when was he planning on sharing that bit of information? Well, it would explain why he was able to buy new clothes and new phones for Luke and Lacey without breaking a sweat. The guy must have a ton of money.

But, Luke thought cynically, that didn't rule out criminal activity. He could be a doctor and still be a criminal. Plenty of people were. And if he was a doctor, when did he see his patients? Uncle Owen hadn't gone to work once since Luke and Lacey had arrived. He hadn't even mentioned work. It was like he didn't have a job. Now if that wasn't suspicious, Luke didn't know what was. Yeah, he would need to do further investigation on this matter. But that would have to wait until later. For the time being, the show before him continued and he didn't want to miss a moment.

"I know you're a doctor," Annika said. (Apparently Uncle Owen wasn't lying about that fact.) "Obviously, you can take care of her, but don't you think she might be more comfortable right now with two women, than with an uncle that she doesn't know very well?"

"I, well I-" Uncle Owen started, then stopped.

"And you're going to make her get up and walk around in pain when she's already resting comfortably?"

"I hadn't thought about that." Uncle Owen then mumbled something incoherent.

"What?"

Uncle Owen sighed like the next words he was about to speak would be pure agony for him. "You might be right," he finally said at normal volume. He spoke the words, but he would not look at her, choosing instead to stare at a fascinating spot on the wall. This was just as well because the smug look on Annika's face would surely have started another fight between the two of them had he seen it. "She can stay here until she's feeling better."

"Okay then. My sister and I will take very good care of her."

"Fine."

"Fine."

"Okay."

"Okay."

After this exchange Uncle Owen seemed to be in a hurry to leave. It probably had something to do with the fact that he'd just lost this round in such an embarrassing way, Luke mused. In any case, Uncle Owen turned and headed back out the door where they'd entered a short while ago without even saying good-bye.

"Come on," were the only words he spoke, or rather grunted toward Luke.

Luke followed after him as he returned to the truck.

It wasn't until after they were both seated inside, that Uncle Owen turned to look at Luke. He had been about to turn the key to start the truck, and now it sat in the ignition abandoned by Uncle Owen's hand.

"You knew," he said, the look on his face indicating that this was a revelation to him. "You knew what was wrong with her, didn't you?"

"Yeah," Luke responded nonchalantly. He had his phone out now and was scrolling through it, barely giving his uncle any attention now that the show had ended. "Happens every month. She'll be better by tomorrow."

"So," Uncle Owen asked, "if you knew then why didn't you tell me?"

Luke shrugged. He was still staring at his phone as he responded. "You didn't ask."

L uke's prediction about Lacey proved true. The next
day she returned home just in time for lunch in good
health and in good spirits. Owen, who was in the
kitchen tossing the arugula salad with the homemade dressing he
had just finished preparing, was startled by her bursting into the
room. But at the sight of her bright face, he immediately broke
into a smile. She answered with a small shy smile of her own.

"I'm back," was all she said, in that quiet voice Owen was
beginning to get used to. "Thanks for letting me stay there."

Owen cleared his throat and turned his gaze back to the food
he'd been working on. "It's nothing," he said quickly. "Just, um,
go and wash your hands. It's time for lunch." He looked back to
her. "You haven't eaten yet, have you?"

She shook her head.

"Okay, well go on and get washed up for lunch then."

Lacey left the kitchen, and Owen went back to his salad,
which at this point was over tossed. He swallowed to try and
remove the lump that had formed in his throat.

He hadn't been prepared for the overwhelming relief that
he'd felt upon seeing her walk into the kitchen, alive and well.
The truth was that when he'd gotten the phone call yesterday

that she'd taken ill, it had frightened him to the core. Owen was a realist. He didn't romanticize situations or gloss over things. He was a direct and honest man who preferred to face reality rather than sugarcoat matters. He always had been and always would be.

That was why when he'd agreed to take in his sister's children, he'd done so only because he knew that they had nowhere else to go. He'd been well aware that he was the absolute worst person for the job. But alas, the job had fallen to him. So, he'd taken them on with the determination to do his best for them. But when he'd gotten that phone call yesterday, it was a feeling he wouldn't wish upon anyone.

Logically, he knew that people got sick and sometimes there was nothing that could be done about it. Lord knows he'd learned that lesson the hard way. Even still, when he'd learned that Lacey was sick, he couldn't help but think that she'd been under his care for only a few days, and he'd already messed up. Is this what it was like to be a parent? Spiraling into a panic every time the kid wasn't feeling well? How did people survive this? He and Natasha had definitely made the right decision by not having children.

"The table's set."

The sound of Luke's voice pulled Owen from his thoughts and back to the present moment. He looked up and saw that Luke had entered through the swinging door that led to the dining room. It was the same door that Lacey had left through moments earlier.

"Set a plate for Lacey," Owen instructed him. "She made it back in time for lunch."

"Yeah, I saw her," Luke said, as he grabbed the tray of grilled chicken sliders that he had helped Owen prepare. He headed back toward the dining room with the food, Owen following behind him with the salad.

"It's real interesting," Luke threw over his shoulder, "how she always seems to show up when it's time to eat but disappear when it's time to work."

Owen, who hadn't noticed this before, let that ruminate for a moment, then replied, "Sounds like I need to make a chore chart."

They placed their dishes on the table where Lacey was already seated and waiting.

"Ooh, this looks yummy," she gushed "I can't wait to eat."

Luke narrowed his eyes at her. "Yeah, I bet," he mumbled.

She either didn't hear this comment or chose to ignore him as she reached toward the tray of sliders. But she stopped herself mid-grab and retreated her hand.

"I think we should pray," she announced.

"What?" Owen, who had been drinking from a glass of ice water, had to set his glass down before he dropped it. "What did you say?"

"I said I think we should pray," Lacey repeated, although dimmed a bit and she sounded much less sure of herself this time.

Luke snorted. "Yeah, we're not doing that," he said as he helped himself to a couple of sliders and moved on to the salad. "You go to church once and now you want to pray. By the way, do you even know how to pray?"

A small no was the answer.

"Thought so. Pass the ketchup."

Lacey handed over the squeezable bottle and Luke set to work, shaking and squeezing the condiment onto one chicken slider after the other.

"It's not hard."

Luke stopped squeezing the ketchup and he and Lacey both looked over at Owen.

"Praying," Owen explained. "It's not hard at all. It's just like talking. Except you're talking to God and you're telling him what's on your mind."

Owen looked up to see two identical pairs of eyes staring at him. That brought him to his senses.

"Not that we're going to be praying. Luke's right. We should just eat before the food gets cold."

Luke didn't need to be told twice. He grabbed a slider and began devouring it. Owen helped himself to the arugula salad, and after hesitating a moment longer, Lacey once again grabbed for a slider.

Once the eating commenced very little talking took place as the food proved to be, as Lacey had guessed, very yummy. Towards the end of the meal, when stomachs were getting tight and the eating slowed down, Lacey brought up her overnight stay at the neighbors'.

"Miss Annika was really nice to me," was how she broached the subject.

"I'm glad to hear that," Owen responded.

"She went out of her way to help me," she continued, and then after a pause said, "so I invited her to dinner. To thank her."

To his credit, Owen didn't react visibly to the bombshell that Lacey dropped. In fact, he didn't react at all. Not outwardly at least. He'd been in the middle of washing down his meal with a large gulp of water when she'd made the announcement. He took his time drinking from his glass before placing it gently back onto the table.

Luke, however, did react. At Lacey's statement, he choked on the last piece of slider he'd been eating. After a moment of violent coughing, he managed to bring up the half-chewed meat. It escaped his mouth and fell back onto his plate. He stared at the mangled food for half a second before grabbing it and shoving it back into his mouth for another try.

Owen didn't bother trying to hide his disgust. Instead, he turned his attention to Lacey, who was looking at him expectantly, with an adorable smile across her face.

"I wish you would have spoken to me about it first," he somehow managed to say, instead of the long line of obscenities that came to mind. "I'm not sure if that's really a good idea."

"Why not?" Lacey persisted.

"Because," Owen fought to keep his voice level as he explained, "because she's unpleasant. From the day she and her sister moved in that woman has caused me nothing but trouble. Every chance she gets she's insipid, she's horrendous, she's volatile, and she's... she's..."

"Unpleasant," Luke finished for him.

"Very," Owen agreed. "Which is why the last thing I want to do is sit across the dinner table from her for an entire evening." Owen grimaced at the thought of it.

"I'm sorry," Lacey looked down at her lap, her smile replaced with a slightly protruding lower lip. "She was just so nice to me, and I didn't know how to thank her."

"You could've just said thank you," Luke said. Lacey shot him a scorching look that, if Owen had blinked, he would've missed. Then her eyes were down again, with her lower lip trembling, followed by what sounded like a sniffle.

Owen sighed before finally relenting. The truth was, he did owe the woman, especially after he'd made a fool of himself the day before. And he'd much rather repay her kindness now, than have her holding it over his head. He didn't know her well enough to be sure, but he just bet she'd be the type to rub it in.

"Alright," he said, "we can have her over sometime."

"How about tomorrow night? Cause that's when I told her to come."

"Okay," Owen forced himself to say, "we can have her over tomorrow night."

"Good," Lacey perked up, no sign of tears or a trembling lower lip now that she'd gotten her way. "And um..."

Owen looked at her warily. What could possibly come out of her mouth now?

"The thing is..."

"What?"

Owen's nerves were on end. What was she so nervous about? Not that anything she said could make things worse. He was already doomed to sit through an entire meal with the world's most awful neighbor. But Lacey's hesitation was scaring him.

"What is it?" he said. "Just spit it out."

"Maybe you could be nice to her?"

"Yeah right. Like that'll happen," Luke offered.

Lacey shot him another look which he shrugged off. Then she turned her smile back to Owen. "I mean, she'll be our guest, right? So, umm, you have to be nice to guests. And...well...it won't be much of a thank you if you're rude to her, will it?"

This got Owen's hackles up. "*I'm* rude to *her*? Try the other way around. She's got the worst attitude-"

"Oh, I know," Lacey cut off his tirade before he could really get going, and Owen was left huffing. "I know it's all her," Lacey assured him, "but maybe, just this once, maybe if you go out of your way to be super nice to her, then she might realize how terrible she's been. Maybe then she'll decide to be nice too." And she ended this request by batting her eyes at him.

Owen gave another huff and a puff. He'd almost rather agree to having his eyes poked out. But another look at Lacey's innocent looking face made him crumble.

"Alright," he relented. "I'll *try* to be nice to her. But if she can't act civilized, then that's on her."

"Unbelievable," Luke muttered.

Lacey jumped up from her seat, ignoring Luke and beaming at her uncle. "Thanks Uncle Owen. You're the best Uncle I've ever had. I'm going to go for a walk now if that's okay." And she skipped out of the dining room and out the back door, taking Nosey with her.

Owen was taken off guard by the sudden emotional display from the girl he'd come to think of as mousy and quiet. This new affectionate Lacey was like a burst of fresh air. And he had to be honest, hearing that he was the best uncle she'd ever had, well, that felt pretty darn good. He was reveling in these pleasant thoughts when Luke snapped him out of it by speaking.

"I see she managed to get out of doing work again," Luke

said, gesturing to the table covered in dirty dishes from the meal they'd just finished. "When are you making that chore chart?"

After lunch, Lacey made sure to duck out of the house and make herself scarce, in case Uncle Owen started having second thoughts and wanted to uninvite Miss Annika. No, Lacey knew well enough to take her win and go. She figured the best place to hide out would be next door, which was perfect because she already had business to attend to with the neighbors.

In no real hurry, she strolled through the woods at a leisurely pace, taking in the scenery around her. Lacey and Luke had been moved around a lot in the past 6 months, but each of those placements had been in a metropolitan area. This marked the first time they'd lived in a small town. It was also the first time they'd ever lived in the woods. For Lacey, who loved nature, this gave her the chance to meet in person the wild plants and animals of Florida that she'd only ever read about in books.

Squinting against the bright sunlight, Lacey admired the deep green of the leaves on the trees and listened to the territorial and mating calls of the birds. She sniffed the air. It wasn't watermelon season yet, but she could almost imagine the smell of the ripe fruit in the air.

Lacey let Nosey lead her through the woods to the cabin

next door, just as he had before. When they reached their destination this time though, Lacey didn't hesitate to step onto the property. She felt comfortable enough to walk across the neighbors' land and head up to the back door and knock. Part of her wondered why she felt so comfortable with these people that she'd only known for a few days.

But it wasn't just the sisters that she had become familiar with. Hadn't she just pulled a fast one over on Uncle Owen? Logically, she should be terrified of him finding out that she'd played him. Because the reality was, she didn't really know the guy. She didn't know what he would do if he found out he'd been had. But knowing this, she still didn't feel frightened or worried that he would try to hurt her. Not really. Not like the others. No, it was different now. Lacey couldn't quite put her finger on what it was, but this place felt a whole lot different than the places they'd stayed before. It felt... better.

The sound of the door opening and Nosey's excited barking whipped Lacey from her thoughts. Miss Olivia held the door open for the two of them. She was dressed head-to-toe in another stylish outfit that made Lacey more than a little self-conscious of the baggy t-shirt and shorts she was wearing with her dirty old sneakers. But Miss Olivia seemed to pay no notice to Lacey's shabby appearance as she greeted her with a smile.

"Come in," she ushered Lacey and Nosey inside. "We've just finished eating lunch. I didn't know you were coming over, or I would've saved some for you."

"That's okay," Lacey said, as she walked through the door and headed to the dining room, "I already ate."

"You sure? I can whip you up something really quick."

"No, I'm stuffed. I couldn't eat anything else."

"Okay," Miss Olivia almost looked disappointed that she wouldn't be feeding her.

"Maybe another time," Lacey suggested.

"Of course," Miss Olivia seemed to cheer up at that idea. Then she asked, "To what do we owe the honor of this visit?"

"Oh, um, well I was hoping to talk to Miss Annika. I needed to ask her something."

Lacey had already decided that it wouldn't be prudent to mention that she was dodging her uncle at the moment. Miss Olivia and Miss Annika may be nice, but at the end of the day, they were still adults, and adults always ratted you out. So, she would be careful what she said to them, and stick to the script she'd come up with the night before when she'd formed this plan.

At the mention of Miss Annika's name, Miss Olivia did what Lacey really could've done herself to summon the woman. She cupped her hands around her mouth and bellowed out, "Annika! Lacey's here to see you!" Then she turned to Lacey and said at a normal volume, "We should probably invest in an intercom system or something."

Lacey nodded in agreement.

"Have a seat while you wait for her," Miss Olivia said, gesturing to the chairs at the dining room table. In the center of the table, there was a pitcher of what appeared to be water with slices of cucumbers and ice cubes floating about the water. Beside the pitcher were a couple of empty glasses. "Pour us something to drink."

Lacey complied, taking the seat nearest her and filling two of the glasses with the cold beverage. A curious sip confirmed that it was indeed the refreshing cucumber water that Lacey had come to enjoy.

Nosey, who at this point was conditioned for a treat whenever he entered this house, walked straight to his area in the corner and examined his dish. Upon finding it empty, he tapped it impatiently with his paw, and then resorted to whining.

"Alright, alright," Miss Olivia said, as she rushed to appease the demanding dog. While she was attending to Nosey's dietary needs, Miss Annika made it into the dining room.

"Must you yell like a banshee every time we have company?" Miss Annika complained. Miss Olivia, who was bent over and occupied with filling Nosey's dishes with water and treats, ignored her sister.

"Lacey," Miss Annika said, turning her attention to the girl seated at her dining room table, "I was just thinking about you. We have so much work to get done here before camp opens next week and I was hoping you wouldn't mind helping us out a little."

Miss Olivia, who had now finished treating Nosey, stood up and joined in the conversation. "She's right. There's a ton of work to do and no time to do it." She took the seat closest to Lacey and helped herself to one of the glasses Lacey had filled with water. After a long gulp she said, "We could really use your help."

Lacey, who had been nursing her own glass of water, responded excitedly, "I'd love to," without even asking for details. She was sure that whatever tasks the sisters planned would be much more interesting than any work Uncle Owen might try to throw at her in the week ahead. She'd just have to find a way to wiggle out of any chores he might dredge up.

"Great!" Miss Annika said, then, as if she could hear Lacey's thoughts, she added, "Just make sure you get your uncle's permission first. And this time, *really* get his permission." She gave Lacey a knowing look that made the girl squirm.

Lacey decided now was a good time to bring up the reason she'd come over. "Speaking of Uncle Owen," she said with as enthusiastic a smile as she could muster. It had worked on Uncle Owen, hopefully it would work on Miss Annika.

"What about your uncle?" Miss Annika's cheery voice had disappeared and been replaced with a menacing snarl. She was definitely not a fan and Lacey was wondering if she would have to break out the fake tears again.

"Well," she said, sticking with the sweet smile for now, "he was talking about how nice it was that you took care of me yesterday."

Miss Annika narrowed her eyes.

"And he was sorry about how rude he was to you," Lacey added.

Miss Annika crossed her arms. "He said he was sorry?" she asked skeptically.

"Yes, he did," Lacey answered quickly.

"Well, he should be sorry," Miss Annika said, a bit grumpily. Then after a pause, she said, "But that's weird though. That he apologized. He never apologizes to me."

"Well," Lacey jumped in before she could linger on that thought, "he's just really, um, grateful, yeah, he's grateful that you helped me, and he wanted to repay you. So, he wanted me to invite you over for dinner tomorrow night, so he can cook for you. It's his way of saying thank you. Because he's grateful."

Miss Olivia, who had refilled her glass and taken another large gulp of water, began choking on her drink. Lacey stared at her in alarm, but after a few rattling coughs she was breathing again. And then she was laughing.

"You said what?" she managed to squeeze out. "Owen Stillwater invited Annika over for dinner?" She was doubled over and wheezing at this point. Lacey wasn't sure if she was laughing or coughing, but she decided that the woman was probably fine.

She turned her attention to the other woman who had been staring at her, mouth gaped open ever since Lacey had extended the invitation. Lacey wasn't sure if this was a good or bad sign, but she was in up to her eyeballs now, so she knew she had to get through it. Besides, she was pretty confident that she could sell it. Hopefully.

Miss Annika gulped, as if she was trying to swallow what Lacey was feeding her but found it hard to digest. Lacey threw her 1000 kilowatt smile back on and beamed at the woman. She was met with silence. And maybe a distrustful glare.

"So, I can tell him you're coming?" Lacey asked.

"Of course, she'll be there." This came from Miss Olivia, who was drying tears from her eyes with the edge of her shirt. Her shoulders still shook in laughter as she answered for her sister. "She wouldn't miss it for the world."

"Fat chance!" Miss Annika found her voice and used it to shut down this operation immediately. "From the moment I met that man he's been nothing but rude to me, and for no reason whatsoever. And every time I've seen him since then, he's insulted me, belittled me, and just been terrible. Now I'm supposed to have dinner with him. Nope. No way. I wouldn't have dinner with him for the world."

Miss Olivia turned to Lacey, "When we moved here last year, your uncle and my sister sort of started off on the wrong foot," she explained. "Let's go over the timeline of events, shall we?" she asked no one in particular. "He was rude and insulting, she yelled back and insulted him, then they both walked away angry. Now repeat that about a dozen times and you'll be caught up to the present day."

Lacey nodded in understanding. Basically, they were fighting without knowing why they were fighting. This was territory she was familiar with. She had a brother, therefore, she knew all about meaningless fights. She was just a little surprised to see adults doing it. To Lacey, they seemed a bit old to be engaging in such juvenile behavior, but that was a thought she would keep to herself.

"Annika," Miss Olivia said, "you have to go. He's trying to thank you. Maybe he's extending an olive branch."

Lacey didn't know what that meant, but she knew she had to say something to change Miss Annika's mind. "He's really sorry about how rude he was. He said that he wanted to try and be friends." Lacey winced, regretting the words once they were out of her mouth. She worried that she'd gone too far with the "f" word. Even to her own ears, it hadn't sounded believable.

But Miss Olivia pounced on it. "Ooh, Annika," she cooed, "you have to go. He wants to be your friend."

"How about you go then," Miss Annika retorted.

"He didn't invite me," Miss Oliva said. "Besides, I have plans."

"You do not," Miss Annika called her on her bluff.

"I do too."

"What plans?"

"Well, umm..."

"Maybe she's going to dinner with Mr. Phillip at the MacPhearsons." This came from Lacey, followed by, "Didn't they invite you to dinner tomorrow? To meet his sister?" She then sat back in her chair to watch the fallout from the grenade she'd just thrown.

Miss Annika gasped. "I'd forgotten about that. Are you going to the MacPhearsons for dinner?"

Miss Olivia shot Lacey a look that branded the girl a big-mouthed traitor before answering. "No, I'm not going. I told you we were done. I don't need to meet his sister cause we're not in a relationship."

"Hmm," Miss Annika said. "See, your mouth says one thing, but your body language says something else. But I won't hassle you about it, although I really think you should go."

"Well, I'm not going, and this isn't about me anyway," Miss Olivia responded. "This is about you finally burying the hatchet with our neighbor."

"I have an idea," Lacey piped up.

"I'll bet you do," Miss Annika said, eyeing the teenager warily.

"Well," Lacey placed a hand against her head, pretending to think the matter over. Then with mock enthusiasm, she said, "I know. What about an agreement?"

"What do you mean? What sort of agreement?" Miss Olivia asked, looking equally suspicious of her.

"Like a pact," Lacey said, and at the blank looks on their faces she explained, "Neither of you want to go to dinner, but you both want each other to go to dinner. So, why don't you make an agreement that you'll both go if the other person goes.

That means you'll have dinner with Uncle Owen," she pointed to Miss Annika, "but only if you have dinner with Mr. Phillip," she said pointing to Miss Olivia.

Miss Annika scrunched up her face at the idea, and Miss Olivia didn't look any more pleased than her sister. But neither of them said a word. They both seemed to be thinking over the proposal. By the growing frowns on their faces, neither of them liked what they'd heard. Lacey began worrying that her plans were falling apart in front of her. She didn't know what she would do if they didn't go for it. This had been her best idea. It had been her only idea. So, she crossed her fingers and wished upon a star and God and all those people in heaven that she'd heard the pastor talk about on Sunday but who she couldn't really remember. She just hoped they were all listening.

Just when she was beginning to think that her plan had failed, Miss Annika said, begrudgingly, "I guess it wouldn't hurt me to just have dinner with him one time, especially if he's going to be cooking. I hear he's pretty good in the kitchen."

"He's a great cook," Lacey bragged. "You won't believe how good his food is."

Both Lacey and Miss Annika looked over at Miss Olivia expectantly. She was sitting with her arms folded across her chest and a scowl plastered across her face. In the end though, she caved, "Oh alright," she exploded. "I was thinking about going anyway. Not because I still have feelings for him or anything like that. It's just that the MacPhearsons are expecting me, and it would be rude of me not to show up."

"Great! Dinner's at 8:00." Lacey said, jumping to her feet. "I'll tell Uncle Owen that you're coming. He's gonna be so happy."

She had already decided that she would take her win and make a hasty retreat before anyone had the chance to change their mind. It had certainly worked with Uncle Owen, and she was gambling that it would work now too.

"By the way," she said casually, while backing towards the

door, "we like to dress up for dinner. You know, like, wear a nice dress, do your hair and makeup and all. It's uh, kind of like a family tradition of sorts. I just wanted to let you know, so you wouldn't feel awkward or anything." She threw a smile at Miss Annika. Then, with a quick call to summon Nosey, who had fallen asleep after finishing his snack, she made her escape in breathtaking time.

Once outside, Lacey slowed her pace again, taking her time to return home. After all, she was still avoiding Uncle Owen and Nosey didn't seem to be in any hurry either. So, the two of them meandered about, enjoying the outdoors. Lacey was rather pleased with her efforts for the day. She'd killed two birds with one stone. But she wasn't under any false pretenses that things would go smoothly from this point. No, she was well-aware that she had only crossed the first hurdle. Now was when the hard work would begin.

.....

AFTER LUNCH ENDED, LUKE AND UNCLE OWEN SHARED CLEAN up duty. Luke grumbled under his breath the entire time, right up until Uncle Owen announced that he would be going fishing. He invited Luke to join him, as their last fishing trip had been cut short before he'd managed to catch anything. This put an end to Luke's complaining at once. Not because he was interested in fishing. He couldn't think of anything more boring than sitting by the lake all afternoon again. No, his thoughts had immediately turned to the fact that Uncle Owen would be absent for an indefinite period of time. It was almost too good to be true.

So, after they'd finished cleaning, and Uncle Owen had left with his gear, Luke rushed upstairs to pick up where he'd left off with his investigation. His first inclination was to finally breach the main bedroom. He knew that this was the perfect opportunity when Uncle Owen was guaranteed to be out of the house, probably for the entire afternoon. (He'd learned yesterday that fishing took a long time, and you weren't even likely to catch anything.)

But even knowing that, he still found himself heading to the spare bedroom turned storage room. He couldn't explain why, but he was drawn to the mysterious boxes as well as the mysterious woman whose belongings filled those boxes. He wanted to investigate further. He wanted to know what happened to her.

So it was, that almost an hour later, Luke was digging through box after box and bin after bin. He'd found more clothes than any one person had a right to own, plenty of jewelry, half-used bottles of perfumes, and even old makeup, all of it presumably belonging to Uncle Owen's wife. Luke had found pictures too – some framed and some not, and he'd even found a photo album, which he'd taken the time to flip through. Inside were pictures of his uncle and aunt engaged in various activities – watching tv, fishing, eating, swimming. It looked as though they'd taken countless pictures of each other during their time together. And in every one of the pictures both subjects looked... happy. Completely and blissfully happy.

Luke was aware at this point that he should be wrapping things up. While he didn't exactly know how long an average fishing expedition lasted, his instincts told him that Uncle Owen could return at any minute, and he was pushing his luck by staying in the room for much longer. Still, he didn't leave. Not yet. Instead, he dug further into the room filled with memories.

He reached for a storage bin that he hadn't been through yet and opened it. Examining its contents revealed more knick-knacks as well as a large accordion folder taking up nearly half the container. Jackpot! This could actually contain some useful information. Luke guessed that it might be heavy to try and lift the accordion, filled with so many papers, and instead opted to open it while it was still in the storage bin. Not sure where to begin with such a treasure trove of information to look over, he just grabbed the first few papers from the front.

Luke wasn't sure what he'd been looking for when he'd started his hunt that day. In fact, he could secretly admit that part of him hadn't been looking for anything in particular. The fun was in the search itself. He rather enjoyed digging through people's personal belongings and discovering their secrets, and he had gotten rather good at it. In this case, he'd mostly let go of the search for dirt on his uncle. He wasn't entirely convinced that the man wasn't a creep, but Luke's instincts were telling him that Uncle Owen might possibly not be a bad person.

Even still, he had been genuinely curious about the mystery of his uncle's wife. Where was she? Did they get divorced? Who gets divorced and leaves all their stuff behind? Maybe she was in jail. No wonder his uncle never mentioned her. Who wants to tell people that their wife is locked up?

Unsure of what to expect, Luke began reading over the documents in his hands. The first was a wedding certificate, confirming what Luke had already deduced himself. Owen Luke Stillwater had married Natasha Jasmine Nez 6 years ago. Although the marriage wasn't a surprise, the name certainly was. Luke? Uncle Owen's middle name was Luke? Did that mean that he was named after Uncle Owen? That was a bit of information that he would need to think about later.

Luke shook his head. Just when he thought he'd figured things out, the surprises kept coming.

He moved to the next document and continued reading. But what he read on this document, stopped him in his tracks. His blood ran cold, and his heart began to crack, first a tiny fissure then with a gaping wound. Following the marriage certificate, was a death certificate for Natasha Nez Stillwater. According to the death certificate, she'd died of breast cancer.

Luke put the documents back where he'd found them, closed the accordion file, and returned the lid to the storage bin. He looked around the room, it was still in disarray from his search, but he didn't care. He got up from where he'd been sitting on the floor and made his way to the door. Without looking back, he left the room. He'd had enough. Enough investigating for the day. Enough investigating for a while.

He made his way to his bedroom and laid across his bed, thankful that Lacey had disappeared to God knows where. He wasn't in the mood to talk. He just wanted to be alone for a while. By the sound of silence echoing throughout the house, his wish was being granted. His uncle apparently hadn't returned yet. But, then again, Uncle Owen didn't make a lot of noise to begin with. It was one of the things Luke was beginning to like about him. And he was beginning to like him. He could admit that, even if it was just to himself.

Luke reasoned that his growing fondness for Uncle Owen must be the reason why it felt like his heart was breaking. Yet again. He was hurting for his uncle. Because he hadn't met Natasha. He hadn't even known she'd existed until a few days ago. So, it made no sense that he should feel so devastated over the loss of an aunt that he'd never had. And yet, his chest ached with a deep pain that he knew all too well. A pain that wedged its way into his being that day while sitting in Principal Forrester's office. A pain that he'd become intimately familiar with the moment he'd heard those words for the very first time – your parents are dead. A pain that just wouldn't go away no matter what. A pain that he felt now for his Aunt Natasha.

❧ 17 ❧

"Explain to me why I have to wear this again?" Uncle Owen grumbled. "I'm in my own home. I shouldn't have to dress up just to eat." He fussed with the tie around his neck and pulled uncomfortably at the sleeves of the suit jacket he'd begrudgingly agreed to wear.

They were gathered in the great room where Lacey had taken it upon herself to officially inspect everyone's attire. And by everyone, that meant Uncle Owen. He had taken her instructions to heart and appeared downstairs in a perfectly tailored navy blue suit and a gray striped tie. Uncle Owen had done his hair too. It was combed back and sleek. Lacey sniffed. He was even wearing cologne. Her plan couldn't fail.

"Like I said," Lacey answered him, while admiring how handsome he looked, "it's for Miss Annika. They dress up for dinner all the time."

"But why do I have to?"

"Because she's our guest and we want her to feel comfortable. Besides," Lacey added, "it's a pretty normal thing to do. I mean, me and Luke are used to dressing up for dinner."

"What?" Luke looked at her in confusion. Lacey had convinced him to wear his best clothes as well – khaki pants and a dress shirt. Or rather the closest thing he had to it, which was a pair of cargo shorts and a plain white t-shirt. Lacey had on her new dress and the pink flip-flops she'd worn to church.

Lacey ignored Luke and continued working on Uncle Owen. "Our family used to dress up for dinner all the time. Almost every night. It was so much fun."

"No we didn't!"

This outburst earned Luke a quick elbow to the ribs.

"Ow! What was that for?" Luke rubbed at the injured area that would surely develop into a bruise, but one look at the glare coming from his sister had him backpedaling from his earlier statement. "Oh. Oh yeah, I mean we used to dress up every night."

Luke and Lacey had discussed the plan for the evening the night before when Lacey had outlined her master plan. Or rather, Luke had cornered her and demanded to know what she was plotting. Initially, Lacey had denied everything and admitted nothing. But Luke wouldn't budge, and she'd wound up telling him everything, which was just as well. She would need his help eventually if she was going to pull it off. At various times, Luke had laughed, looked at her like she was a crazed lunatic, and shook his head in pity as she told him the details. In the end though, he had agreed to go along with it, not because he thought she stood a chance of pulling it off, but because as he'd said, "I'm bored and this is going to be hilarious."

That was how she'd gotten him to dress his best for dinner this evening. It was also why he'd helped her to persuade Uncle Owen to do the same. He was a recruit, but he was a reluctant recruit.

Their explanation seemed to be enough to appease Uncle Owen, as he stopped tugging at his tie, and settled himself into an armchair to wait on their guest.

"What time is she supposed to get here?" Uncle Owen grumbled again. He looked at his watch impatiently.

"She should be here any minute now," Lacey assured him.

Then she figured that now might be a good time to remind him of his promise. "And remember, you're going to be nice to her."

Uncle Owen plastered a fake smile across his face that made him look unhinged.

"Perfect!" Lacey said.

"You look like The Joker," Luke said.

Uncle Owen dropped the smile. Then he said, "I'm surprised you didn't make me put out hors d'ovures for her. That's what people usually do when they have these kind of fancy dinner parties."

"They do?" Lacey's face fell. She turned to Luke who nodded in confirmation. "I didn't know that," she said quietly.

But Lacey didn't have time to lament over her faux pas or her lack of knowledge of fancy dinner etiquette because the doorbell rang at that moment, and it was time to spring into action.

Uncle Owen began heading toward the front door, but Lacey zipped past him. "I'll get it," she called as she raced to the door. She could hear Luke behind her doing his part, "You should stand right here Uncle Owen," Luke said, as he guided the man to the center of the room where the lighting was best.

Lacey made it to the front door and took a moment to catch her breath. In that moment, she sent up another wish to God and those people in heaven that Miss Annika had indeed dressed up for dinner. Part of Lacey was worried that the woman would show up in tattered and dirty clothes just to be spiteful to Uncle Owen. It was the kind of thing Lacey would've done herself.

The doorbell rang again prompting Lacey to act. She didn't want Miss Annika to get annoyed and leave. She hurried to open the door and was rewarded with the sight of Miss Annika in a form-fitting black dress that fell to her knees. Her straight brown hair sat on her shoulders and was curled at the end. And she had even worn make-up. The soft color across the eyes and lips complemented her brown skin and made it glow.

"Am I late?" Miss Annika asked, as Lacey stood in the doorway gaping at her.

The question brought Lacey to her senses. "Nope, you're right on time. Come in," she said, and ushered the woman into the house, closing the door behind her. "Everyone's waiting for you" she announced as she led Miss Annika from the foyer and through to the great room. Then she stood aside and let Miss Annika enter first.

Indeed, Uncle Owen was standing in precisely the right location so that he was the first thing Miss Annika saw when she stepped into the room. Luke had even made sure that Uncle Owen was facing the opposite direction so that he had to turn around when she walked into the room. Just like in the movies.

Lacey held in a squeal of delight. It was absolutely perfect.

It was perfect the way Uncle Owen looked over Miss Annika and said in a deep voice, "You look lovely."

It was perfect the way Miss Annika smiled at the complement and then said, "Not too bad yourself. You clean up well."

And Lacey knew she wasn't imagining the way Uncle Owen's face went slightly red at Miss Annika's words. Then he cleared his throat and said, "Well, shall we?" And he held out his hand to Miss Annika to lead her toward the dining room.

It was absolutely perfect.

That is until Luke said loudly, "We don't have any hors d'ovures cause Lacey didn't know to make 'em and we didn't care."

.....

A SHORT WHILE LATER, THEY WERE SEATED AT THE DINING room table with the meal Owen had cooked (with Luke's help) spread out in front of them. Owen had broiled the fish that he'd caught just the day before. Paired with fresh greens, the meal looked and smelled delectable. Owen had to admit that he had gone the extra mile with this meal, and maybe wanted to show off his cooking skills just a bit. Not that he was trying to impress anyone though. Still, he couldn't help feeling pleased when Annika took a deep inhale of the delicious aroma, then looked at him and said, "This looks incredible."

"Wait until you taste it," he responded. Then he gestured for her to try it.

When she picked up her fork to do just that, Lacey made a sound.

"Umm," Lacey said, "I umm, I don't feel so good. I think, maybe I should go lie down."

"Well, you haven't eaten," Owen said, trying not to be alarmed that she was sick again. How fragile was this girl? "Eat something first. You'll feel much better once there's food on your stomach."

"Ohhh," Lacey moaned, "my head hurts so bad." She put a hand across her forehead and began to sway back and forth. "I'm just so tired. I think I should go lie down." This was followed by a groan.

Owen frowned, his anxiety increasing with each sound she made. "Maybe I should give you a checkup."

"Oh no," she said. "I'll be okay if I can just go now."

"But you haven't eaten anything." Owen wouldn't let the matter rest.

"It's okay. I'll eat something later if I get hungry." Then she gestured to Luke, who was sitting across the table from her, and said, "Luke isn't hungry either."

"What do you mean? I'm starving? Ow!" Luke reached under the table to rub what looked like his leg, as Lacey moved about in her chair. Then he said, "Oh, oh yeah. I uh... I guess I'm still full from lunch. I'd like to go to my room too." He mumbled the words with much less enthusiasm than Lacey had shown. In fact, his lips were saying one thing, but his eyes were greedily devouring the food in front of him.

This gave Owen pause. Since when did Luke turn down a

delicious meal? He may not have known the boy long, but he knew that Luke appreciated good food. Just as he was beginning to wonder what was going on, Lacey hit him with the pout. The same one from yesterday that had him agreeing to something he never would've agreed to before. Then came the trembling lip, and Owen felt himself caving.

"I guess if you two want to go, it's alright," he heard himself say.

Lacey leapt from her chair and threw her arms around him. "Thanks Uncle Owen! You're my favorite uncle."

And Owen couldn't help the smile that spread across his face as she skipped out of the room and Luke followed at a much slower pace, as if he was reluctant to leave.

Once they were alone, Owen turned his attention to his dinner guest. Annika was holding her glass of water and looking at him with a smirk on her face. But Owen didn't care. He felt like the Uncle of the Year and said as much to her.

"Did you hear that?" he asked, reaching for his fork to begin his meal. "I'm her favorite uncle." He grinned as he took a bite of the tender meat. It was seasoned to perfection.

"I heard," Annika said, picking up her own fork. "Tell me," she said, "how many uncles does she have?"

"Well," Owen stopped chewing as his mind processed the question and the answer. He swallowed his food before mumbling, "Just one."

18

"What are they saying?"

"Shh! I can't hear."

Luke shoved Lacey, who shoved him back in return.

They were huddled in the kitchen just off the dining room, spying on the two adults having dinner. After leaving the dinner table, they'd made their way to their hiding spot by running up the stairs in the front of the house, racing towards the back of the house, and tiptoeing down the back staircase that led into the kitchen. Now they were perched at the slightly cracked door to the dining room, peering at their subjects like scientists studying specimen in a laboratory.

"Move over, I want to see too."

"You move over."

Truthfully, as small as they were, they probably could've both shared the peeping space quite comfortably, but they wouldn't stop fighting to test that theory.

"This was my idea," Lacey pointed out. "You didn't even want to do it."

Luke made a face at her which she ignored as she returned her attention to the dinner table.

"Awww," Lacey said, "Look how he's looking at her. I told you he liked her."

"Of course he likes her." Luke rolled his eyes. "He practically told us that himself, but that doesn't mean that she likes him."

"But she will," Lacey argued, "once she gets to know him."

"You don't know that."

"Yes, I do. And then they'll fall in love, and he'll be happy. Don't you think he deserves to be happy?"

Luke had no argument for that. He thought about the man he'd spent the last few days getting to know. Then he thought about the man in the wedding picture in the room upstairs. It was as if they were two different people. Before and after. One was the man that he was. One was the man that he could be.

Luke looked up at Uncle Owen. He was laughing. Head thrown back, eyes closed, uninhibited laughing. Luke would bet money that he didn't have that Uncle Owen didn't laugh very often.

"Yeah," Luke said, "he deserves to be happy."

.....

"So, TELL ME AGAIN," ANNIKA SAID, ATTEMPTING AND FAILING to stifle a laugh. "She talked you into dinner by pretending to cry?"

Owen, who was beginning to feel more than a little foolish, tried to defend himself. Tried but failed. "Well, it wasn't really crying. It was more like she was about to cry."

"Wait," Annika said, "please tell me it wasn't that pouting act she put on just now. Tell me you didn't fall for that."

Owen decided to remain silent.

Annika abandoned all pretenses and outright laughed.

They had finished their meal and were now conversing over

empty plates and half empty glasses of water. The subject had naturally come to the evening's origins in which the case of the manipulating teenaged girl had been brought to light. However, it was Owen's retelling of the invitation that had Annika in stitches.

"It was very convincing," Owen said, and then gave in and laughed himself. He'd been had and they both knew it.

Annika shook her head. "She's got you wrapped around her little finger already. You'd better watch out for that one."

Owen had to agree with her. Lacey really had worked a number on him. More than once. And he wasn't even upset about it. How could he be mad at her when he'd been the one to fall for her charms. Yep, he would have to stay on his guard with her.

"Hey, don't feel bad," Annika said, as if she could sense what he'd been thinking. "Anyone could've fallen for it. She knows what she's doing."

"At least one of us does," he'd meant for the remark to be flippant, but it had come out more brusque than he'd intended, the intonation revealing his true feelings on the matter.

"What does that mean?"

Owen didn't respond right away. He hadn't intended to open himself up to her. But he could feel her watching him, waiting for an answer. He shrugged his shoulders. "Nothing, it was just a silly joke."

Annika looked as though she didn't believe him, but thankfully she let the matter go.

"What would you say to going out onto the deck?" Owen asked, eager to change the mood that had suddenly shifted. "It's a clear spring night. The stars will be nice and bright."

"Why don't I help you clear the table?" Annika responded, "And then we can do some stargazing."

Owen agreed to her suggestion and together they cleaned the table, then headed toward the kitchen with the dishes.

.....

"OKAY," LUKE SAID, "I GET WHY YOU'RE DOING ALL THIS FOR Uncle Owen. Sort of. I guess. But what I don't get is why you're messing with Miss Annika's sister. What's she got to do with anything? Why are you messing with both of their lives?"

"Because," Lacey began to explain, even though she'd already told him all this last night when she'd laid out the plan for Project Adult Happiness. (The title was a work in progress.) "Miss Olivia and her boyfriend are fighting and it's making them both sad. So, if I can get them to see that they love each other then they'll stop fighting and be happy together." After a moment she added, "And I'm not messing with their lives. I'm helping them."

Luke looked unconvinced of her interpretation of the situation but didn't press her on it.

"What are they saying now?" Lacey said, peering through the crack in the door.

Luke leaned closer as well, hoping to catch a few words.

"I can't hear," Lacey began a complaint, which turned into a panicked, "They're coming! They're coming!"

Luke hadn't needed her to tell him that. He'd seen the adults headed their way and deduced the same thing as Lacey – time to run for it.

They both made a mad dash for the staircase, bumping into cabinets, counters, and the trash can along the way. Luke was in the lead, but as he rounded the banister, he could feel Lacey hot on his tail. He took the stairs two at a time with leaps that could rival the best Olympic hurdler. Once at the top, he turned to see Lacey with several steps left, doomed to get caught. But with guts and determination, she closed her eyes and flung herself across the remaining stairs, falling halfway onto Luke. He extricated himself and they both took a moment to catch their breaths.

While out of view, they could still hear the two adults below as they entered the kitchen and stacked the dishwasher together. Luke was especially attentive when he heard Uncle Owen say that he would place his and Lacey's uneaten meals in the refrigerator in case they got hungry later. Luke's stomach rumbled in response, as if to say that he was hungry now.

They listened carefully as the two adults finished in the kitchen and left the way they'd entered. After waiting a moment to make sure the coast was clear, Lacey tiptoed back down the stairs, through the kitchen, and back to their lookout door. After a peek into the dining room, she called over her shoulder to Luke. "They're not here."

"That's because they're outside," Luke said.

Lacey turned around to see that Luke had followed her into the kitchen and was now looking out the window over the sink, which provided an impressive view of the deck area and the backyard. She joined him at the window and saw for herself that Miss Annika and Uncle Owen were both seated in the wicker chairs out on the deck. They had drinks in their hands and were deep in conversation.

"Aww, now I can't hear what they're saying," Lacey complained.

"You couldn't hear what they were saying before," Luke pointed out. He had left the window for the fridge where he was searching its contents for the promised leftovers. "Score!" He reached into the fridge and retrieved a wrapped plate of food. Not even bothering to reheat the meal, he grabbed a fork and dug in, standing next to the fridge that he hadn't bothered to close either.

"I wonder what they're talking about," Lacey said.

"Well," Luke said around a mouthful of food, "you got three options." He scraped more food into his mouth. "Boy this is really good. Can you hand me a glass so I can get some water?"

Lacey, who was standing near the cabinets, reached inside for a glass. Instead of handing it to him, she poured him a glass of cold water from the pitcher in the fridge, and then shut the door that he had left open.

"Thanks," he said, taking the glass that she held out to him. After a gulp of the water, he set the glass down, wiped his mouth with the back of his hand, and then continued to speak. The plate of food never left his hand the entire time.

"Like I said," Luke reached for the fork again. "You got three options. One. You can go out there and ask 'em what they're talking about." He took another huge bite and continued talking with his mouth full of food. "Two. You can stare at 'em out the window until they turn around and bust you. But you still won't know what they're saying. Or three." He swallowed the food in his mouth. "This is really good. You want a bite?"

Lacey shrugged. She took a fork from the utensil drawer and helped herself to some of Luke's meal. Then she helped herself to a bit more. When she went in for a third time, Luke pushed her away.

"I said a bite, not the whole thing."

"I'm hungry."

"Then get your own food. You're not eating all of mine." He held the plate away from her and shooed her with his fork.

Lacey frowned but did as he said and grabbed her own plate from the fridge. She opted for a warm meal though and placed it in the microwave to heat. At the ding, she rescued her food and tucked into her meal with as much enthusiasm as Luke had shown to his. That is until Luke appeared in front of her with his fork and began taking food from her plate.

"Hey!"

"It's only fair. You took some of mine."

"I didn't take that much. You took way more food than I took from you."

Luke wasn't prepared to admit to this, although the evidence was clearly on Lacey's side, with the gaping hole on her plate where food used to be. As somewhat of a truce (and not in any way admitting to his guilt), he handed her the half-full glass of water.

"You can have the rest of my water," he said.

Lacey took the glass for the peace offering that it was. She continued eating her meal while Luke rinsed his now empty plate and stacked it into the dishwasher.

"Well?" she asked.

"Well what?" Luke asked in confusion.

"You didn't finish telling me what I should do."

"Oh yeah." Luke closed the dishwasher and leaned against the counter. "Your third option. You could always just wait until tomorrow and trick them into telling you everything."

Lacey puckered her lips, considering her options as she finished her meal. Once she was done eating, she had a smile on her face, having chosen the best plan.

Finished with his meal as well, Luke turned to leave but Lacey stopped him.

"Can you put my dishes in the dishwasher for me?" she asked, shoving the now dirty dishes toward him.

"Really?"

"Luke please, you're right there."

"You're right there. You can't rinse a couple of dishes and stack them in the dishwasher? Have you suddenly forgotten how to do work?"

Lacey pouted. It didn't work. It never worked on Luke.

He crossed his arms and stared her down.

"Luke."

"Lacey."

"I am asking you would you please put my things in the dishwasher just this once for me?"

Luke rolled his eyes. "Fine!" He grabbed the dirty dishes from her.

"Stop shouting," Lacey admonished, "They'll hear you and then they'll know we're in the kitchen." She peeked out the window at the adults one more time, as if she could tell by looking whether they'd heard Luke or not.

Luke snorted. "They already know we're here." He was busy loading the dishwasher, so he didn't see Lacey turn to look at him, aghast.

"What do you mean? How would they know we're in the kitchen?"

Luke started the dishwasher before looking at her. "Well, I'm sure they heard you using the microwave earlier. It's not exactly quiet, is it?" He walked past her stricken face and headed up the stairs, but not before calling over his shoulder, "That's why I didn't heat my food up."

.....

OUTSIDE, OWEN AND ANNIKA SAT NEXT TO EACH OTHER ON the deck in his favorite wicker chairs. Owen had lit two citronella candles to ward off mosquitoes and positioned them on the small glass table between them. The sky was cloudless, providing a perfect view of the moon and the stars clustered together to form somewhat identifiable constellations in the night sky over the trees. Thus, although the air was muggy with the customary Florida humidity, it was a pleasant atmosphere with pleasant company. It had taken a bit of time for Owen to come to this realization but once he'd given it some thought he'd had to admit to himself that his neighbor made very pleasant company indeed.

"So," she said, after taking a sip from the glass of water in her hand, which was thankfully bug free due to the effectiveness of the candles, "since her scheming worked and the two of us are alone together, now what?"

"Are you implying that my niece didn't really become so overcome with exhaustion that she suddenly had to leave the room just as we sat down to eat?"

"She really wants us to be friends, doesn't she?"

"Yes, she does." Owen said with a laugh. Then he said, "So, what do you say we give her what she wants? Do you think we could just start over?"

"She did go through a lot of effort." Annika thought for a moment. "I think I could live with that."

Owen extended his hand. "Friends?"

Annika accepted the handshake. "Friends."

After a moment she asked, "Do you hear that?" She looked back toward the house. "What is that?"

Owen took a sip from his own glass and answered without looking back. "I believe that's the microwave. Luke's probably heating up his dinner. I figured he'd be back to get it sooner or later. Actually, he held out longer than I thought he would. That boy doesn't miss a good meal."

Annika smiled at him. "It sounds like you're really getting the hang of this."

Owen scoffed. "I guess looks really can be deceiving."

"What do you mean by that?"

Owen sighed. He looked out across the perfectly manicured lawn illuminated by moonlight and stars. If he squinted, he could almost see the boat dock in the distance, leading to the adjoining lake. But maybe that was just his imagination.

"What's on your mind?" Annika asked him quietly. "You can talk to me you know. I mean, I know you don't know this about me, but I'm a really good listener."

Owen finally looked at her and told her what had been rattling around inside his head for days. "I'm in way over my head here. I have no idea what I'm doing with these kids. It just seems like the more I try, the more I screw up. And this is one time that I can't afford to blow it." He let out a breath that he didn't even know he'd been holding.

He wasn't sure why he'd opened up to her, only that it felt

good to release some of the frustration and anxiety that had been troubling him since the moment this rollercoaster ride had begun. Since the day that he'd learned of his niece and nephew's existence and that he would become their legal guardian, Owen had been plagued with nothing but fear and doubt about his ability to do the job properly. After they'd been through so much, all he wanted was to help them to feel safe again, maybe find some closure, and if at all possible, find their way to happiness. Only Owen was worried that he was making things worse for them, not better.

Annika sat in silence for so long that Owen became worried that he'd said too much too soon. They'd only just agreed that they would no longer be mortal enemies. In the very next breath, he'd dumped all his personal problems onto her. She was probably freaked out by the extreme amount of oversharing she'd just endured. He'd just decided to apologize for making things awkward when she spoke.

"Okay," Annika said, looking at him. "I just prayed about what to say to you and now I'm ready to respond."

"You prayed about what to say to me?"

"Absolutely," she said, looking directly at him. "You need advice and I'm certainly not qualified to give it, but I really want to help you in any way I can."

Owen didn't know what to say to this. He was dumbfounded. This woman that he'd loathed the entire time that he'd known her, who he'd made very mean statements about just 24 hours ago, was praying about how to help him. Not that he believed prayer helped anything. He knew firsthand that it didn't. But still, it shook him that she'd taken the time to pray for him. It shook him to the core. And her next words shook him even more.

Annika set her glass down on the small table between their two chairs before continuing. "There are two things that I want to say. First of all," she ticked the point off on her finger, "I don't have kids and I'm not a guardian or anything. Sure, I run a camp for pre-teen girls for one week every season, but that's hardly the same thing. Not even close."

Owen silently nodded in agreement. He was familiar with the camp next door, having thrown the biggest hissy fit known to mankind when he'd learned about his neighbors' plans to open it. He only hoped that she didn't bring up that incident now. It wasn't exactly his finest moment.

Thankfully, she continued, leaving the camp behind. "The point is, I don't know what you're going through. I can't even fathom what it is you're experiencing right now. Second," she said as she raised two fingers to indicate her next point. "You showed up."

He blinked at her, not registering her meaning.

"You showed up," Annika said again, this time more forcefully. "Fully invested, fully committed. And that's all they need right now. Just showing up and being there makes a huge difference."

Owen tried to swallow, but it couldn't get past the lump that had formed in his throat. For the past few days, he'd felt like he was drowning. He'd worried constantly that with his many blunders he was doing his young charges more harm than good. He wanted desperately to help them, but he just didn't know how. Now, it seemed as if Annika could see into his mind or read what was behind his eyes.

"Look," she said, "it's clear to anyone with eyes that you care for these kids. So let that be your guide. Whatever mistakes you make, and from what I've heard every parent makes plenty, just use them to grow and learn. It will all work out in the end. Just keep doing what you're doing."

Owen sat in silence, too rattled to speak. He turned her words over and over in his mind. He wasn't sure how long he'd sat there thinking, but apparently enough time had passed for Annika to grow uncomfortable with the silence.

She gave what sounded like a nervous laugh and said, "But you know that's just my uneducated observation."

Owen smiled. "Hardly. More like expertly targeted advice."

She smiled back at him and looked into his eyes. "I just hope I helped a little."

Owen was in the middle of trying to come up with a clever and impressive response to her statement when Annika looked away and then stood abruptly.

"It's getting late," she announced. "It's time for me to go."

"Oh." Thrown off by her announcement and more than a little disappointed, that was the only thing Owen could think to say.

Without any further explanation, Annika headed toward the door to go back into the house. Owen (slightly delayed due to his confusion over the sudden turn of events), grabbed both glasses of water and followed. By the time he'd made it inside and closed the door behind himself, he'd thought of something to say.

"Well, let me walk you to your car."

"No, no, I'm fine, but-" Annika paused her speedy exit and walked back to him. When she reached him, she looked like she wanted to shake his hand, but he was still holding the water. She placed her hand gently on his arm instead.

"Owen, I just wanted to say thank you for dinner, and also tell you that you're doing great. You *will* do great. So don't doubt yourself."

Her words were touching, but all Owen could think about was that it was the first time she'd ever called him by his name.

After that, she turned and walked away again, just as quickly as before. Owen followed her wordlessly to the foyer, both glasses still in hand. When she got to the front door, she threw out, "Oh, and Lacey really needs some clothes. Let me know if you want me to take her shopping sometime." Then she opened the door and left.

Owen stood at the door and watched her get into her car and drive off. Then he closed the door. It was a struggle to lock it while balancing two glasses of water in his hands, but he managed. As he walked back to the kitchen, he decided that he would clean out the fridge and maybe rearrange the pantry while he was at it. Why not? He had time. Owen knew he'd be up late into the night processing the things Annika had said to him, and the things she hadn't said. And he would be wondering why he liked the sound of his name so much when it came from her lips.

19

Back at her own cabin, Annika let herself in, kicked off her heels at the door, and immediately began calling out for her sister.

"Olivia!"

She knew that Olivia was home because she'd seen her hot pink SUV parked in the driveway. The sight of it was disappointing to Annika, because the fact that Olivia had beaten her home meant that dinner with the MacPhearsons must not have gone well. Annika had hoped that Olivia and Phillip would reconcile, as it was clear that they both still cared for each other a great deal. And while she wasn't naïve enough to think that one dinner with his family would be enough to fix all their problems, Annika had hoped that it would be a start.

"Olivia!" Annika shouted as she walked through the foyer towards the back of the cabin. They really needed to get an intercom system installed. This was getting ridiculous.

Just as Annika was opening her mouth to belt out her sister's name again, she heard Olivia's voice beckoning her toward the dining room.

"I'm in here!"

Annika followed the sound of the voice and found Olivia

sitting at the table, nursing the world's largest slice of chocolate cake. Annika sighed. Dinner must have gone even worse than she'd imagined.

Without preamble, Annika went and grabbed herself a fork from the kitchen and plopped down across the table from Olivia. She then proceeded to help Olivia with the burden of eating her cake.

"Mmm," she said, licking chocolate icing from her fork. "This is really good cake."

"Meredith made it," Olivia said, referring to Phillip's mother. "She's the best baker in the world."

Despite her praising Meredith MacPhearson's skills with the oven, Olivia made no attempts to indulge in the treat herself. Instead, she sat slumped in her chair, somehow looking morose and furious at the same time.

"So?" Annika prompted.

"So what?"

"So, what happened?"

Olivia groaned. "What didn't happen?" She leaned forward, put her elbows on the table, and put her head in her hands.

"Well," Annika said, trying a different tactic, "did you meet Phillip's sister?"

Olivia nodded her answer but didn't lift her head to look at Annika.

"What's she like?" Annika persisted.

Olivia sighed, lifted her head, and said, "Well, I didn't' get to talk to her much, but she seemed nice and normal."

"Good, but why didn't you talk to her? Wasn't that like the whole point of going? To meet her?"

"Because it, I...I don't really want to talk about it." With that she put her head down on the table, effectively ending the conversation. Then she lifted her head and restarted it. "Do you know what he did? Can you believe what he did?"

"Phillip?" Annika asked around a mouth full of chocolate. She eyed the glass of milk that Olivia had evidently prepared for herself to wash down the cake. After just a moment of consideration, she seized the drink. If she was enjoying the cake, she may as well enjoy the milk too.

Olivia didn't answer the chocolatey question but instead proceeded to tell Annika exactly what he did.

"I can't believe the nerve of that guy. I get there and everything's all fine, right? But then he decides he has to introduce me to his sister. Like, Don or Meredith can't introduce me. I mean, she's their kid, you know. Well anyway," she continued without a pause and seemingly quite willing to talk about it despite her previous claim, "so anyway, do you know what his *introduction* was?"

She used her fingers as quotation marks at the word introduction, leaving Annika somewhat confused. But before she could ask about the meaning, Olivia continued her story. "He said, and I quote, 'April, this is Olivia, the woman that I've been dating.' And then she said, 'so this is your girlfriend'. And then he said, 'yes.' Are you kidding me? Are you kidding me?!" Olivia threw up her hands in exasperation. "Can you believe that creep?"

After a moment, Annika realized that the last question had not been rhetorical, so she did her sisterly duty and agreed with everything Olivia said. Her support may have been delayed but it was enthusiastic. This response satisfied Olivia, but only momentarily. After thinking it through she eyed Annika warily, her arms folded across her chest.

"Wait a minute," she said. "You're agreeing with me? You never agree with me. You're always trying to be reasonable and think things through. But you're agreeing with me now?"

"About Phillip being a massive jerk?" Annika nodded her head while licking chocolate frosting off her fork. "Yep, I agree wholeheartedly."

"So, you don't think that my sitting through dinner in a silent protest and then bailing the second I saw an opening was a bit immature and kind of uncalled for?"

"Nope. It was a perfectly appropriate response to the situation that he put you in," Annika answered before returning her attention to the cake.

"But I didn't even tell him. Like, he probably still doesn't know why I'm mad at him."

"So what? He made his bed and now he has to lie in it."

Olivia frowned at that response. Then she said, "But shouldn't I at least talk to him or something and tell him why I won't talk to him? I mean like tell him why I'm mad at him?"

Annika paused, as though considering the question, then shook her head. "Nah, there's no point. You guys were never gonna last. You weren't good together. Just cut your losses. He's a loser and you're much better off without him."

Olivia gasped at Annika's words. Then her brows furrowed in anger. "He's not a loser. And we're great together. It's like we were meant to be."

"But you're totally over him."

"I'm not over him," she argued. "I'm just mad at him."

"Why?"

"Because he put me on the back burner. At first, he couldn't spend enough time with me. Then it was like he was always busy, and I never got to see him. And it felt like I didn't even have a boyfriend. And then he has the nerve to tell his sister that we're dating? How can we be dating if we never even see each other?" She ended on a pitiful note, her rant burning off the anger from before.

Annika nodded. "Yes, I see," she said sagely. "These are all good points. You did the right thing by ignoring him all this time. It's a shame that he thinks you two are still together. Well, he'll get the picture when he sees you with someone else. Someone *much* better."

"I'm not going to date someone else," Olivia sounded offended. "And I haven't been ignoring him. I'm just mad at him."

"Ooh, even better. If I can't figure out what's going on, he

certainly can't either. Keep the silent treatment going. The guy's
gonna be so confused. I mean even more confused than he is
right now. Cause think about it. One day everything's going great
as far as he knew, since you never actually told him you were
unhappy. Then, the next day, bam! Silent treatment. Genius play.
I mean, you should teach classes on how to get rid of a guy
you're finished with."

Olivia narrowed her eyes at Annika.

"I'm not finished with him," she said through gritted teeth.
"And I'm not stupid. I can see what you're doing."

"What am I doing," Annika asked, "other than being
supportive of your life decisions?"

Olivia smirked at her. "Yeah, real supportive."

She reached over and reclaimed her now half-eaten piece of
cake. Then, she took the nearly empty glass of milk as well.
After shoveling a large chunk of cake into her mouth, Olivia
pointed her fork accusingly at Annika.

"You're trying to get me to see that if I really care about
Phillip like I claim, then I should grow up, stop playing games,
and just talk to the man about what's bothering me," Olivia
grumbled around a mouthful of chocolate.

Annika put her hand over her heart and gasped. "What do
you mean?" she said. "Do you think that chances are that if
Phillip actually knew what the problem was, he'd do his best to
fix it? You know, because he's a really great guy, but he's got a lot
of commitments, but if you told him you were feeling unappreci-
ated then he would bend over backwards to make sure that you
knew that you were his number one priority?"

"Yeah," Olivia swallowed, then said, "all that stuff."

"Nope," Annika said quickly, "I wouldn't dream of telling you
any of those things. Or that it's your own fault that you had a
miserable time tonight."

Olivia opened her mouth to say something else to Annika,
and by the look on her face, it was going to be a scathing
comment about Annika's opinion about her night. Then she

seemed to think better of it and returned to her cake. After another bite, she brought up another topic.

"Speaking of disasters," Olivia said. She stopped to swallow the chocolate in her mouth before continuing. "According to Don MacPhearson, we might have a problem with the camp."

Annika looked at her quizzically, pausing her consumption of cake.

"He heard from a couple of council members that Brian Felton is trying to get us shut down."

Annika snorted. "What else is new? He's had it out for us since the day we met him."

Brian Felton was the local carpenter that the sisters had met the year before. Not counting their neighbor, he was the only true enemy they had made since they'd arrived in Port St. Annabelle. To be fair though, Brian Felton didn't get along with anyone in town. It seemed he was much more skilled at making enemies than making friends.

"Yeah," Olivia said, "but according to Don, he's really coming after us and he's doing it through the law. Something about a change in zoning codes or whatever. Don thinks the city council might have their hands tied on it."

They both sat in silence thinking about the ramifications of that statement. They'd only just started their camp the prior year, but it had already become dear to both of them, along with the girls who attended. To lose the camp would be a devastating blow.

"Don thinks that could really happen?" Annika whispered. Her mood had plummeted, and she felt the threat of tears.

Olivia nodded slowly, then added optimistically, "But nothing is certain. It might be alright."

Olivia's optimism, although forced, was enough to shake Annika out of her defeated spirit. She sat up straighter and pushed back the desire to cry. In the last year she had moved to Port St. Annabelle, begun a new (surprisingly fulfilling) career as a waitress, and started a seasonal camp with her sister. Through all of the upheavals she had learned that things almost never go according to plan, but you can't wallow in misery whenever something doesn't work out the way you want it to. She reminded herself of this now, and made the conscious decision not to fret about their situation.

"Oh well," she said, "we can't do anything about that. We can only make sure that we have the best camp anyone's ever seen for as long as we're allowed to be open."

Olivia nodded in agreement, taking strength from her younger sister's encouragement.

"And," Annika added, "we won't feel all miserable about what's out of our control."

Olivia nodded again, then she said, as if just remembering, "Oh yeah, speaking of miserable, how'd the dinner party of your nightmares go with the maniac next door?"

"Oh."

Annika was caught off guard by this conversation shift. She wasn't prepared to talk about her evening. It had been pleasant. Very. Which was an immense surprise and extremely confusing. She needed time to herself to sort out what had occurred and how she felt about it. What she didn't need was Olivia's involvement. No. Definitely not.

But even as she decided not to divulge anything to her sister, Annika heard herself saying, "Don't call him that. He's not a maniac." This, she realized belatedly, was a mistake.

Oliva stared at her. She blinked once. She blinked twice.

Annika squirmed under the scrutiny. "I'm just saying that he's a nice guy. He doesn't deserve you having him talk trash about him."

More silent staring.

"You don't know him okay. He's actually really nice and the way he cares for his niece and nephew is admirable."

The more she talked, the deeper the hole she dug for herself. Annika had spent an entire year despising Owen Stillwater. She had loudly and vocally informed anyone within earshot that he was the worst human being on the planet. The word maniac was quite mild compared to the names Annika had called him in the past. Now, she was telling Olivia that she had been mistaken all along, and that Owen was a decent guy. Olivia would never take this complete turnabout at face value. She would dig and dig until she got to the bottom of it. Annika realized all of this far too late of course. It wasn't until Olivia's staring and blinking transformed into a wide-toothed grin that she knew she was in trouble. Annika's stomach sank as she wondered what she'd just done.

"You like him!" Olivia screeched, before bursting into hysterical laughter.

Annika bristled and immediately launched into the denial game.

"No, I don't!"

To Olivia, this was just confirmation. "Yes, you do! Your arch-nemesis? Oh, this is so poetic." She leaned back in her chair and sighed, all other troubles momentarily forgotten.

"I don't like him," Annika insisted. "I just think he's a great guy, and now that I've gotten to know him a little better, I think that we could be friends."

The look on Olivia's face made it clear that she didn't believe Annika's claims, but thankfully she didn't say as much. Instead, she said, "Yeah, well you were the one who hated him, not me. I always thought he was okay." Then she added, "And how does he feel about you? Cause the animosity went both ways. Has he changed his mind too?"

Annika shrugged, "I don't know. Yeah, I guess. He said he wanted us to start over."

Olivia's eyes lit up.

"He wants us to be friends," Annika clarified.

Now her eyes were dancing.

"You're making something out of nothing. Believe me, there is absolutely nothing there."

Annika's argument might have held up, it might have been

convincing, if her phone hadn't started buzzing right at that moment. She grabbed her handbag that she'd slung onto the table when she'd first sat down and retrieved the phone from inside.

"Who's calling you this late?" Olivia asked, scraping the last remnants of chocolate from the plate with her fork. She licked the fork clean and then downed the remainder of the milk.

"It's not a call," Annika said, looking at the phone screen, "it's a text."

"From who?" Olivia asked, wiping away her milk moustache with the back of her hand.

Annika didn't answer but read the text silently to herself. When she finished, her mouth transformed into a smile on its own accord. This was reason enough for Olivia to sneak up behind her and read the message over Annika's shoulder. Annika, who was quietly reading the message over and over, was so absorbed that she didn't even notice Olivia until it was too late.

"Thank you for the wonderful evening. I hope to get the chance to repeat it again very soon. Until then, have a good night and sleep well."

Olivia read the words out so quickly that Annika didn't have time to hide her phone away before she could see the message Owen sent. Annika shoved the phone back into her purse unnecessarily. Olivia had already seen the message and formed her opinion. The damage was done.

"Whoa," Olivia said.

"It's rude to read over someone's shoulder," Annika said, refusing to meet Olivia's stare.

"Thank you for the wonderful evening?"

"It's an invasion of privacy."

"It's a guy who's into you."

Annika refused to take the bait. She stood up and grabbed her bag. After glancing under the table for her shoes and not finding them, she remembered she'd left them at the door. Oh well, they could stay there for now. What was of chief concern was getting out of the room before Olivia could hurl more blind accusations her way.

Olivia continued surmising the situation as Annika prepared to leave. "Judging by the way you were smiling at that phone, you're into him too," she said.

Annika threw her a look before announcing, "I'm going to bed." Then she began marching from the room, barefoot with her handbag shoved under her arm.

"Okay," Olivia responded to Annika's retreating back. "Have a good night and sleep well."

20

The following week went by much too quickly for everyone involved. At the same time a routine developed that helped the twins and Owen begin to adjust to their new lives. Every morning Owen rose well before the sun. Upon waking, he would go for a long walk with Nosey before showering and settling down with his journal and a hot cup of tea. It was his time to reflect and center his thoughts before starting a new day. He found that this routine, which he'd been following since shortly after he married Natasha, had become even more crucial since the twins had come to stay with him.

Luke, who had now taken to waking early as well, although not as early as Owen, would shower and dress for the day before heading to the kitchen where he always found Owen preparing to cook breakfast. Luke would silently join him as sous chef without needing to be asked. The two soon realized that they'd found a fellow foodie in one another and began cooking all meals together. Owen would teach Luke new techniques and proudly watch over him as he attempted and mastered them. Luke, who'd paused his investigation of Owen (not that he trusted him now, he just hadn't quite gotten over the last bit of information that he'd found out), now spent hours each day looking up recipes on his phone for them to try out together. He soon learned that Owen's food knowledge was vast, and there were few things that he didn't know how to cook.

It was during these cooking sessions that Owen found Luke to be the most candid. While the teenager remained tight-lipped about his time in foster care, Owen discovered that when Luke was fully absorbed in perfecting a recipe, he relaxed more and let his guard down. Those were the moments when he would talk about their lives before the accident. He didn't divulge much, just snippets here and there, snapshots of the family that he'd lost. Owen saw them as precious moments that Luke was choosing to share with him, and something told Owen that Luke didn't share this part of himself very often, if at all. It made those moments that much more important to Owen. It gave him a glimmer of hope that he was breaking through the wall that surrounded Luke.

It was during one of these conversations that Luke revealed to Owen his father's dream of traveling the world as a family. Luke shrugged it off after mentioning it, but Owen pressed him further.

"You know," Owen said as he corrected Luke's handle on the knife he was using to dice an onion, "you could still travel and taste the cuisines of the world. If that's what you want to do."

Luke scoffed. "Yeah? With what money?"

"I-"

"Not like that matters. It was supposed to be a family trip and in case you didn't notice, my parents are dead. So, what, I'm supposed to go with just Lacey? That would be lame. Anyway, it was just some stupid dream of my dad's. It was probably never gonna happen."

"Well," Owen spoke hesitantly. "if you wanted, I could travel with you. I mean, the three of us could travel together. Obviously, it wouldn't be the same but..."

Owen let the remainder of his sentence trail off and they

both stood in silence, staring at the food on the island they'd been preparing. Owen's offer hang in the air between them.

Finally, Luke shrugged his shoulders. "Just forget it," he said roughly. "Forget I even said anything."

Owen nodded, swallowing back the hurt at Luke's rejection. He reasoned that it was unfair of him to think Luke might want him to take part in a family trip meant to be shared with his parents. Feeling like he'd upset Luke by overstepping, Owen made sure not to bring up the matter again.

As for Lacey (who was never an early riser and never pretended to be), she took to the habit of sleeping soundly every morning until Luke came to wake her (sometimes by banging on the door, sometimes by shaking her mercilessly, and sometimes by shouting in her ear, but never gently). Lacey would angrily arise from her side of the bed (they were still sharing a room, more out of habit now than anything else), and get herself ready for the day. After breakfast, she would find some reason why she had to leave, each excuse wilder than the other, and conveniently manage to disappear before any cleaning began. Luke gave up on wording his feelings about the matter and took to staring daggers at Owen, who would shrug and solemnly vow to produce a chore chart sometime in the near future.

Lacey, often with Nosey in tow, would hop over to the neighbors' cabin with a full stomach and a light heart. She knew that she'd been avoiding her share of household work. She had yet to pull kitchen duty, either to cook (which no one in their right mind would ask her to do anyway) or to clean. Since she and Luke were still sharing a bedroom and an adjoining bathroom, she'd managed to get out of cleaning those as well, leaving Luke to keep both rooms tidy. She'd even thrown a couple of her clothing items into the washing machine after Luke had started a load for himself.

Lacey reasoned that she wasn't a very messy person to begin with, so her contribution to the mess was minimal. Therefore, her contribution to the cleaning should be minimal as well. It wasn't as though she were lazy or anything like that, it's just that she didn't feel that she should have to clean an entire room, say the kitchen for example, when she'd only dirtied a plate and a fork. Okay, she did feel kind of bad about the laundry thing. That may have been over the top.

But it wasn't as if Luke really cared. He didn't seem to mind at all. Not really. She didn't think. Uncle Owen certainly didn't care because if he did, he'd say something, wouldn't he? Or assign chores to them or something, right? And he hadn't done anything like that, so obviously he was okay with it.

Besides, she'd make it all up to Luke later, somehow. She'd start doing her fair share of cleaning, but not until after the camp had ended. Right now, that was what took priority.

The Big Happy Camp (probably not it's real name but that was what Lacey called it in her head), was scheduled to open next week and the two sisters, with Lacey's help, were neck deep in preparations. Every day Lacey went next door, where she was put to work by one or both sisters. There was a never-ending to-do list that they were working from, and both sisters were more than happy to hand out tasks to their new recruit. Each day was spent cleaning rooms, organizing craft supplies, and troubleshooting solutions to new problems that arose. From the moment she arrived until the moment she left their cabin, Lacey was kept busy. She didn't mind the work though. Possibly, because it didn't feel like work to her. As grueling as scrubbing bathroom floors and making a dozen beds was, she enjoyed every minute of it. Knowing why she was working so hard, and what was about to come made the work exciting. She couldn't wait for next week when she'd see the fruits of their labor. She only hoped the campers liked the crafts and games she and the sisters were planning. She hoped they would have as much fun doing them as she'd had planning them.

With all the hard work she'd been doing, Lacey barely had the time or energy for Project Adult Happiness. On one particularly grueling day of scrubbing toilets, Lacey had almost considered setting it aside until camp was over. Almost. But she quickly overcame that moment of lunacy and began planning her next move. (She couldn't fake being ill again. Uncle Owen might send her to a hospital.) Whenever she wasn't thinking about the camp and all the work that needed to be done, she was brainstorming ways to move forward with her secret project.

Of course, things would go a lot easier if her brother were more invested. She had told him her plans with the expectation that he would agree with her idea, then they would join forces and tackle the project together. Just like they always did. But that hadn't been the case at all. He hadn't offered his help. Instead, she'd gotten only resistance and doubt from him. Sure, he'd helped her plan and execute the dinner with Uncle Owen and Miss Annika (which had gone even better than Lacey had hoped), but he'd done so begrudgingly. She'd basically had to beg and plead for his assistance.

That's not the way these things usually went. They usually worked together on an operation, regardless of which one of them had come up with the idea. That was the way it had always went. Or that was the way it used to go. Before.

Never mind. Lacey was confident in her mission, and sure of her success. Although it would be nice to have Luke's help, it looked like this time she would be flying solo. And she was perfectly capable of doing that. After all, she didn't need Luke to speak for her. She didn't need him to fight for her. She certainly didn't need him to think for her. Not anymore. She would see this through on her own. She just had to figure out what her next move would be.

Lacey was in the middle of pondering this problem Thursday afternoon, while simultaneously organizing fingerpaints and sorting bottles of glitter, when she discovered that the next move had already been made for her. She was sitting on the floor in the corner of the kitchen, surrounded by bottles of paint and glitter, and trying to decide whether the mixture of pink and silver glitter should be sorted with the pink glitter or the silver glitter, when she overheard (or eavesdropped on) an interesting conversation.

Miss Annika and Miss Olivia entered the kitchen with arms full of grocery bags. Miss Olivia had gone to the store earlier to stock up on food supplies. Now, the two of them were shelving the food in the freezer, fridge, and pantry. Lacey was wondering if she should offer to help or continue with the project that she'd been told was of the utmost priority.

Neither woman had seen her when they'd entered the room, as she was tucked away in a far corner that wasn't easily visible from the countertop where they had placed the bags of groceries for sorting. Also, Miss Annika had instructed her to perform the task in the third floor attic turned art room, but Lacey had made the executive decision to relocate to the kitchen. This was in case she got hungry and needed a snack while she worked. Thus, neither sister could've expected that there was a third party present.

It was lucky for Lacey that they were unaware of her presence because they likely wouldn't have had such a conversation had they known she was there. And as it just so happened, they were discussing a topic that was of great interest to Lacey.

"I'm gonna have to bail on dinner tomorrow," Miss Annika said, rifling through a bag of groceries that she had just set on the counter.

"What? What do you mean bail?" This came from Miss Olivia, who had her own arms full of food and had been about to open the door to the walk-in pantry. She stopped in her tracks at Miss Annika's statement though and turned to her with a confused look on her face.

"I mean," Miss Annika said, grabbing a few items and heading towards the pantry as well, "I won't be able to have dinner with you. I have plans."

"You have plans?" Miss Olivia asked, disappointment in her voice. "But it's taco night. We always make tacos together on Friday. How could you have plans-"

PAMELA BROWN

Miss Olivia stopped abruptly as the saddened look on her face slowly morphed into a grin. "Do you have plans, or do you have a date?" she asked.

Instead of answering, Miss Annika marched past her sister, opened the pantry door, and went inside. Miss Olivia simply followed after her. "And who would this date happen to be with? Could it be a mysterious and handsome doctor that lives next door?"

Luckily, they'd kept the door open while they worked inside. It may have been a few feet away and essentially a closet, but with the door open and neither of them thinking to lower their voices, Lacey was able to hear every word. That was how she caught Miss Annika's answer.

"I'm having dinner with a new friend," was Miss Annika's stilted response. "who just so happens to be of the male persuasion. And wears nice cologne. And looks great in a suit."

"Yes!" was Miss Olivia's triumphant response, which mirrored Lacey's silent fist pump in the air.

"But it's not a date," Miss Annika insisted. "It's just two friends having dinner. That's all."

"Okay, sure," Miss Olivia said, sounding unconvinced of Miss Annika's claim. "You go ahead and have your not-date. But I want all the juicy details afterwards."

Lacey was of a like mind with Miss Olivia. She didn't buy Miss Annika's claims of friendship either. And she couldn't help but feel pleased with how well things were progressing, and even faster than she'd anticipated. That only left her with the other sister to work on. She needed to know how things were coming along with that part of her project, and she needed to figure out what to do next.

As if reading her mind, Miss Annika brought the subject up herself. Finished shelving their pantry items, they both exited the room and shut the wooden door behind themselves.

"Enough about my love life," Miss Annika said. "What's going on with you and the handyman?"

Miss Olivia went to retrieve more food items from the bag and began handing them to Miss Annika who was standing near the fridge. She opened the door and began putting the food away as she received it.

When Miss Olivia didn't answer, Miss Annika pressed her on the matter. "Well? Did you talk to him yet? Are you two back on track?"

Miss Olivia shrugged. "I don't know."

"What do you mean you don't know?"

"Well," she sighed. "I mean we talked, and he said he would try harder to make me a priority, but hose are just words, you know."

"So, give him time to prove it."

"Yeah, okay. I guess I'll have to wait and see." Then she perked up. "What are you going to wear on your date? We should go and pick out an outfit right now."

"Yes!" Lacey momentarily forgot herself at the prospect of going through the sisters' elaborate wardrobe. She already knew they had amazing taste by the nice clothes that they wore, and she found the idea of looking through their closets far more exciting than sorting paint. That was why she had mistakenly shouted out at Miss Olivia's suggestion.

The sound of her voice startled the two women. They both jumped and nearly dropped the groceries they'd been holding. They spun around to the corner Lacey had been holed up in and spotted her instantly, surrounded by paint and glitter.

"Lacey?" Miss Annika said, sounding as though she was confused as to why a teenager would be sitting on the floor in the corner of her kitchen, holding a jar of glitter in each hand.

"What are you doing down there?" Miss Olivia asked the question that was on Miss Annika's face.

"Sorting," Lacey answered, and held the two jars higher.

"How long have you been there?" Miss Annika asked.

"Not long," she answered evasively. "I mean, I was just..." Her mind raced to come up with something, and when it did, she couldn't help the smile that took over her face, because it was simply brilliant. "I was just wondering, I mean I couldn't help but overhear that you won't be able to have your taco night," she said to Miss Olivia, as she attempted to control her voice, trying not to sound too eager. "Well, I think that's a shame, but, well, if you want, if it's okay, um, me and my brother love tacos, and we haven't had them in a really long time. So, we could have dinner here with you that night, if you wanted, if that would be okay."

"Hmm..." Miss Olivia seemed to ponder the suggestion while Lacey crossed her fingers behind her back and hoped for the best. "Well, I guess that could be fun. Okay. That will work, but only if your uncle agrees."

"Oh, he won't have a problem with it," Lacey said. "I'm sure of it." More like she was sure she could get her way with him. Besides, she was secretly hoping that he would want to spend the evening alone with Miss Annika. That would be a good sign that her plan was working.

As predicted, Uncle Owen gave her no trouble whatsoever. The trouble came in the form of her twin. Sure, he went along with her plan, but he intentionally made things more difficult than they needed to be. He was grumpy, argumentative, and just an overall pain. He scowled at Lacey the entire night and would barely speak to Miss Olivia when she asked him questions. He refused to play any of the games that Miss Olivia had planned for the evening which Lacey thought sounded fun. Lacey found herself apologizing to Miss Olivia repeatedly for his terrible atti-tude and regretting dragging him along to what had now become her favorite place.

For her part, Miss Olivia didn't seem too put out by Luke's bad mood. She brushed off Lacey's apologies and assured her that she wasn't offended by the withering glare Luke had given her when she'd suggested that they all do makeovers.

The evening ended with Lacey hoping it had all been worth it, which in her mind meant that Uncle Owen had at least declared his undying love for Miss Annika, if he hadn't already proposed. That would have been worth putting up with her brother's sour mood. In the end though, she was just grateful that she hadn't been banned from ever returning to the neighbors due to Luke's behavior.

But, as she'd dropped them off at home, Miss Olivia had confirmed with Lacey that she would come over the next day to help wrap things up before the big week ahead. Lacey had assured the woman that nothing could keep her away before skipping ahead and beating Luke to the front door. He glared at the smile she threw him over her shoulder before entering the cabin.

However, Lacey decided that she wouldn't let his bad mood ruin her good mood. Whatever was bugging him, whatever had him in such a foul way would hopefully pass and he would become his old self again. She was sure of this, because even though they hadn't been in Port St. Annabelle for long, things were going well. Things were going really well.

In fact, everything was looking so promising that Lacey had begun to wonder if it might be possible to allow herself to begin to hope. Hope that this new home of theirs might work out. Hope that Uncle Owen might be the good guy that he seemed to be. And hope that she and Luke might find a way to start to feel some sort of happiness again. Not like before. She wasn't foolish enough to think that things would ever be like they were before. But maybe, just maybe, they might figure out a new kind of happy. Maybe it could be here, with Uncle Owen, in his cabin in the woods.

❦ 21 ❦

Owen wasn't nervous. Not exactly. But he couldn't pretend that he was calm either. Maybe he was calmly nervous. Was that even a thing? He wasn't sure, but it was the closest description to what he was feeling at the moment. He was standing in his closet, studying the tie section, torn between which tie would be most appropriate for the occasion and which would be most appreciated by his dinner guest. Stripes were bold but plain showed decorum. Owen snorted. If he'd learned anything about her over the past year, it was that she was seriously lacking in decorum. She would most likely prefer the stripes.

But as he reached for the tie that he'd settled on, he began to question that decision as well. Should he wear a tie? A tie was formal. Was that the impression that he wanted to give? Sure, the last time they'd had dinner together, he'd worn a suit, but that was because Lacey had insisted. This time neither Lacey nor Luke would be present, as they would be having dinner next door. So, Lacey's dress code no longer applied. That begged the question of what should he wear? A question that he spent an hour turning over in his mind, as the stack of clothing items tossed haphazardly across his bed testified.

Nope. He wasn't nervous at all, and he certainly wasn't over-thinking things.

In the end, Owen chose a pair of khaki trousers and a light-weight cashmere sweater. He'd even gotten the thumbs up from Lacey, who'd peeked her head into his room at some point during his wardrobe crisis to inform him that she and Luke were leaving for dinner, and to assure him that Olivia would be driving them back home at the end of the evening so that they wouldn't have to walk in the dark.

Although, if Owen had taken the time to think about it, he might not have held her opinion in such high regard, considering the way that she dressed herself. He really needed to get her some new clothes. He wasn't sure how he would manage that when she seemed averse to buying things for herself. Also, school was just around the corner. Both Luke and Lacey would be needing clothes that met the dress code, and school supplies and everything else that teenagers were supposed to have. The list was never ending. It was enough to bring on an anxiety attack. No wonder he and Natasha never had kids.

The sound of the doorbell rescued Owen from his mental anxiety. But it also served the purpose of plunging him back into his earlier nervousness. No, not nervousness. Eagerness? No, definitely not. It was just dinner with a new friend. A potential new friend who happened to be a very attractive woman. But that was certainly coincidental. Possibly. Maybe. This was the silent conversation that he held with the reflection in the mirror until the doorbell rang again, prompting him to sprint to the foyer. Not because he was eager, but because he was worried that she might think he wasn't home and leave. Also, it was rude to make her wait.

Once in the foyer, he took a moment to gather himself together and catch his breath from his sprint down the stairs. When he did open the door, he found himself short of breath again. Only this time it had nothing to do with any physical exertion on his part and everything to do with the woman in front of him. Owen had thought that she'd looked beautiful the other night in the form fitting dress that she'd worn, but this evening she took his breath away.

Annika wore a sleeveless jumpsuit in a bright shade of red that stood out against her brown skin, and her brown hair was pulled back in a casual but sleek ponytail. With his house facing the west, the setting sun threw arcs of color between the trees of the wooded area surrounding his home. Annika stood in the doorway in the midst of the sunset and the last of the sun's rays danced off of her skin, making it appear to glow.

Owen stood there, transfixed by the sight before him. It wasn't until after Annika spoke that the spell was broken, and he regained his senses.

"I know I'm a little late," she said. "I'm sorry. It took me a little longer than expected to find my right shoe." She dangled the leg wearing the errant shoe, as if to offer him a visual to her story.

Owen, who hadn't noticed that she was late and certainly didn't care, shrugged off her apology. "It's fine," he said, coming out of his stupor. "Come in." He stepped back from the door and allowed her to enter. "I hope you brought your appetite. I made lasagna."

Annika's eyes lit up at this information. "I love Italian food," she confessed, as she followed Owen's lead through the great room and into the dining room. Then she scrunched up her nose. "It's not one of those frozen lasagnas from the grocery store, is it?"

Owen stumbled in his tracks at her words, and then held a hand over his heart like she'd physically wounded him. "I can't believe those words came from your mouth. I don't think I've ever been more offended in my life."

"Okay," Annika said, laughing. "Does that mean you made it from scratch?"

He stood up straight and jutted out his chin. "Of course I

did. Luke helped me create the pasta. It was his first time making pasta from scratch."

Annika blinked. They had reached the dining room and stopped walking, so she was able to stare at him, dumbfounded. "You...you made the pasta yourself?"

"Is there any other way?" Owen winked at her, and then left to get the food from the kitchen.

.....

"ALL I'M SAYING IS THAT YOU MUST HAVE CONSISTENCY. Continuity is key to success. Otherwise, there's chaos. What's the point in having any rules? We may as well throw them all out the window."

"See, you're wrong. You're just wrong." Annika adamantly declared. "Of course, there's rules that must be followed, but that's the beauty of the genre. You get to bend those rules, just as long as you offer some sort of explanation for bending them."

"Chaos is what you're advocating. Chaos and madness." Owen shook his head. "Nothing good can come of it."

They were lounging outside on his deck as they had before, having finished their Italian meal, which had been just as delicious as he'd promised. Now they were surrounded by citronella candles and having a very heated discussion about Doctor Who, a passion which they'd learned over dinner that they both shared. At least that was how it started. At some point the discussion over the show's plot points had evolved into a conversation about the Science Fiction genre as a whole, it's rules and limitations. Now they were both standing firmly in their own corner and neither refused to budge on their beliefs.

"You can't use the same actress to play different characters during different time periods for different story lines." Owen stated firmly.

"You can if you give a plausible excuse to explain it away." Annika folded her arms, telling him that she had given her final word on the matter.

Owen watched her and chuckled. "You're stubborn," he said.

She lifted her chin and stared at him, as if to say, 'Yeah, and so what?'

And it was at that moment as she stared him down over the rules of a fictional show that had no effect on either of their lives that Owen realized he liked her. A lot.

He cleared his throat to try and dislodge the lump that had suddenly formed there and said, "I don't think either of us are going to change our opinions, so let's agree to disagree."

She shrugged and unfolded her arms, a sign of concession. Then she said, "It's okay. Star Trek is better anyway."

Owen nearly fell from his seat. "What? Oh, no. That's a deal-breaker for me!"

Annika threw her head back and laughed at the predictable reaction of any diehard Doctor Who fan upon hearing those words. Her laughter was infectious and soon Owen was laughing as well. It was then that it occurred to him that it had been quite some time since he'd done so. It had been a long time since he'd had a reason to laugh, or even smile for that matter. But it felt good now, stretching his lungs, hearing his own voice ring out in the night air, mixing with the sound of her softer laugh. It felt really good, and it made him realize that he missed it. He missed this - this version of himself. It was someone he hadn't seen in a while. Part of him believed he'd never see this version of himself again. Part of him had accepted this. But now-

"What are you doing tomorrow?" Owen asked once the laughter died down.

Annika released a huge sigh. "Preparations. Just like all week. Gotta get ready for camp. Honestly, if I didn't love this so much, I would hate it."

They both laughed lightly at her joke.

Then Owen asked, "Do you think you can carve out a little time in your busy day?"

She tilted her head and gave him a quizzical look.

"I was thinking about taking the boat out on the lake, and I was wondering if you wanted to come."

Annika's face transformed to a look of surprise.

A rare spring breeze blew over them offering the briefest respite from the stifling humidity. The clouds finally parted and revealed the full moon underneath. Out across the yard and further into the woods beyond, every nocturnal creature of Florida produced their finest vocals, delivering a roaring chorus into the night. Owen registered none of these things because when Annika turned to look at him the light from the candles around them illuminated her eyes, making them dance as her surprise turned to joy.

"I've never been on a boat," she said, "Never. Not once." She shrugged. "I can't even swim. Is that a problem?"

He couldn't help but smile at her enthusiasm. "For the boat? Not so much. That's what the life jackets are for. For living on a lake on a peninsula? Yeah, that might become a problem."

"What do I bring? What do I wear?" She carried on, her excitement building by the moment.

"You don't need to bring anything. I have everything we need. And you can just wear shorts or whatever you'll be comfortable in."

"Oooh, I should go shopping!"

"Why? I just told you that you don't have to bring anything."

She rolled her eyes. "To get cute boating clothes, of course."

Owen chuckled. "Of course. I don't know what I was thinking."

"Oh, and shoes," she said almost dreamily. "And maybe a new bag to match."

"So, does that mean you'll be able to join me?"

She grinned at him and nodded. "I can't wait."

He smiled back. "Good. Then it's a date."

Her eyes grew wide which made Owen realize that his choice of words may not have been the best.

"I mean, it's not a date. It's a day that we're going to spend together, but not a date. Not that I wouldn't want to date you. I mean, just not tomorrow."

As he stuttered and backtracked, she began to laugh.

"I was only using that term as a colloquialism, not as its actual definition." His explanation only made her laugh more.

Finally, she stopped his nervous ramblings. "Let's just say that we'll see each other tomorrow. As friends. And after that, we'll see how it goes. But it's not a date."

Owen nodded. "Yes, that's good. It's not a date," he affirmed.

And he meant it. Because despite finding her attractive, he knew he wasn't ready. Not yet.

Later that night, as he performed his nightly routine before bed, Owen thought about the situation. He thought about it as he changed into his pajamas, he thought about it as he brushed and flossed his teeth, he thought about it as he attempted to read for an hour from the book he kept on the nightstand by his bed. Attempted, but failed. He gave up on it. The words seemed to have no meaning and he found himself re-reading the same sentence multiple times without comprehending any of it.

Owen returned the book to the nightstand, no further along than when he'd picked it up, and sank down into the mattress to pretend to sleep. He knew real sleep would be impossible while his mind was so preoccupied.

The crux of the matter was that in order to pursue what he wanted, he would have to face what he didn't want to face, think about what he'd spent the last two years intentionally not thinking about, and talk about what he promised himself that he would never speak to anyone about.

Because he was interested in Annika, that much was clear to him, and he wanted to be able to move forward to the next step – asking her for a real date. But Owen knew that if he was going to look to the future, he would have to reconcile with the past. That started with removing his wedding ring. Finally. He just didn't know if he *could* do it. He just wasn't sure.

Owen held his right hand in front of his face. The silvery moonlight squeezed through the almost non-existent openings of the closed Venetian blinds on the large bay window of his bedroom. The light was sparse, but it was just enough to illuminate the gold band around his finger. It reminded him of the light that had dazzled in Annika's eyes and taken his breath away earlier that evening.

The memory of that moment made his chest tighten. Owen thought he would never feel that way again. He was certain he would never be interested in anyone else. But-

Owen held his breath and slid the ring off his finger. And he waited. And waited. Then he finally released his breath, because he didn't feel the agony in his heart that he'd expected to feel. He just felt sad. It felt like something that had been the center of his life for such a long time had come to an end. But it also felt necessary, as though its time had come, as though it were the end of an era. It was beautiful while it lasted, but it would be wrong to hold onto it and try to make it fit where it no longer belonged. He could accept this.

But Owen knew that he would also have to do something else that would be much more difficult, something he'd vowed to never do. Up until this point, he'd kept to his word and never spoken about it. But he wanted to be an open book. Thus, he would have to tell Annika about his wife. He would have to talk about Natasha.

🧩 22 🧩

Saturday proved to be the perfect day for boating. The warm spring weather, which in Florida was nearly identical to summer weather but with a bit more rain, had Owen in high spirits as he boarded the vessel. Well, the weather and the company.

Annika had arrived at his front door at the agreed upon time, wearing her new boating clothes. Owen examined the woman at his door, grinning excitedly. She was wearing navy blue shorts covered in white anchors and a white top covered in navy blue anchors. Navy anchors dangled from her earlobes, and she even had an anchor-shaped handbag slung across her shoulder.

Owen chuckled. From her smile to her themed clothing, Annika's enthusiasm could not be denied.

"I'm ready to go sailing," she announced.

"Well, I don't own a sailboat so that might be difficult, but I do have a deck boat. If you don't mind going boating with me, then we could do that."

Annika nodded, the anchors in her ears bobbing along with her head, and her grin still firmly in place.

"Okay," Owen said, ushering her through the front door. "Let's go boating."

Owen had purchased the 20 ft deck boat shortly after his marriage to Natasha. She'd told him not to buy it, warned that it was a waste of money, and brought up the fact that he'd never even been on a boat, let alone known how to operate one. It was true, he hadn't been on a boat before because although he'd been born and raised in a cabin on the lake, his parents had been paranoid about boating accidents and had never owned a boat, never even considered purchasing one. Owen, who loved fishing, and dreamed of being out on the water had been determined to buy his own boat as soon as financially possible. He'd researched and priced them and finally settled on a deck boat mainly because someone locally was selling one for cheap. Very cheap. So, he'd purchased it and spent countless hours refurbishing it. In the end, Natasha had come around once she'd seen how determined he was, especially when he'd learned how to drive it. In fact, she'd grown to love spending afternoons on the boat just as much as he did. It was one of the few things he'd shared with Natasha that he'd been able to continue after he'd lost her.

As he started the boat and pulled away from the dock, headed out onto the lake, Owen watched Annika's reaction to her first boating experience. He saw her initial trepidation of the unfamiliar surroundings, followed by fear at the rocking motion caused by the waves, and then delight as she relaxed and allowed herself to enjoy the new adventure.

Owen couldn't help but note how similar her reaction was to Natasha's first time out on the water, although the two women were dissimilar in every other regard. Natasha had been mild mannered, slow to anger and quick to forgive. Even when she was upset, there were no visible signs of the emotion, at least to the untrained eye. To Owen, who'd grown to know her so well, she was an open book. He'd learned to read her distress in the way she folded her hands, make out her unhappiness by the way she avoided eye contact. She had been a riddle to be deciphered and he had diligently worked out every clue.

Annika, on the other hand, hid nothing. She displayed her

emotions openly to everyone, not leaving the interpretation of her feelings to chance. Where Natasha was harmonious, Annika was a spitfire. She angered easily and held a grudge for so long that she rivaled Owen's own record length of time.

Once he'd driven a fair distance and the coastline was no longer visible on the horizon, Owen cut the engine and allowed the boat to drift. He joined Annika on the bench seat at the rear of the boat, stopping along the way to retrieve two ice cold beverages from the cooler he'd brought along. He handed her the drink and opened his own.

"I was wondering what was in there," Annika said, gesturing to the white cooler sitting on the deck. She took a sip of her drink. "You really came prepared, but how did you know I love Coke?"

Owen shrugged. "Everyone loves Coke." He drank from his own soda. "I also brought food if you're hungry."

"Well, I am feeling peckish, and I haven't had lunch yet."

"Peckish?"

"I'm hungry and I want food! Is that better?"

Owen laughed and went back to the cooler. "Alright then. I have a few things that you can peck on." He opened the cooler again and began retrieving items. "And for the record," he added, "I'm feeling peckish too."

They distributed the food evenly and had a lavish feast of corned beef sandwiches, potato salad, deli pickles, and blondies. They ate in silence, relishing every bite until the last blondie had been devoured. When lunch was over and the plastic containers put away, they both leaned back in their seats feeling the stuffed contentment of a good meal eaten.

"Those blondies turned out better than I thought," Owen remarked. "I was afraid that I might've overbaked them, but they were perfect."

Annika shook her head and smiled.

"What?" he asked.

"Do you ever really overbake or burn or mess up anything in the kitchen? Ever?"

"Sure I do."

"Yeah right," she challenged.

"I do," he argued back. "I just don't tell anyone, and I get rid of the evidence quickly and quietly."

"You what?!" Annika laughed out loud. "You destroy all the evidence?"

"Well," Owen defended himself, "I do have a reputation to uphold." Then he started laughing as well.

"It's nice to know my hard work is appreciated though," Owen said once their laughter had died down. "I take it you enjoyed lunch."

Annika nodded, then said, "The best part was the pickles. They had an odd taste. I've never tasted pickles like that. What brand were they?"

Owen smiled at her, but it was a melancholy smile that didn't quite reach his eyes. "I didn't buy them. I made them."

Annika's mouth dropped open, and Owen gave a soft laugh at her reaction.

"You made them? What do you mean you made them? Like... how?"

He shook his head. "It's not that hard. People do it all the time. You cut up the cucumbers, make the brine, seal it all in a jar, and leave it for it to, well, pickle."

Annika stared at him, as though he'd done something amazing, like solved a Calculus problem in his head (which he had been known to do back in college, but that wasn't the point), so he decided to tell her. He figured that this was as good a segue as any to bring up what he really wanted to talk to her about.

"Look," Owen said, "I'm pleased that you liked them, but I really can't take the credit. The flavor is all in the brine and the recipe for that...well...those were Natasha's pickles."

"Natasha?"

He nodded slowly, and then spoke wistfully, remembering.

"It was one of the things she was most known for. She won a couple of times with them at the County Fair. Everyone loved Natasha's prized pickles. She used to give away jars as presents. I told her she could probably sell them and make a fortune, but she didn't want that. She just liked making them for the people she loved. That was the kind of person she was – simple, kind, generous."

"Your wife?" Annika asked soberly.

Owen nodded again. "Yeah."

"I heard that you'd been married, but I didn't know her name."

"Natasha Nez. Her name was Natasha Nez."

They sat in silence for a moment. Owen gathered his thoughts and his courage. Annika sat patiently, waiting for him.

The boat rocked in the water, bobbing gently to the natural ebb and flow of the lake. Overhead, the sun barreled relentlessly on the water, the boat, and Annika and Owen. In the boat, Owen breathed deeply and focused on his surroundings rather than the pounding in his chest – the feel of the waves rolling the boat, the heat of the sun warming his skin, the sound of the various species of birds far above him calling out to one another, the smell of Annika's perfume.

When he finally felt ready, Owen told her his story. Annika listened attentively, and if his voice trembled or even cracked at times, she ignored it and for that, Owen was grateful.

"We met in college," he began. "My parents had passed, one after the other, right after I left for school, and by then I wasn't on speaking terms with my sister. I guess I was craving something resembling a family or maybe I was just missing my culture, so I joined the Native-American student group. There were so few of us there that we were all on a first name basis right away. That's where I met her, and it was love at first sight, at least it was for me anyway. She, on the other hand, made me work hard for that first date. I thought she was playing hard to get, but later I learned that she was just really shy and reserved. I took her bowling and at the end of the night I told her that she was the woman I would marry."

Annika laughed at this, and Owen chuckled too.

"Believe it or not, that didn't send her running. But I was serious. Later on, she told me that she'd gone straight to her roommate and told her that she'd met the man that she was going to marry."

Owen smiled to himself, cherishing the memory.

"We got married right after I finished medical school, and considering we were both straight out of college and broke, it just made sense for us to move back here into my old family home. I was happy because I loved it here, but I was worried Natasha wouldn't want to live in such a remote area. She followed me with no complaints though, and she took to the town immediately. While I set up my practice, she started volunteering at every charity, organization, and event she could find. She was always trying to save something. She just always wanted to help."

After a moment, Annika said, "It sounds like she was a really sweet person."

"She was," Owen said, unable to keep the anguish from his voice. "She was the sweetest soul that I've ever met. I think that's why it hurt so much when she got sick. How could someone who loved everyone get dealt a blow like that? To have to go through all of that, the diagnosis, the treatments, the pain, the constant uncertainty, and then just to die in the end. It felt so cruel. I just couldn't understand it. Of all the people in the world. It made no sense. Why her? Why?"

"And you couldn't do anything to help her," Annika said, empathizing with the ordeal he must have suffered.

"I was a doctor," he said to her, pleading with his eyes. "Prestigious medical school. Top of the class. But what good was I? Huh? In the end all I did was watch. She was the love of my life, and I just watched her die."

Saying the words aloud that had echoed in his head felt like re-opening an old wound. The pain was so familiar, even if it had been dulled somewhat by time.

"That's why you stopped practicing, isn't it?" she said, finally understanding.

"If I couldn't save her, then what was the point? What was the point of any of it? How could I help anyone when I couldn't even help my own wife?"

Owen held his head in his hands and tried to concentrate on breathing. He hated this part, the remembering, the feeling. It was painful, but he could live through it. He *had* lived through it and come out on the other side. And he was relieved that he'd gotten it all out. He'd confessed to Annika what he hadn't revealed to anyone else, what he'd barely been able to say to himself. And now that it was out, he felt exhausted and emotionally drained.

He felt Annika slide closer to him on the bench seat. They were so close that their knees were almost touching, but he didn't look up. Annika slid her hand into his and squeezed it.

"Owen," she said quietly, almost imperceptibly. "That. Really. Sucks."

Owen let out a rough laugh and looked up at her. "Yeah," he agreed, "it really does."

"Like a lot," she said, causing him to laugh even more.

She smiled at him, a sort of half smile.

"You still love her." It wasn't a question but a statement of fact.

Owen nodded. "I will always love her," he said, smiling back at her. He chose his next words carefully. "But...I think...it's time to let her go." He looked into Annika's warm brown eyes, her hand still tucked into his. "I'm ready to move on," he said with a certainty he hadn't known he'd felt until that moment.

Annika's half smile turned into a whole smile, and the remnants of ice that had been covering his heart defrosted, as if melted by the sun. He lingered there a moment longer, indulging in her smile, before getting to his feet.

"I do believe," he said, if a bit reluctantly, "that we should be getting back. Don't you have a camp to get ready for?"

Annika groaned, causing Owen to chuckle.

"Oh please. You love that camp."

"Yeah, I do. But you hate it. You completely flipped out when you first found out we were going to open it."

Owen grimaced. That wasn't exactly his finest moment. Annika either didn't see his discomfort or decided that she wasn't going to let him off the hook because she continued on.

"You made a big scene at the diner and everything. You were screaming and throwing fliers. You were actually kicked out of the place."

Yep, the wicked grin on her face was evidence that she was enjoying his embarrassment.

Owen decided to tell her the truth. He didn't want to admit it, but he figured he was in too deep at this point. "Well, actually, I didn't hate it last time."

Annika gasped, "What?"

"It wasn't as horrendous as I thought it would be. Some of the kids were actually kind of cute from a reasonable distance and for short lengths of time."

Annika stared at him.

Owen shrugged. "I may have overreacted."

Annika stared at him a moment longer, and then shrugged. "Well," she said, "I'm glad you finally came around. Too bad this might be our curtain call."

Owen frowned. "What do you mean? You aren't closing, are you?"

"Not by choice."

Owen sat back down and watched her, waiting for her to explain. He wanted to give her the time she needed to gather her thoughts and put them into words, just as she'd done for him earlier.

Finally, she sighed. "Do you know Brian Felton?"

"The contractor? Yeah. I went to school with his son,

Richard. Well, Richard was a couple of years ahead of me, but I knew of him. What's Brian got to do with your camp going bust?"

"So, last year when my sister and I moved here, our cabin was in shambles."

Owen nodded. He vividly remembered the sad state that the property next door to him had been in for years. If what he'd heard around town was true, the previous owners had bought it with the intent to rent it out, but they'd never seemed to get around to it. The place had been abandoned and neglected for so many years that it had fallen into total disrepair. In fact, the property was so bad that Owen had assumed that it would have to be demolished.

"Well," Annika continued, "we were going to hire Felton to fix it, but he was way too expensive, so Phillip MacPhearson did it for us instead."

Owen was well aware that Phillip had done the work as he'd seen the hardware store owner next door during that time. He'd even patched up the scrapes and bruises that Phillip and the friends he'd brought to help him, had incurred during the renovation phase.

"Anyway," Annika said. She was talking faster now, eagerly explaining. "It seems that Felton got all bent out of shape that we didn't hire him, and he's been making trouble for us ever since."

"What?"

"Yeah. He threatened to get us shut down last time we opened camp, but we didn't pay much attention because we had done everything correctly. All of our paperwork was in order and everything. So, we figured that there was nothing he could really do, right?"

Owen nodded in full agreement with her. He certainly didn't see how Brian could stop them. Short of badmouthing them, there was no way for him to ruin their business. But even that probably wouldn't work, as from what Owen had seen, the sisters had made quite an impression on Port St. Annabelle. Since the moment they'd arrived, together they'd charmed the residents with their tenacity and their spirits. Even he, the supposed town grump, hadn't found too much to complain about with Olivia. And he was warming to Annika more and more each day. So, what exactly did Brian Felton think he could do?

Annika answered that question for him.

"We were feeling pretty confident, but I think he outsmarted us. He's gone to city council and pushed his weight around to try and get us shut down. It looks like he might succeed too due to some new zoning laws."

"That's ridiculous."

"Oh, and get this, the council tried to get him to drop the matter and everything. Even they don't have a problem with us being open. But Felton is determined, and due to those stupid laws, he's likely to get his way. All because his feelings were hurt when we didn't hire him. The whole thing is so silly. Anyway, there's nothing anyone can do as long as Felton insists on pursing this, and his mind is made up. We tried talking to him. Phillip tried talking to him. Even his own son tried to get him to back down. But...well...it was really fun while it lasted."

"Don't give up," Owen told her. "You never know, he may have a change of heart."

Annika snorted.

"Hey, it ain't over til it's over."

She rolled her eyes but didn't bother to argue with him.

The ride seemed to go much faster on the way back, probably because Owen was reluctant to return. Although the day had been difficult and he felt drained from their conversation, he also felt a sense of peace. Perhaps, he'd needed to get some of that stuff out. Perhaps, he should have talked about it sooner. Now, Annika sat next to him in the passenger seat, with her head back and the wind blowing her ponytail about. She looked radiant as she smiled into the afternoon sun and lifted her hands to catch the wind. Owen was sorry that they had to return. He wouldn't have minded spending another hour out on the water with her. He wouldn't have minded spending several more hours there with her.

After docking and removing their life jackets, they climbed back onto land, and headed to Owen's cabin.

"Did you have a good time?" Owen asked, carrying the cooler as they walked next to each other through the grass.

"I did," she said softly.

This drew a sharp look from him. "Is something wrong?" He could hear it in her voice. It wasn't the same carefree tone that she usually spoke with. When had he learned the differences in her tone of voice?

"Nothing's wrong," she said, "I've just been thinking."

"About?"

They were nearing the cabin now, the deck only a few steps away. Owen was hesitant to take those steps, not wanting the afternoon to end.

"You want to come inside?" he offered. "You can tell me what you were thinking about."

He climbed the steps to the deck and turned around, waiting for her to join him.

"I was thinking about you," she said, as she climbed the steps after him, "or rather about what you said."

When she reached his level, Annika stopped and faced him. "Owen, I don't know how to say this."

Owen's insides began to churn as his stomach did an incredible impression of a platform diver. Never in the history of the world did those words precede anything good. He set the cooler onto the deck and braced himself for her next words, certain that he wouldn't like them.

Annika wringed her hands, worried her bottom lip, and effectively sent his anxiety levels through the roof. Was she actually going to break up with him before they'd even started dating? It was the blondies. He was sure of it. He shouldn't have bragged so much about how well they'd turned out. Now she thought he was arrogant and wanted nothing to do with him.

"The thing is," she said. "Well, you're wrong. You're just wrong. The measure of your worth to the world isn't predicated upon your inability to save one. No matter how incredibly significant that one might be."

Owen nodded in agreement, as if he had any idea what she was talking about. He didn't tell her she was speaking in riddles though. He thought it best to just agree in hopes that she would stumble upon an explanation.

"Don't you see that?"

"Not really," he admitted.

She sighed, and then stepped closer to him and gently placed her hand on his arm, which was a darker shade of brown than normal, due to his day out in the sun.

"I can't comprehend the level of pain you felt, knowing that you couldn't save your wife. But not saving her and not helping her are two completely different things. You helped her through the most difficult thing she ever had to face, just by showing up and being there for her."

Owen stiffened, a visceral reaction to the shock of her words. But he didn't pull away, which Annika must've taken as a signal to continue.

"I know it's none of my business and you didn't ask my opinion, but I just can't stand the thought of you torturing yourself over something that you had no control over. Especially, considering everything you've told me about Natasha, I think that she would've told you the same thing."

Her words took the breath out of him, and he would've thanked her for saying them if he hadn't heard screaming coming from inside the house.

L acey breathed a sigh of contentment. No, not contentment. Certainly not. Happiness? Hmm...no, not really that either. More like the possibility of happiness. Lacey breathed a sigh of the tentative possibility of foreseeable happiness. It was the fact that she was permitting thoughts of some sort of future happiness to burrow into her heart that made it that much more painful when things came crashing down. When the colloquial other shoe dropped, she was unprepared and taken aback, not just by when it occurred but mostly by where it came from.

It was Saturday afternoon and Uncle Owen was off on his romantic boat ride with Miss Annika, falling in love and preparing to live happily ever after. Lacey couldn't help but sigh at that prospect.

She was sitting on the bed in the room that she shared with Luke. She'd just finished doing her laundry (Well, Luke had done his laundry and she had thrown the few items of clothing that she owned in with his), and now she was carefully folding her wardrobe.

She was considering whether she should place her clean

clothes in one of the drawers of the ornate wooden dresser set against the wall across from the bed. Lacey couldn't believe she was even considering it. It was one of the cardinal rules that they had agreed upon – never unpack. Never unpack because this isn't home. Never unpack because we won't be staying long.

Up until now, she'd been keeping her things in the trash bag that she'd brought them in. Storing her clothes in the dresser drawer made it seem as if she were moving in. Permanently. It felt so final, as if it were all settled. And she and Luke had both learned as foster kids that no placement was final. No placement was home.

But still...

Lacey glanced over to the floor and saw Luke's trash bag sitting next to the door, as though he wanted to be ready to leave at any moment. But he'd promised her that he'd make this placement work, that this time they would stay. She'd known even as he said it, that it was a ridiculous promise for him to make. There was no way he could ensure things would work out, but that didn't mean she didn't want it to be true.

Lacey liked it here. She liked the town. She liked the church. She liked the neighbors. She liked the cabin. And she liked Uncle Owen. Out of all the placements, this one felt the most like home. Or something close to it. Lacey shook her head, as if to dispel it of the absurd thoughts floating around inside. No place was home but home. Which meant that no place would be home again because home was gone. She knew this to be true.

But still...

Without another thought and before she could talk herself out of it, Lacey rushed across the room, laundry in her hands, to the oh-so-inviting dresser. One drawer should do. She didn't have many clothes after all. Lacey picked a drawer at random and began shoving her things inside.

"What are you doing?"

"Eek!"

The sound of Luke's voice in the previously quiet room startled Lacey so much that she jumped, while simultaneously making a sound similar to that of a mouse. Lacey spun around to face him, hoping she didn't look as guilty as she felt. Why did he have to come in here at this particular moment? She should have closed the door the moment she'd first considered using the drawer.

"What are you doing?" he asked again.

Luke stood in the middle of the room with his own folded laundry in his hands. Lacey could have smacked herself. She'd forgotten that he had clean clothes to put away too. She should've predicted that he would be coming into the room. She should have locked the door as well.

This time when she didn't answer, Luke walked over and peered into the still open drawer behind her. He glanced down at her things tossed inside and then looked up at her. Then he turned his back and started walking away. For one moment, Lacey thought she saw betrayal in his eyes, and it made her feel as low as a worm. Even worse than a worm. Amoeba. She was amoeba.

"I - I just thought it was time. I mean I know it's only been like a week or so, but..." she trailed off. She didn't know how to finish that statement anyway. What could she say to him? I like it here? I want to live here? I know we promised each other that we'd never call anywhere else home, but I think I want this to be home? No, she couldn't say any of that to him, so she reverted to her old nature and remained quiet.

Luke, although he'd initially appeared hurt by what he'd caught her doing, seemed to revert to his old ways as well. The betrayal Lacey had caught a glimpse of was extinguished, only to be replaced by cold hard resolution. Luke balled up his fists, squared his shoulders, and turned back around to face her.

"It's okay," he said. "I should have guessed this would happen."

Lacey looked at him in wonder. Had he really said it was

okay? Filled with relief at his reaction, and a tad bit of disbelief, she smiled at him. Her relief, however, would be short-lived, and her smile would have an even shorter life span, because in the very next breath, Luke let his true feelings be known.

"You've changed," he said, accusingly.

"What?"

"From the moment we got here. I've watched you get worse and worse."

"What are you talking about?"

"It's that lady next door. Every time you get a chance you go running over there, following her around, doing whatever she says."

"That's not true!" Lacey argued, and then bit her lip because it felt just a little true.

He scoffed. "Yes, it is. All you care about is trying to be just like her. She's not your mother, you know."

Lacey gasped at the cruelty in Luke's words.

She knew Luke could be mean. She'd watched him turn his tongue and his fists on people at least a dozen times. But she'd always witnessed it from the sidelines. He'd take on a man twice his size without hesitation to keep her out of harm's way. She'd watched him do it and had tended to his bruises after the monumental beating he'd suffered, the whole time feeling extremely grateful that he was her brother.

Lacey had heard him shout down and tell off more people than she could remember with his quick wit and sharp tongue. Most of them had deserved it, and the others had really deserved it.

Lacey, whose tongue got tied the moment she became flustered or frightened or even angry, had never had to worry about bullies or anyone else because she'd had Luke. Luke had always been there, ready to fight for her with his fists or his words. He had always fought for her, but now he was fighting her.

As usual, Lacey, couldn't speak. Her eyes filled with tears –

out of hurt or anger, she wasn't sure, but the tears came just the same.

But Luke wasn't done. No, it appeared he was just getting warmed up.

"She's not your mother, as much as you wish she was."

Lacey shook her head, either to deny Luke's accusations or to banish his words from her mind.

Luke ignored her and pushed on. He seemed intent on making her break.

"You're trying so hard to be just like her. You're talking like her and everything. *Let's go to church.*" On the last line, he mimicked her voice. Then he shouted at her, "You don't even have clothes to wear to church!"

"Shut up!" Lacey shouted back. She had somehow found her voice and said the only thing that had come to her. "Just shut up!"

But Luke carried on and this time he went for the jugular.

"Look at you. You're like a complete stranger. I don't even recognize you. If mom saw you like this, she'd be ashamed of you."

Lacey didn't think, couldn't think. She just reacted. Her hand reached out towards the dresser and closed around the first thing it touched, Luke's flashlight. Without hesitation, she grabbed the flashlight and chucked it at Luke's head. Luke, whose reflexes were faster, saw the projectile coming and managed to duck out of the way. The weapon narrowly missed him, went sailing across the room, and shattered against the wall.

Lacey didn't hear it break, and in that moment, she wouldn't have cared even if she had. All she cared about was getting as far away from Luke as she could. She headed towards the door. Luke moved as if to block her passage. "I hate you!" she screamed through her tears and shoved him out of her way.

"You're crazy!" he shouted after her while rubbing his midsection where he'd caught an elbow when she'd shoved him.

Lacey didn't respond to him. She ran to the bedroom door,

desperate to be away from him and sobbing the whole way. She paused momentarily once she'd cleared the threshold, shocked to discover that they'd had an audience. Uncle Luke and Miss Annika stood just outside the door in the hallway. One look at their horrified faces told Lacey that they'd heard the whole fight.

Humiliated and ashamed, Lacey took off running again, a fresh wave of tears hitting her eyes. She ran downstairs, through the cabin, and out the back door. With no clear destination in mind, she let her feet take her wherever they chose – past the backyard and through the woods.

As her feet pounded across the earth, she could hear Luke's words reverberating through her mind. She couldn't make it stop. She couldn't remember ever feeling so angry at a person as she did at that moment. But as angry as she was at Luke by the things that he'd said, she was far more hurt.

How could Luke say those things to her? And how could he ever think that she'd want someone else to be her mother, even someone as amazing as Miss Annika. No. Her mother was gone.

Lacey finally stopped running. Out of breath and exhausted, she collapsed in a pile by a tree. She had no idea where she was as she hadn't been paying attention to where she was going. At the moment, she didn't really care. She was far too overwhelmed with her grief to be bothered by such a thing.

So, she sat by the tree and cried her heart out. She cried the way she hadn't cried in ages, the way she hadn't even cried when her parents had died and her whole world was turned upside down. She'd wanted to cry then. She'd wanted to scream and wail at the universe at the injustice of it all. But there hadn't been time with the caseworker rushing them to collect their things from their home, and then shooing them along to her office, and to the shelter. Then there were the foster homes, all of which were so unpleasant that they themselves were reason enough to cry. But she didn't cry. Not even then. There didn't seem to be any point. It wasn't like crying or grieving or even thinking about it would bring her parents back. Besides, Luke hadn't cried, and she'd felt that if he could be strong then she needed to be strong as well. So, she didn't dwell on it. She didn't think about it.

But she thought about it now, sitting alone under a massive oak tree in the middle of the woods in the late afternoon sun. She thought about it, and she cried.

❧ 24 ❧

Owen reached the second floor, following the shouting to its source. It was coming from the twins' room. They were in the middle of a heated argument, that much was obvious. What wasn't obvious was why. As far as Owen had seen, the two of them were thick as thieves. He couldn't imagine why they'd suddenly turned on each other.

He reached their bedroom and stood outside the door, trying to understand what had set the two of them off, and trying to figure out what he should do about it.

"Maybe you should break this up."

Owen turned around to find that Annika had followed him. She stood just behind him with a pained expression on her face, as though it hurt her to hear the twins fighting each other. As usual, she was offering up sound advice to him. Owen intended to follow that advice. Before he could intervene, however, he heard something that made his blood run cold.

"If mom saw you like this, she'd be ashamed of you!"

This came from Luke. Owen couldn't believe his ears. Next to him, Annika gasped.

"Did he just say-"

"Yeah," Owen clipped, equal waves of shock and anger over his nephew's words washing over him.

Lacey, quite naturally, threw the first thing she could grab at her brother. Then she burst into tears and ran from the room. She rushed past both Owen and Annika in a blur before Owen could even think of stopping her.

"That poor girl," Annika said, her thoughts mirroring Owen's own.

Still inside the room, Owen could hear Luke muttering to himself. Owen knew and could sense that this was a key guardianship moment. More than that, a key uncle moment. Too bad he had no idea what to do. His heart was torn between going to Lacey and comforting her and going to Luke and throttling him. He ran his hands through his hair, wracked with frustration. It felt like he was being tested for a subject he hadn't studied for. In fact, he didn't even know that he was registered for the class. If this was what parenting was like, he and Natasha definitely made the right decision to not have kids.

"Owen," Annika said, startling him. He was so lost in his own thoughts that he'd almost forgotten she was there.

"Owen," she repeated, but then stopped when she saw his face.

He looked at her openly, vulnerably and told her what he'd come to realize.

"I can't do this." He released a deep breath before continuing in a shaky voice. "I tried to. I wanted to. I wanted to so bad, but I can't." He swallowed and said, "I think I should call their caseworker. Let her know that it's not going to work. I just-"

He looked at the floor, the wall, anywhere but at Annika. He didn't want to see her face as he admitted to her that he'd failed to help someone he cared for. Again. Owen stared at his hands. His useless hands. They hadn't saved Natasha. And now, when his niece and nephew needed him most, he couldn't do a thing to help them.

Well, he could do this. He would send them back to their

caseworker and she could find them a good home. They deserved that. They would have real parents who knew what to do when they imploded and went at each other's throats, not the town recluse who was rooted to the spot, unable to act. No, they deserved someone else. Anyone else. Because anyone else would be better suited for the job than him.

"Look," Annika said, shaking him out of his thoughts. "Right here. Right now. We need to do something."

"I don't know what to do," he told her, finally meeting her eyes.

"Well," she said, returning his gaze, unwavering, "neither do I. So, we're going to go with our guts. My gut is telling me to go after that girl. What's your gut telling you to do?"

Owen thought for a brief moment, but really, he knew the answer to her question. It was the obvious choice. "I need to talk to him." He nodded, certain of his decision.

"Okay. Then I'm going to go find her."

"And maybe," Owen said, pausing her retreat, "maybe she could stay with you tonight. I think some time apart might be good for them."

Annika nodded. "I think you're right."

.....

LACEY HAD JUST ABOUT CRIED HERSELF OUT BY THE TIME THE afternoon sun melted into the evening sun. She was still slumped against the tree, who she now considered her only friend. Perhaps she could even live there. She wondered if Uncle Owen would mind her moving into a tree on his land. Was this even his land?

She looked around and grew alarmed. Where was she? She hadn't followed any path. She'd just run aimlessly, and now she was getting the sinking suspicion that she might be lost. She couldn't even tell for sure which direction she had come.

Just as the panic started, she heard barking in the distance. And then it wasn't in the distance. She stood up, listening carefully. Yep, that was barking, and it was getting closer.

It could be a serial killer, she thought briefly. But would a serial killer have a cute dog? Then again, who said the dog was cute. It was too far away for her to see it, so far all she knew it was one of those rabid murderous dogs that attacked people on sight. Now she was more afraid of the animal (which had almost reached her, judging by the sound of its barks) than any human that might be escorting the animal.

Lacey backed up to the tree. She had few options available to her. She certainly couldn't outrun a dog. She didn't have a weapon and even if she did, Lacey doubted that she'd be able to use it on an animal, even one that was trying to attack her. Maybe she should try and hide. It sounded like a weak plan to her, but she was desperate and no other ideas were forthcoming, so hiding it was. But where? She could climb the tree. A dog couldn't follow her up there. Sure, she'd never climbed a tree before and wasn't quite sure how to go about it, but no better time to learn than now.

She quickly examined the tree and tried to deduce the best way to scramble up it. However, before she could even begin her ill-advised climb, the dog broke through the trees and rushed toward her, and Lacey saw with unquantifiable relief that the rabid animal she was so afraid of was Nosey.

He circled her excitedly, sniffing at her feet, tail wagging with unbridled enthusiasm. She bent to pet him and let him lick her hands in affection. After a moment of this, Lacey looked at the dog with a frown, confused at his presence. Not that she wasn't pleased to see him. She was delighted that he'd found her in the woods and not the rabid animal she had feared, but she had no idea why he was there. How had he even found her?

The answer to her question came trampling through the woods.

"Oh, there you are," Miss Annika said, breathing heavily. "That dog," she pointed at Nosey as she took time to catch her breath. "That dog runs too fast. It's like he doesn't even care if someone's trying to follow him. He just takes off as soon as he gets the scent of his target."

She walked over to Lacey and the dog in question while Lacey stared at her, dumbfounded.

"But I guess I can't be too mad at him," Miss Annika said. "He did lead me here." She reached down and pet him for a job well done.

Lacey opened her mouth, but she wasn't sure which of the dozen questions running through her mind she should ask first. "What are you doing here?" was the one that came out.

Miss Annika stood up straight and looked at her. "Looking for you," she said, as if that were the most obvious thing in the world. "And not too soon either. It's starting to get dark, and I definitely don't want to be in the woods at night." She looked up at the sky and Lacey followed her gaze, noting the disappearing sun. "Come on," Miss Annika said. "Nosey can help us find the way to my cabin. As often as he sneaks over there, he should be able to find his way in the dark." She snapped her hand to get Nosey's attention. "Okay, Nosey. Lead the way," she told the dog, and he took off, as if he understood exactly what was expected of him. "Let's go before he gets too far ahead of us," she told Lacey and then took off after the dog.

Lacey ran after the two of them. It wasn't like she was too keen on being in the woods after dark either. She was, in fact, thrilled that she was no longer lost. She just had not expected Miss Annika to come and rescue her. Not after the way she'd behaved.

Once they reached the cabin next door (to Lacey's surprise because although she'd been confident that Nosey could find the way, she'd had her doubts that he'd understood where he was supposed to be leading them), Nosey far ahead of them and sending back barks like echolocation, they slowed their run, and both nearly collapsed on the ground with exhaustion. Chasing after an enthusiastic dog was not for the weak. Somehow, they managed to move their tired limbs to the door and inside the cabin to the dining room. For his hard work, Nosey was given dog treats and cold water, while the two humans received the luxury of sitting in an air-conditioned home in comfortable chairs. They were extremely appreciative of this.

Once they'd recovered from their ordeal, Miss Annika said. "I'm afraid we're on our own for dinner tonight. Olivia went out with Phillip. That means the worst possible thing – we're going to have to cook for ourselves." She cringed when she said this, which brought a small smile to Lacey's face.

"I'm actually kind of afraid we might give ourselves food poisoning," Miss Annika said, and mimed vomiting. This brought about a full smile. "Or worse." She pretended to have a seizure and then rolled from her chair onto the floor and under the dining room table. Lacey laughed at this. "Stop laughing," she called from the floor. "This isn't the way I wanted to go. What will they say at my funeral?"

"That you cooked yourself to death?" Lacey offered.

"Death by dinner," Miss Annika said in a dramatic voice. "It will be so embarrassing."

"But you'll be dead. You won't know."

"Oh, I'll know," Miss Annika said. "I'll know and I'll be embarrassed to death."

This caused Lacey to laugh again. "That was so corny," she said through her laughter.

Miss Annika laughed along with her.

"Well, I know how to make spaghetti," Lacey offered.

"You do?" Miss Annika got off of the floor and returned to her chair.

Lacey nodded.

"Okay. I guess we'll have spaghetti then."

An hour later they were seated back at the dining room table eating a dinner of peanut butter sandwiches, pop tarts, and baby carrots (to ensure they were getting their vegetables). A generic brand of grape soda had been chosen for their beverage.

"You know," Miss Annika said while eating a pop tart, "this meal isn't bad at all. It's actually quite tasty." She took a gulp of the grape soda in front of her to wash down the pop tart.

"It's pretty healthy too," Lacey pointed to the baby carrots sitting in front of her, which she had no intentions of touching. Then she pushed the officious items a little further away to make sure that she didn't accidentally put one into her mouth.

Miss Annika, who had been the one to insist on the carrots, noted Lacey's avoidance of the vegetable. "I don't know about healthy," she said, "but it gets the job done."

Lacey cringed. "I'm sorry about the spaghetti," she said for the hundredth time. "I don't know what went wrong."

Miss Annika shook her head. "Nope. We're not talking about that experience. Ever."

Flashbacks of the disaster that had transpired and the house fire that had nearly resulted from their kitchen experiment threatened to overtake Lacey until Miss Annika pulled her from the terrifying thoughts.

"No. We cleaned the mess and threw out the ruined food. All traces of that...experience are gone, and we will never speak of it again."

Lacey nodded. That sounded like a good idea.

They continued with their meal until they'd both had their fill of junk food (the carrots remained untouched and eventually were returned to the fridge). Then they cleaned up behind themselves and at Miss Annika's suggestion and Lacey's enthusiastic agreement, they went to Miss Olivia's bedroom to go through her jewelry and try on the best pieces.

A short while later they were both covered in a ridiculous amount of costume jewelry and fake diamonds. They'd taken the necessary dozens of pictures and posted them to social media.

Now Lacey, who was wearing a tiara and pink lipstick (because if they were going to wear her jewelry it only made sense that they should wear her makeup as well), was admiring herself in the vanity mirror. Miss Annika joined her and they both began posing like models.

"Fabulous darling. Fabulous," Miss Annika said in a terrible French accent causing Lacey to burst into laughter. Once she stopped laughing, Miss Annika asked her a question that took all the joy from her.

"Are you feeling better?"

Instantly the bubble of happiness that had been forming around her heart deflated along with her smile, and she found herself struggling not to cry again.

"Come sit down," Miss Annika said, and she guided Lacey over to the queen sized four poster bed that was set against the wall directly across from the vanity. The bedding was hot pink (which Lacey was beginning to suspect was Miss Olivia's favorite color) and there was an interesting assortment of pillows and stuffed animals arranged against the headboard. Lacey ran her hand across the soft comforter and wondered if the bed was as comfortable and cozy as it looked. She sat on the edge of the bed and Miss Annika sat next to her.

"I hope you don't mind but I overheard the fight you had with your brother."

Lacey stared at the floor. She tried to concentrate on the furry pink rug under her feet and not on the lump in her throat or the pain in her heart.

Miss Annika took her hand and held it as she spoke.

"You do know, don't you, that every word he said is complete baloney. None of it's true."

Lacey did cry then. First the tears came slowly. Then, Miss Annika pulled her into her arms and the silent crying turned into a sob.

"I miss my mom," Lacey cried into Miss Annika's arms.

"I know you do princess. I know you do."

"I had the best mom in the whole world."

Lacey thought she'd cried herself out in the woods earlier, but here in Miss Annika's arms, fresh tears poured out as the pain rolled over her. It was as if six months of grief had caught up to her in one day.

"I wish I could make this easier for you, but I don't think that there's any way around this pain. There are no short cuts to get to the other side. I'm afraid you have to go right through it. But I'm here with you. I won't let you go through it alone."

Miss Annika's words of comfort did little to salve the wound in her heart. Her mother was gone. Lacey would never hug her again. Lacey would never smell her perfume again. Lacey would never see her mother again. She was gone.

Lacey felt the sorrow wrap around her like a blanket, covering every inch of her in pain. All she could do was cry. Neither of them said anything else. Lacey cried out her anguish and Miss Annika held her.

Later that evening, long after Lacey had exhausted herself with tears and fallen asleep on the bed, Olivia returned home and the two adults stood next to the bed, discussing the situation. Annika filled her in on the day's events, and Olivia was appropriately heartbroken over Lacey's pain.

"Poor thing," she said, looking over at the teenager asleep on her bed.

"She'll be okay," Annika said with certainty. She reached over and picked up the tiara that had fallen from Lacey's head at some point, probably when she'd fallen asleep. "She got dealt a really hard blow, but she's a tough kid and as smart as they come. She'll get through this and come out on the other side." She handed the tiara to Olivia.

"I know she'll get through it," Olivia said as she walked over to the vanity and placed the tiara back on its custom-made stand. "The thing is, what will she be like once she gets to the other side?"

Annika sighed. "I guess we'll find out." She looked back

down at the sleeping girl. "Do you want me to wake her and move her to a guest room?"

"No, let her stay here. I'll sleep with you tonight."

Annika nodded her agreement with the idea. She took the throw blanket folded across the bottom of the bed and spread it out over Lacey.

"You know," Olivia remarked, "she really needs new clothes."

"Yeah, I mentioned it to Owen, but we should take her shopping before she starts school."

"Definitely. I guess tomorrow she could borrow one of our dresses to wear to church. I'm sure we can find something here to fit her."

With that, they left the room and left Lacey to sleep off the day's troubles.

❧ 25 ❧

Owen counted to ten before entering the room. He was sure he'd read that somewhere. When you were angry you were supposed to count to ten before speaking. After ten he still wanted to yell at Luke, so he tried counting again. At fifteen he gave up and stormed into the room.

He found Luke sitting on the bed with his back to the door. Luke was slouched over and as Owen crossed the room, he could see the boy's shoulders shaking and hear the soft sobs coming from him. This made Owen falter in his step. He had expected Luke to be angry, irrational. He had expected to receive the same Luke that Lacey had tangled with. Owen had intended to march into the room and knock some sense into the boy.

This, however, this was something he hadn't anticipated. Owen never expected to see Luke broken, and he couldn't have predicted the way the sight of his nephew crying would affect him.

Everything he had intended to say was forgotten and the only thought left in Owen's mind was that he must protect this boy no matter what. It was remarkable really. Later, when Owen was alone and had more time to think it over thoroughly, he still

PAMELA BROWN

wouldn't be able to come up with a rational explanation. He'd spent a little over a week with the twins. He barely knew them at all. Yet, he knew with certainty now that he loved them fiercely and that he could do, would do anything for them. Including learning how to be a good uncle.

Owen continued his approach to the bed, more slowly this time, his anger gone. He sat next to Luke on the bed and attempted to place a hand on his shoulder, but Luke shrugged him off, so Owen tried to reach him with words.

"Listen Luke, I know you're upset but you don't have to go through this alone. I'm right here for you, for both of you."

"Liar!" Luke yelled through his tears. "You don't care what happens to us. I heard you tell that neighbor lady that you're gonna send us away. You said all that stuff when we got here about us being family, but you didn't mean any of it, did you? You're just like all the rest of them. You can't wait to get rid of us."

Luke's accusations pierced Owen's heart. He had no idea that his voice had carried from the hallway. His conversation with Annika wasn't something that he'd ever wanted Luke to hear. Now he attempted to do damage control.

"I meant every word I said. We are family. An address doesn't change that. I mean, we don't have to live together to spend time together. I plan on being a part of your lives forever."

Luke turned around then and faced Owen. His face was tear-stained, and his eyes glistened with fresh tears yet to be shed. He stared Owen in the eyes and said, "If you send us away, we'll never see you again." His voice tremored as he spoke, but his gaze held steady.

Owen met his stare for a moment and then looked down at his own hands. The truth of Luke's statement cut him like a knife. He'd heard about the cruelty of the foster care system. He'd even caught a glimpse of it when the twins had arrived – malnourished, hand-me-down ill-fitted clothing, and the bruises

216

(both internal and external). However, he'd had the privilege of never having to witness the foster care system up close. Now he was being confronted with the reality of it through Luke, who was all too familiar with it.

Luke's words rang true. What were the odds that Owen would be able to keep in touch with them if they were shipped off to the other side of the state? For that matter, would he even be permitted to know where they were? If he was no longer their guardian, would he even have that right? He wasn't sure how these things worked.

"Maybe that's what you want," Luke said, "to be rid of us for good." He turned back around and faced the wall. "Well, now you get your wish. You won't see us anymore. We won't even see each other." Once he said that, fresh sobs racked through his body.

At first, Owen was confused. Then, as the memory surfaced, a fresh horror struck Owen. He closed his eyes as understanding dawned on him. With everything that was happening, he hadn't paid close attention at the time, but now as he remembered the caseworker's words thrown so cavalierly during her departure, Owen realized the reality of the situation they were facing.

"Is that why you're crying? You're afraid of being separated from your sister?"

Luke didn't answer at first. Then he confessed through his tears. "I messed up. I was supposed to make this work, but I messed up. And now you're kicking us out and it's all my fault."

"I-"

Owen searched for words but found none. He thought for a moment, then tried again.

"It's not your fault Luke. It's my fault."

Owen took a deep breath. He knew he had to lay all his cards out on the table. It might be the only way that Luke could ever understand and stop blaming himself for something that he didn't do, something he had no control over.

"It's me Luke. I'm broken. Damaged goods. I can't take care of you. I'm too messed up. I thought the worst thing that could ever happen to me was when my parents died, but then I lost my sister. After that, I was sure that nothing could ever hurt worse. But then my wife was diagnosed with cancer. I had to watch her slowly slip away and there was nothing I could do about it. There was no medicine that would cure her. There was just... nothing. And I don't...I don't think I've ever recovered from losing her."

Owen turned to Luke, who had stopped crying at some point while Owen was speaking, and was now watching him with interest.

"Don't you see," Owen said, pleading with him to under-stand. "I can't take care of you when I'm barely hanging on myself."

Luke looked down at the floor, appearing to think about what Owen had said. After a moment of thinking he looked back at Owen.

"That's why you stopped being a doctor?"

"Well, I didn't stop being a doctor. I just stopped practicing."

"But that's it, isn't it?" Luke said, his tone shifting to accusing.

Owen shrugged. "I just didn't see the point."

"Man," Luke scoffed, "you just give up on everything, don't you?"

His reaction shocked Owen so much that he didn't respond immediately. Once he'd registered it though, he became offended.

"What's that supposed to mean?"

"Just what I said." Luke stood up and looked down at Owen with disdain.

Owen, who was baffled at the sudden mood change, stared back at Luke, at a loss for words.

But Luke had plenty to say.

"You give up on everything. Your sister doesn't do what you want her to, so you write her off and give her up. You can't cure your wife, so you give up on medicine. Me and Lacey don't act how you thought we would, so you give up on us. Like, you don't even try."

Owen stared at him open-mouthed, too stunned to speak.

"My dad," Luke continued, even though his eyes began to cloud with tears again, "he never did anything right. He would always say the wrong thing. He could barely cook. He was terrible at cleaning. He couldn't even remember our birthday. But he would never ever give us up. Not in a million years. He would fight for us."

His tears were falling now, and his voice was no longer clear, but shook as he cried. "And you tried to make us think this was home? This was never gonna be home. Home is where the people fight to keep you. And you're just giving us up."

He paused to wipe his tears with the back of his hand. Then he shook his head, as though he had come to a decision. He told Owen, "If that's what you think family is, then you're right. We're better off without you."

When he'd finished speaking, Luke turned his back to Owen, as though he couldn't stand to look at him anymore.

Owen stood. He didn't know what to say, what he could say in this moment. But he felt he had to do something. He placed a hand on Luke's shoulder, but Luke shrugged it off, this time more aggressively, more resignedly.

"I..." Owen began, with no clear idea of what would come next.

He didn't get a chance to form the thought, however, because Luke said brusquely, "I don't want to talk anymore. I just want you to leave me alone."

Owen could feel the door shut on their conversation just as clearly as if it were a physical door in front of him. And in that precise moment, he knew that he had lost Luke. The ground that they had gained, the tiny bit of trust, every bit of progress that had been made was gone just that quickly.

Not sure what else to do, Owen granted Luke's request. He left the room quietly, shutting the door behind him. Out in the hallway, he could hear Luke's muffled cries resume.

26

The sound of Luke's cries was like a battering ram to Owen's heart, and he had no idea how to fix it. He forced himself to walk away from the door. He went downstairs and out the back door with no clear destination in mind. Outside, the afternoon was bowing out as the evening took its place, and the sun shifted from a bright yellow death star into a beam of melted gold. It was the perfect time to take Nosey for a walk, before night fell and Owen could no longer find his way through the woods, except Owen had no idea where his dog had run off to.

So, instead he walked out onto the deck, and he came across the cooler that he'd taken on his boating trip with Annika earlier that day. (Had that really been the same day? It seemed like a lifetime ago.) He must have dropped it there when he'd heard the twins fighting and rushed inside. Owen took the cooler now and began cleaning it out. Once he'd stored away the leftovers and cleaned the empty containers, he set about cleaning the cooler itself, ensuring it would be ready the next time he wanted to use it. After that was complete, he decided his boat could use a good cleaning, so he began gathering the tools he'd need for that job. It was while he was in the middle of this task that it hit him what he was really doing – keeping himself busy with mind-less tasks so that he wouldn't have to think, because stopping for just a moment would bring Luke's words to the forefront of his mind and he'd have to face them.

With a resigned sigh, Owen stopped what he was doing. He was in the supply closet downstairs, where he had been stacking his arms with cleaning supplies from the shelves. He slowly returned everything back to its correct place and left the closet. Cleaning wouldn't solve his problems, and it wouldn't bring him peace. It was only a tactic to hold his thoughts at bay.

Owen walked past the great room and into the den. It was his favorite room in the house, and the place where he did most of his heavy thinking. Once in the den, he sat in his much-loved recliner with his feet resting upon the Persian rug.

He supposed he should call the caseworker – he still had her business card stapled to the front of the paperwork she'd given him when she'd first arrived with the twins. He should call and tell her that he'd had a change of heart and that it wasn't going to work out. He *should* call her. But he didn't move from his spot. Owen couldn't bring himself to think about making that call, let alone actually saying the words.

The problem was that he wanted them to stay. He genuinely liked them both and wanted to get to know more about them as individuals, and he was dying to know what they were conveying to each other whenever they did their silent "twin speak". They were growing on him, and he didn't want them to leave. The two of them had brought nothing but chaos and disorder into his life, and if he were being completely honest, he'd loved every minute of it.

But did that make him selfish? He wasn't up to the task of caring for them for all the reasons that he'd mentioned to Luke. So, was he selfish for wanting to keep them anyway, when the responsible thing would be to let them go in hopes of them finding a better home?

Home.

Luke's words cut through Owen like a knife. They bounced through his mind, reverberating, echoing. He couldn't drown the sound out. *Home is where the people fight to keep you.*

Owen couldn't stop hearing it. And each time it tore at his heart. Did Luke really believe that Owen wouldn't fight for him? He'd fight for him. He'd been fighting for him this whole time.

In fact, Owen had been fighting his whole life. He didn't just give up, as Luke put it. The same way he wasn't giving up now. It's just that sometimes you had to know when it was best to walk away, no matter how much you might want to keep going. That's what being an adult was about – knowing when to throw in the towel.

But of course, Luke couldn't see that. All he saw was Owen giving in when things got hard. Owen could imagine that to Luke it looked like he was letting them down, just like every other adult in their life had done.

Throwing Owen's own words back into his face was low though. Owen had meant what he'd said when the twins had arrived. They were family. In fact, the three of them were the only family they had left. The rest of Owen's family had passed years ago. His sister had been his only remaining relative, and now she was gone. As for the twins, their father had been an only child. Owen had learned that from the caseworker. Their father's parents had died as well, and he had no other relatives. That was why they had gone into foster care – because they had no one else. Just as he had no one else. Owen swallowed hard as the reality of that statement hit him. There were no other family members – they only had each other.

And he was going to send them away.

Owen didn't want to think anymore. He didn't want to spend another moment following this train of thought because he didn't like where it was leading, and he didn't like the way it made his heart constrict.

But did he really have that luxury? To shut it out and move on? Sure, he could send the twins away and shut the door on them forever, but...isn't that what he'd done with his sister? Didn't he do that when he'd lost Natasha? Locked himself up inside this log cabin in the middle of the woods and growled at anyone who dared to speak to him. He'd shut out the thoughts, the feelings. He'd thought he was doing what was best for himself, but hadn't he still lost in the end?

He'd lost years with his sister. Years. And now she was gone, and he could never get that time back. He couldn't even apologize for driving her away. He'd thrown away his medical practice which had meant so much to him. He'd worked hard to build it into the success it had become. Natasha had been so proud of him, so happy for him, standing right by his side and encouraging him along the way. Then, because modern medicine refused to bend to his will, he'd shut down the practice that he'd loved dearly.

Owen held his head in his hands. He'd lost so much. So much. Some of it had been out of his control – his parents, Natasha. But he was now starting to realize, some of it may have been his own doing. He wasn't sure. He just knew that he was tired of losing.

27

L uke had a restless night. He alternated between pacing the room and lying on the bed. It was an enormous mattress. This was more obvious to him with the absence of Lacey, who always drifted over to his side of the bed in her sleep, crowding him into the corner. But even without the human boulder lying next to him, he couldn't sleep. He tossed fitfully, making a mess of the bedding.

He'd finally stopped crying, but his thoughts hadn't stopped. Neither had his fears. Uncle Owen would be sending them away, thanks to him. Lacey had done her part and behaved like a well-adjusted kid. But as usual, he'd blown up and ruined everything.

He'd meant what he'd said to Lacey when he told her she'd changed – she had changed, granted it was only a little, but Luke knew her so well that he could spot the differences from a mile away. The way she held her head up, the way she spoke up, and the way she'd ventured out on her own. She was different. Stronger. Happy. Luke could see it clearly. She was adjusting, moving on. Without him.

Then, she'd broken the rule. Seeing Lacey's clothes inside that dresser drawer had been the final straw for Luke. And it wasn't that she'd decided to break the rule, it was that she hadn't even talked to him about it first. She had made the decision without him, like she didn't even need him. It had hurt more than Luke could've imagined. But he didn't tell her that. No. True to form, Luke fought back. And as always, he'd swung with everything he had – at the person he cared about the most.

To make matters worse, when Uncle Owen had tried talking to him, Luke had gone and insulted him as well. It was probably the only chance Luke would have to try and talk him out of ditching them, and Luke had done the opposite. He'd pretty much guaranteed that they'd be kicked out by the morning. This was the best place they'd lived since their mom and dad had died, and now they would have to leave. And after he'd made that promise to Lacey.

What was he going to tell her? Would he even get a chance to talk to her before they separated them? Would she even want to talk to him? Luke wasn't sure.

Where would they send her? Would she be okay? Luke wasn't worried about himself. Whatever happened to him, he'd deal with it. But Lacey. People tended to pick on her, mess with her. Guys tended to. Luke's stomach clenched into a ball thinking about her being alone and facing those creeps on her own.

It was something he hadn't had to worry about here. Sure, he'd been wary at first. Uncle Owen may have seemed nice, but that didn't mean anything. Luke had learned that the nice ones were often the worst ones. But then Uncle Owen had told him that he didn't have to worry about it anymore, and Luke believed him. He could see it in Uncle Owen's eyes, he wasn't like those other men. And Luke had started to feel something he hadn't felt in six months – safe.

Sure, he'd pushed Uncle Owen. He'd had to. Luke had needed to be sure that he was for real, because he'd seemed too good to be true. And Uncle Owen proved to be one of the weirdest people Luke had ever met. He was really messed up too. But he was nice. And honest. A little too honest. Some of the things he said he really should keep to himself. Also, it was kind of pathetic the way he just stayed out in these woods with his dog all the time. The guy didn't have one single friend. Luke bet he didn't even realize how lonely he was. Yep, he was definitely a sad case.

But Luke liked him. A lot. And he didn't want to leave.

All at once, Luke felt the weight of his troubles fall upon his shoulders. He'd tried to be strong. He'd tried to be the pillar, just like his dad had demonstrated countless times, but he'd failed miserably. He felt so scared and helpless and all he could think was that he really missed his dad. He missed him with an ache so deep that it felt like a physical wound. Luke knew, he just knew that if his dad were here then everything would be okay. He curled up into a ball on his bed while sobs racked through his body, and as the longing intensified, Luke wished and hoped and prayed to anyone who would listen to send him his dad.

.....

"BREAKFAST IS READY," UNCLE OWEN SAID.

At some point during the night, Luke must've fallen asleep because he woke to Uncle Owen standing over him and shaking him awake. As Luke blinked away the sleep in his eyes, he noticed the sunlight streaming through the blinds on the bedroom window. He never slept this late anymore. It must've been because he'd been up most of the night worrying. With that thought, the memory of yesterday's events came back to Luke, and he pulled the covers over his head in an attempt to hide away from the world.

"Get up," Uncle Owen said.

"I'm not hungry," Luke mumbled from beneath the covers.

"It wasn't a request," Uncle Owen said. "Come downstairs.

We need to talk." Then he left the room, closing the door behind him.

Luke couldn't imagine what was left to talk about. Uncle Owen had made himself pretty clear the day before. He didn't want them. He didn't care about them. He was throwing them away like garbage. Just like everyone else had done. Throw their belongings in a trash bag and shove them out the door. Then never think about them again.

These were the thoughts going through Luke's mind as he angrily brushed his teeth and furiously washed his face. Then he marched down the stairs, stomping as loudly as he could. At some point he'd gone from feeling sorry for himself to feeling enraged. Enraged at Uncle Owen, the foster care system, and the whole world who seemed to have it in for teenagers.

When Luke reached the dining room, he found Uncle Owen sitting at the table, waiting for him. There was a healthy spread of French toast and sausages for breakfast even though it was just the two of them. Luke's stomach growled, reminding him that he'd skipped dinner. This only served to make him angrier. Uncle Owen thought he could buy him with food. Well, that didn't mean he had to eat it. Luke had gone hungry before and he could do it again. Would do it again, he thought as he remembered the likely future ahead of him within the foster care system.

Luke took the seat opposite Uncle Owen and sat with his arms folded, refusing to touch the scrumptious looking food laid out in front of him. He also refused to look at Uncle Owen. Not because he was afraid he might cry. It was because he was angry. And if he did cry, it was because of how angry he was.

"How did you sleep last night?" Uncle Owen asked. He began filling his own plate with a large helping of food, his appetite clearly not affected by the thought of tossing two helpless teenagers out on the street.

And why was he asking about Luke's troublesome night? Was that supposed to be a joke? Or did he just want to hear all about how Luke suffered through the night? Well, Luke wouldn't give him the satisfaction. He clenched his mouth shut even tighter and glared at the man across from him.

Uncle Owen poured himself a large glass of orange juice from the pitcher on the table. "Did you sleep at all," he asked, seemingly unbothered by Luke's silent treatment, "because I didn't."

Luke watched as Uncle Owen picked up his glass of orange juice, stared at it for a moment, and then said, "I didn't get a wink of sleep. I was up all night thinking."

He set his glass back on the table without drinking. Before him, his food sat on his plate untouched.

"I think," Uncle Owen said, staring down at the plate of food before him. "I think you've made a lot of mistakes," he said to Luke.

Luke rolled his eyes. He should've known that a lecture was coming. Wasn't that in the adult handbook somewhere? It was their go-to move. He prepared himself to be blamed for everything under the sun.

"But," Uncle Owen continued. "I think I've made even more mistakes than you." He sighed. "I also think that you made a lot of good points, although you really need to work on your delivery."

After he said that, Uncle Owen looked up at Luke, who was staring back at him, baffled. This wasn't like any lecture he'd heard before. And it didn't sound like Uncle Owen was rubbing it in that he was kicking them out. In fact, Luke didn't know what the man was saying. He blinked at him, trying to understand what was happening.

"I may not have liked the way I received it, but I can't deny that it was something that I needed to hear. The truth is I've been locked up inside of this cabin for so long, that I think I forgot what it was like to live. It's like, after Natasha died, that was my wife by the way, I don't know if I ever told you her name, but after she died, it's like I just stopped. I boxed all her stuff up and put it away. I just couldn't bring myself to get rid of it. I mean, you saw the storage room. It's piled with her belongings."

Taken off guard, Luke couldn't keep the guilty look from his face. He thought he'd been so careful.

"Yes, I know you've been snooping around the house. Don't look so surprised. It's my house, you think I wouldn't notice that someone searched it. Besides, you weren't exactly subtle about it."

"But you never said anything."

"Because it was harmless." Uncle Owen waved away his concern. "And if it made you feel better to search the place, then have at it. What were you looking for anyway?"

"Evidence of criminal activity," Luke said steely. He didn't think he liked the way Uncle Owen was blowing off his investigation, and he really didn't like the way he was laughing under his breath.

"Well, what did you discover?" Uncle Owen asked, not even attempting to hide his grin.

"The evidence is inconclusive," Luke answered, mainly out of annoyance that his important work was being treated as no more than a kid's game of hide-and-seek.

"Right," Uncle Owen chuckled. "Well, you didn't go snooping in my room and I appreciate you respecting my personal space."

"I didn't get to it. I was saving it for last cause I knew that's where the worst stuff would be. Criminals always hide the stuff in their room somewhere. Plus, my flashlight died."

"Oh," Uncle Owen responded. Then he said something that wiped the scowl off Luke's face. "Well, there's plenty of flashlights around here. And I suppose it wouldn't hurt if you looked around my room a bit whenever you feel like it, if it would help put your mind at ease that I'm not running a drug cartel. Just put everything back the way you found it."

Luke stared at Uncle Owen.

"What do you mean? How am I going to search your room if I don't live here?"

Uncle Owen stared back at him.

"I told you. You were right. I was very wrong."

Luke thought he understood, but he had to be sure. He wanted to hope, but was afraid to. Hope was dangerous. Hope was cruel. He took a moment, cleared his throat, and then asked in a small tentative voice.

"Do you mean we can stay?"

He continued to stare at Uncle Owen. He would meet his gaze, no matter what the answer would be. That was how he saw the definitive nod his uncle gave him.

But that wasn't enough for Luke. He had gone through too much, been let down by too many adults, and had felt the hope crushed from his heart more times than he could count.

"How do I know that?" he demanded. He shook his head, trying to frame his thoughts correctly. He tried again to form the words, to get the answers he desperately needed to hear. "How do I know you're not gonna change your mind again? How do I know that you're not just gonna get rid of us tomorrow, or next week, or next month?"

Uncle Owen started to speak, but Luke cut him off before he could offer up a meaningless platitude.

"And don't say it's cause we're family either, cause that's what they always say at first. Then you break something or get bad grades on your report card or get into a fight with your sister and the next thing you know you're off to your new *family*. So how do I know this time it's for real, and you're not just gonna give up on us?"

Uncle Owen met his gaze steadily. "Because I'm tired of losing. Aren't you tired too?"

Luke wiped at the tears that had fallen as he spoke and nodded slowly.

"Then let's start winning."

28

The morning had been long and difficult, time passing at a snail's pace. But that's often how time goes when there's work to be done. Owen and Luke had eaten breakfast, both of their appetites renewed after their talk. In fact, Owen had insisted that they both fill up, because as he put it, they would need their energy.

"We have a lot of work to do today," he'd said, as Luke shoveled French toast into his mouth, "starting with you apologizing to your sister."

Luke scrunched up his nose at that. Thankfully, his mouth was full though, so he couldn't argue back. Owen spoke quickly before he could swallow and start complaining.

"You said some hurtful things to her. Things that never should've been said. I know you were only pushing because you were upset. She's been spending a lot of time next door, and not so much time with you."

Luke's face turned somber. He lowered his head and finished chewing his food slowly. Owen didn't need him to acknowledge what he'd said though. He knew that he'd gotten it right. He recognized what was happening because he'd seen it before. He'd lived it before.

Owen sighed. "You need to give her space. It doesn't mean she's forgetting about you. Regardless, you can't push her away when you're upset. You push too hard, and you'll lose her. For good." Owen swallowed deeply. "Trust me. I know."

Luke looked back up at Owen and nodded.

Then Owen said, "Actually, that could probably wait until later on today because it's Sunday. She's probably in church right now, so you get a reprieve. We'll tackle the other job first."

Luke stabbed a sausage with his fork. "What's that?" he asked warily before taking a giant bite.

"I think we need to clear out that storage room."

So that's what they spent the morning doing – going through so many boxes and bins that Luke lost count of them all and lost track of the time as well. He only became aware of the hour when his stomach started growling, signaling time for lunch.

"No offense," Luke said, shoving aside a plastic storage container full of colorful skirts to get to the cardboard box underneath, "but your wife sure had a lot of stuff."

"Actually, it's not all hers." Uncle Owen retrieved the container that Luke had tossed to the side and carefully went through the items.

"Well, then who else did all this junk belong to?" Luke poked at the findings inside the box – jewelry and knickknacks. They were no more impressive than the rest of the things he had uncovered so far.

"Your mother."

Luke stopped poking at the items and looked up at Uncle Owen. "What? This stuff was mom's? But I don't recognize any of it. And how'd you get it?"

"When she left here for the final time...when I drove her away, that is, she barely took anything with her. Just a couple of pieces of clothes. Everything else was left here. Once I came to accept the fact that she wasn't returning, I packed everything up and put it in here."

Luke sat quietly for a moment, thinking about the fact that

he'd been surrounded by his mother's belongings this entire time and hadn't known it. The clothes and jewelry began to look different to him now. He touched the items carefully, almost reverently.

"I know it's probably weird," Uncle Owen said, looking at the skirts the same way that Luke looked at the jewelry. "Keeping all this stuff for so long. But I just couldn't bring myself to get rid of any of it. To tell you the truth, it's still really hard. I can't throw it away, and donating it? Well, the thought of a stranger with this stuff just feels kind of wrong."

Luke nodded. Now that he had a personal connection with the items, he understood exactly what Uncle Owen meant.

They spent a few more minutes there, staring at the containers, no decisions being made until Uncle Owen announced, "I'm really hungry. Isn't it lunch time yet?"

That led to them sitting back at the table with cold cut sandwiches on thick slices of bread from the local bakery and fresh brewed sweet tea to wash it down. They were both starved after a morning of rummaging through boxes, and they did justice to their lunches.

"You know," Luke said, looking at his half-eaten sandwich, "for a doctor, you really don't eat very healthy."

Uncle Owen laughed. "I don't think my diet is that terrible."

Luke waved his half-eaten sandwich as evidence to the contrary. Then he added hastily, "Don't get me wrong. I'm not complaining. This is the best I've ever eaten." He took a large bite of his sandwich to prove his point.

"Well, I guess I really do need to cut back on the fried foods, and the cold cuts, and the white bread. Perhaps, add in more fresh salads and drink more water. After all, I'm not in any hurry to get to heaven." Uncle Owen chuckled again and went back to his own lunch.

Luke rolled his eyes. "You don't even believe in heaven."

Uncle Owen frowned. "Of course I do. Don't you?"

Luke shrugged. "I never really thought about it." Then he

said, "How can you believe in heaven when you don't believe in God?"

Uncle Owen had been about to take a drink from his glass of tea, but he stopped to respond to Luke, his glass halfway to his mouth. "What? I believe in God. Why would you assume that I didn't?" He set his glass back down, thirst unquenched.

"Because," Luke answered, "you practically said it when Lacey asked you go to church."

"I didn't say that I don't believe in God."

"Yeah, you did."

"No, I said I wasn't going to church."

"Because you don't believe in God."

Uncle Owen pushed his now empty plate aside with an exasperated sigh. "Look. I believe in God. I believe in heaven. Got it?" Then with the matter laid to rest, he picked his glass back up, ready for that drink.

"Then how come you don't go to church?"

Uncle Owen placed his glass back on the table slowly, again without drinking. He took his time responding. Either he was gathering his thoughts or his patience, maybe both.

"I don't go to church because I don't want to."

"Why?"

"Because I don't. Where is all this coming from?"

"I'm trying to understand because it doesn't make sense," Luke said. His meal now finished as well, Luke stacked his empty plate on top of Uncle Owen's. "When Lacey asked about church you practically bit her head off. It was like you hate God or something."

"I don't hate God. It's more like we had a falling out."

"Huh?" He looked at Uncle Owen in confusion.

"I guess you could say that I was upset with him for a while."

"But you're not upset with him now?"

Uncle Owen stared at Luke for a moment, considering his question. Then he answered him honestly. "I don't know how I feel now."

"That's kind of weird," Luke said. "I never heard of someone being upset with God. You make it sound like he did something to you."

"In a way, he did."

Luke's eyes got big at this. "He did? What did he do?"

"He didn't... are we really talking about this?"

Luke nodded eagerly, his eyes glued to Uncle Owen.

"He gave my wife cancer."

"*He* gave her cancer?"

"Well maybe, or maybe not. I don't know. He certainly didn't stop it from happening, did he? And then he let her die. So yeah, I was pretty upset with him. And you know what? I think I still am."

Uncle Owen sat back in his chair. He pushed his drink away just as he'd done his plate. Evidently, he was no longer thirsty. It probably had something to do with the subject matter. A thoughtful intuitive person would have left the topic alone, as it clearly was upsetting to him.

"So, let me see if I understand," Luke continued with his interrogation. "You believed in God, then something bad happened, so you got mad at him and stopped going to church and stuff."

"Well, I just-"

"Quit?" Luke filled in for him. "Gave up? Yeah, that seems to be a pattern for you."

"Listen," Uncle Owen said through clenched teeth. The small amount of patience he'd found earlier apparently had shriveled up several questions ago. "Not that it's any of your business, but I didn't just quit. When Natasha got sick, I prayed for weeks for her to get better, but it didn't happen. God could've cured her, but he didn't. Instead, he just let her die."

"Sooo," Luke asked, "whenever you pray for something you're supposed to get it?"

"Not necessarily."

"And you only like God if he gives you want you want?"

Owen scowled at him. "No, that's not what I'm saying."

"Sure sounds like it," Luke muttered.

"Look-"

"I'm just saying that it seems kind of shallow. Like you only like God when everything is going your way. But then as soon as something bad happens or he stops giving you stuff, you don't really like him anymore. It sounds like you were a fake friend."

"I-"

"Just something you should maybe think about."

Luke finished off his own tea and sat back in his chair.

"Well... maybe." Owen said quietly, and reached for his drink again. Then he told Luke, "You really need to work on your delivery."

Luke shrugged before begrudgingly agreeing, "Well... maybe."

Owen gave a small smile, but then asked, "Does it seem a little warm in here to you?"

"Well, yeah, but it's the middle of the day. Of course it's hot. We should turn on the a/c."

"The a/c *is* on."

"Oh. Well, that can't be good."

❧ 29 ❧

After a quick check of the thermostat to double check that it was indeed switched on and that it was not cooling the house, Owen called the only company in town that could fix the broken air conditioning unit and was open on a Sunday afternoon – Felton and Son. He was told that it would be a couple of hours before a serviceman could get there at which point Luke protested loudly to being stuck inside of a house with no air conditioning. For once, Owen agreed with him. With the Florida sun directly overhead, and no cool air to save them, the house felt like a furnace. So, they left a key under the mat and a note on the door for the serviceman to let himself inside. Luke was skeptical about trusting a complete stranger to be alone in the house, but Owen told him that he knew Felton and he knew Son, and he assured him that it would be okay. Then they bolted from the place.

That was how they found themselves next door, just in time for the official Spring opening of the camp, which was pretty much the last place on earth that Owen wanted to be. Judging by the scowl on Luke's face and his awkward fidgeting, he was pretty sure that his nephew felt the same. After explaining their dire situation to the women next door (including Lacey, who seemed to have jumped ship and joined their side), it had been decided that Owen and Luke would be permitted to kill a few hours as junior camp counselors. They had both been appalled at the very idea, but accepted the offer, knowing that the alternative was far worse.

As a line of cars arrived, one after the other, Owen and Luke stood on the front lawn with the women (and Lacey) as official counselors, to welcome the campers. Lacey, Annika, and Olivia held enthusiastic grins and said hello to each newcomer. Luke grumbled under his breath. Owen tried to keep his frowns to a minimum in an attempt to not look as miserable as he felt.

.....

LUKE WAS STANDING JUST ABOUT THE LAST PLACE HE WANTED to be. Things couldn't get much worse than this. Immediately, his thoughts turned to the previous night and where he'd thought he'd be at this moment (in the backseat of Miss Abigail's car being carted off to a new foster home or children's shelter). Just the thought was enough to sober him up and get him to offer up a smile. Or at least attempt not to scowl.

"Okay," Miss Annika said. "We are the official welcoming committee, and the campers will be arriving at any moment now. So, everyone put on your game faces."

Luke's scowl deepened, and if he grumbled just a little it couldn't be helped.

"This is gonna be a great week. I can feel it," Miss Olivia said.

Luke had serious doubts about that statement, but decided to keep those thoughts to himself. He looked over at Lacey, who was standing aloft. Her frown seemed to match his in size and attitude. This was peculiar to Luke because he knew that she'd been looking forward to this day since she'd learned about the camp. She'd spent every waking moment working and helping to prepare. Now that it was opening day, she looked like she didn't even want to be here.

Lacey looked up at him briefly before diverting her gaze and frowning even deeper. That was when Luke realized that he was the cause of her misery.

Luke had thought that maybe she'd get over the fight after their time apart. But even thinking that now, he realized how ridiculous that sounded. Lacey didn't get over things. She dwelled and stewed and ruminated and drove herself crazy over it. And now she couldn't enjoy this moment that she'd been so excited about, all because she had a jerk for a brother.

Luke could feel Uncle Owen's gaze on him and looked up to see the man giving him a look that said more than words ever could. Right. He needed to apologize. Now. Luke shoved his fists into the pockets of his cargo shorts and scooted closer to Lacey. When she didn't stomp away from him, he took that as his cue to walk over to her.

When he reached her, he could see on her face that she'd been crying. A lot. He wondered if his night of tears showed on his face as well.

"Hey," he said.

"Hey," she repeated softly.

She was talking to him. That was a good sign.

"Umm-"

"I'm not talking to you," she said to him.

"Oh, okay."

They stood next to each other in silence for a moment, both of them staring at the ground.

Luke decided to just get the words out, whether she was talking to him or not.

"I didn't mean any of it. I really-"

"You always do that. You always fight. Even when you don't

have to fight. Why?" She turned to face him, waiting for his answer.

Luke told her the truth. "I don't know."

"Even when everything is going good. Even when it's working out you fight."

"What? When's it ever worked out?" he demanded.

"Here. It was working out here. And then you had to go and pick a fight. For no good reason. Why?"

He shook his head. "Because it never works out Lacey. And you forgot that. You forgot that it never ever works out. No matter what we do. It always ends the same way."

Another silence overtook them. Lacey chewed on her lower lip while Luke pondered over his own words.

It was Lacey who broke the silence when she said quietly, almost as a whispered hope, "I think it could work out this time. Don't you?"

Luke didn't answer her at first. He stared at the ground, stuck in his own head as he thought about everything that had happened. Then, finally, he looked at her and nodded. "Yeah," he said. "I think it could."

Lacey nodded in return.

They both returned their gazes to the ground. Lacey hugged herself while Luke kicked at the grass with the new sneakers he'd bought with Uncle Owen's money. This time, he spoke first.

"I'm sorry about that stuff I said. I didn't really mean to hurt you."

"I'm sorry I threw your flashlight at you. I did mean to hurt you, but you were mean to me though, so it doesn't count."

Luke nodded, accepting those terms as fair.

"It's not true, you know. What I said about mom. I mean, you have changed, but like, kind of in a good way. I think mom would like the new you."

This was enough to return the smile to Lacey's face.

"Oh, and I really don't mind that you hang out here all the time," Luke added.

"Well, I really don't hate you," Lacey told him.

"Okay."

"Okay."

"Look alive people!"

Miss Annika shouted, startling both Luke and Lacey. They turned to look at where she was pointing and saw the first vehicle come bouncing up the dirt path towards them.

"It's time!" Lacey squealed.

Luke looked over at his sister and saw that her entire demeanor had changed. She was no longer frowning but was positively giddy at the sight of the car approaching. Luke, however, had the opposite reaction towards the newcomer. Although he was pleased that his sister was enjoying herself once more, he couldn't help the scowl that returned to its customary position on his face.

.....

OWEN WAS RELIEVED ONCE ALL THE CAMPERS HAD FINALLY arrived (9 girls in all, aged 7-13), and Annika gave the order for everyone to head inside to the cool a/c. That is, he was relieved until he heard Annika's next announcement. He was loading his arms with the overnight bags, blankets, and stuffed animals brought by the girls as Lacey and Olivia ushered them all towards the front door. Luke, who was supposed to be helping Owen carry the luggage, was hanging back and kicking at the dirt and grass. He was making a lousy counselor so far. Annika was reading from a chart on the purple clipboard in her hand, which she'd used to check off each girl's arrival.

"Okay girls," she called out, a little louder than necessary considering there weren't very many of them there and everyone was standing close together. "Follow the counselors to your rooms. Go ahead and take a few minutes to get settled in and then we'll start our first activity for the day – face painting."

There were a few excited cheers at this news, but Owen paid no attention. He made his way to Annika and whispered, "Face painting? Are you serious?"

"What's wrong with that?"

"Everything. Do you know how big of a mess that's going to make? There'll be paint everywhere. Why not something a little safer, like silent reading?"

Annika chuckled. "Something tells me they'll enjoy painting more."

Owen huffed. Admittedly, it wasn't very becoming of a grown man, but he huffed.

Annika gave a small laugh at his reaction. "I'm pretty sure you'll survive."

"That remains to be seen."

Annika moved to follow the others inside, but Owen stopped her.

"I wanted to tell you," he began, "that is, I thought that you should know or that you would want to know."

"What is it?" She looked at him puzzled.

"I've decided they should stay. Luke and Lacey, I mean. I think...I know that they belong here with me. No matter what."

Annika released a breath. "Thank goodness," she said. "I know this wasn't an easy choice for you and I didn't want to sway you one way or the other, but...Owen Stillwater if you had sent those kids away you would have made the biggest mistake of your life."

Owen cocked an eyebrow.

"Do you hear me?"

"Loud and clear. Message well received," Owen said with a smile. He adjusted the load of luggage in his arms, repositioning a giant stuffed unicorn that was poking him in the chin with its pink horn.

Annika folded her arms and gave a nod of assent. "Good.

Now that you've come to your senses and are in control of your mental faculties, we can go paint."

That wiped the smile off his face. Owen hung his head. For a moment, just a moment, he'd forgotten what awaited him inside the cabin. But his temporary reprieve was over and now he'd have to face it.

"Okay, fine," Owen said. "But does it have to be the face?"

"Well, we tried rock painting last time, but that turned into face painting. So, we thought we'd just cut to the chase this time."

And that's what they were doing in the sunroom an hour later. They were split up into groups, sitting at the folding tables and chairs spread throughout the room, and smearing each other with face paint. That was actually a misleading term considering the paint seemed to land everywhere but on their faces.

Owen looked down at his favorite polo shirt that had been dry cleaned and pressed at an exorbitant cost. This morning it had been a pristine white, now it was splattered with pink and purple paint, creating a tie-dyed effect. It also shimmered with glitter. Glitter? How was that possible? They weren't even working with glitter.

He looked up at the two girls he'd been paired off with. The first was a red-head named Ginny that he'd met during the previous camp session when she'd wandered over to his place. He made a note to himself to keep a close eye on her; she liked to wander off. The other girl, George, had to be the youngest one there. She was a tiny blonde with pigtails and teary eyes. She'd already cried once and camp had only just started.

"We need to finish your giraffe," Ginny announced, and the two girls advanced on him with paint covered hands. Technically, everything on them was covered in paint, from their hair to their shoes.

"Oh, I think it's good enough," Owen pointed to the dot of pink on the side of his face. He had no desire to resemble the two painted monsters before him. The shirt was a loss. That was a given. But that didn't mean the rest of him had to be pink as well. He looked down again at the miserable state of his shirt, still confused about where the glitter had come from.

"Okay, who needs more glitter?" Annika called out. She walked back and forth from the groups with an enormous plastic jar of the horrendous stuff, pouring it out like candy.

Everyone but Owen asked for more.

Everyone.

Owen gaped at Luke who was sitting to the right of him. The boy who hadn't even wanted to be there held his hands out greedily as Annika poured him a heap of glitter. Luke seemed to feel Owen looking at him because he turned to him with a sheepish look on his face.

"I need it to finish my choo-choo train," Luke gestured to the cheek of the little girl he was paired with. "It's gonna be the smoke, billowing up. You know, out of the smokestack." He looked proud. He actually looked proud of his idea. "It's gonna be awesome," he said with a grin.

Owen shook his head in disgust and returned his attention to the girls in front of him. Unfortunately, while he'd been distracted by Luke and his choo-choo train, Annika had paid his group a visit and loaded the girls up with glitter and renewed enthusiasm.

"Oh no," he said.

That was all he managed to get out before they pounced on him.

"**K**nock knock. Anyone home?"

"We're in here," Annika called out without taking her eyes off the bottles of paint she was collecting. "It's Phillip. He said he would stop by today." She said this to Owen who was helping her with clean-up duty.

Owen nodded absently. He was preoccupied with the impossible task of trying to clean an ocean of paint and glitter from the floor, and the folding chairs, and the portable table that had been set up in the center of the room, oh and also from the ceiling. How'd it get on the ceiling? Owen decided he didn't want to know the answer to that question. Still, he'd volunteered for clean-up duty. It had been either this or helping Olivia, Lacey, and Luke wash up the little nightmares, children, they were washing up the children. Yep, he'd gotten the better deal.

"Man," Annika said, taking a moment to survey the damage. "I don't think we bought enough paint. And we're definitely going to need more glitter."

"Are you serious?" Owen balked at her statement. She was joking. She had to be joking.

"Well, we're finger painting tomorrow," she said. "This won't

246

be nearly enough." She held up the jar of glitter for him to assess the situation as well.

Owen blinked at her. The jar was at least a gallon and looked to be about half full.

"What do you think? We're going to need more, right?"

"I think it'll be okay." Owen said. "Worst case scenario, maybe you can salvage the glitter from the ceiling and reuse it." He pointed upward and Annika looked up to the spot he was indicating.

"How'd it get on the ceiling?" she asked.

They were staring at the anomaly and trying to come up with scenarios that could explain it away when they heard a voice at the entrance of the sunroom.

"Excuse me."

They turned to meet the owner of the voice that did not belong to Phillip after all. At the sight of the owner of the voice, they both had a distinct visceral reaction – one relief, one fury.

"Thank goodness," Owen said.

"What are you doing here?" Annika demanded.

Brian Felton, Annika's archnemesis (now that she and Owen were on good terms) walked further into the sunroom. He waved a slip of paper in his hands as he entered.

"This is business sweetheart," he answered Annika. "Believe me I wouldn't be inside this death trap otherwise. Knowing that clown your sister is seeing rebuilt this place is enough reason for me to steer clear."

Annika clutched the giant jar of glitter in her arms with a death grip. Owen thought he saw steam coming from her ears. This was a new experience – seeing her anger directed at someone other than himself. Owen wasn't sure whether he should feel relief that he wasn't the one in the crosshairs, or concern over Felton's safety.

Meanwhile, Annika was fuming at Felton's jab at Phillip. "Phillip is an excellent handyman," she retorted. "And – and this house is perfectly safe."

Felton snorted. "And you would be an expert judge of that? Forgive me if I don't take your word for it."

"You are an evil critter," was her comeback.

"Calm down sweetheart. I didn't come here to fight with you. I just came to talk to him." Felton walked over to Owen and handed him the slip of paper. "Here's your bill."

Owen took the bill from him. "I thought I told you to leave the bill in the door. In fact, I'm certain I wrote that in the note."

"Yeah, well, let's just say I felt more comfortable handing it to you in person," Felton said.

Owen took the paper from Felton and read it.

"Your system was backed up. The air duct needed to be cleaned out." Felton explained as Owen read over the bill.

"You're a contractor," Annika said. "Since when do you fix air conditioners?"

"Felton and Son is a construction company," Felton said, "but I have other companies – one of 'em fixes a/c units. Why? Is your system shot too?"

Annika scoffed. "Like I'd hire you if it was."

Owen looked up from his bill and stared at Felton. "Is this really what you're charging me? To clean out the air duct?"

"It took a lot of work because it's an old system."

"I just got that system last year."

"Like I said, it's old. Now if you want me to, I could install a brand new top of the line–"

Owen held his hand up to cut off Felton's sales pitch. "I'm good with the one I have, thanks." He turned the bill around to show Annika, who gasped audibly.

"You're a crook!" She pointed an accusing finger at him.

"Why? Because I know the value of my work?"

"No, because you overcharge for everything."

"Do you expect me to go around fixing stuff for free? I have to make a living." Felton picked a piece of lint, or possibly a crumb from his shirt, examined it momentarily, and then flung it onto the floor. Owen watched its flight path and landing, and wondered if it too would become covered in glitter as everything else in this room was.

"This is price gauging. You ought to be ashamed of yourself!" Annika yelled.

"And yet, I'm not," Felton replied smugly.

"Well, you should be," Annika retorted. "Don't pay him Owen. That price is ridiculous, and he knows it."

"Does the a/c work?" Owen asked, cutting to the chase.

"Of course it does," Felton answered, looking somewhat offended. Owen noted that he'd seemed indifferent when Annika had called him a crook, but he was insulted at the questioning of his handiwork.

Everyone's values were different.

"I'll pay what you're asking," Owen said definitively, "because you did what I hired you to do."

Next to him, Annika gave a dissatisfied harrumph, while Felton's face held a grin.

"But I'm glad you're here," Owen said. "I need to talk to you about something."

Felton's grin left his face, like he could sense where this was going and he didn't care for it at all.

Owen blew out a breath and then stated his piece. "This agenda you have to close down her camp," Owen jerked his thumb at Annika, "it needs to stop."

Felton looked at Owen for a moment, and then burst out laughing. "What's that supposed to mean? It needs to stop? Are you serious?"

"I mean it Brian," Owen said, not backing down. He had known the older man his entire life and he knew that Felton was a lot of things, most of them unpleasant. But one thing Owen knew for certain was that Brian Felton was a man of his word. This was why Owen was so confident as he stared him down.

"You can hate her and her sister all you want, but leave them and their camp alone. Just back off," Owen said.

Felton wasn't laughing anymore now. What he'd found so

funny just moments earlier, now enraged him. His face turned red as his mouth twisted into an angry scowl. "Look here. You're not the boss of me. So, I don't know who you think you're trying to tell what to do–"

"You owe me."

Those three little words cut off Felton's rant. The color drained from his face as he met Owen's unwavering gaze.

"That's a low blow," Felton whispered.

"And now the slate is wiped clean."

Felton closed his eyes and nodded. "Very well then. We're even." He turned and stomped from the room.

"I'll be by tomorrow to pay my bill," Owen called after him.

Owen didn't hear a reply or any indication that Felton had heard him. The only sound Owen did hear was Felton's work boots trampling through the house and out the front door, which he slammed behind him. And although he was too far away to hear it, Owen could imagine that Felton's truck made quite a noise as he floored it down the long driveway to the road.

"Um, what just happened?"

Owen turned to look at the woman next to him, confusion in her pretty brown eyes.

"What was that?" Annika asked. She stood in her paint covered clothes, her hair messy and askew. She had paint smeared on the side of her face and she was still clutching her jar of glitter in both arms. She looked beautiful.

Owen smiled at her. "That was the end of your troubles with Brian Felton. He owed me a favor and I just cashed it in."

Annika looked unconvinced. "Just like that. He's going to back off just because you told him to?" She shook her head. "That must have been some favor. What did you do?"

"I saved his son's life."

"Oh, um, that's a pretty big favor."

Owen took a seat in the folding chair closest to him. it was covered in paint, but so was he. He gestured for Annika to sit as well and she took the chair across from him, finally setting her glitter down on the table.

"It was a long time ago. His son, Richard, stopped breathing. He was unresponsive. And I-"

"Saved his life?" Annika offered.

"Well, yeah," he responded. "In my book he didn't owe me anything. I was happy just to see that Richard lived. But Brian was so emotional and he vowed to pay me back somehow. I just held him to that promise."

"To...save our camp?"

Owen shrugged.

Annika still seemed confused by this and needed clarification. "But you hate this camp, right?"

Owen looked down at his ruined clothes, then surveyed the disaster area the sunroom had become. The mess would take a considerable amount of time to clean, and even then, Owen doubted that they would be able to remove all of the paint stains splattered about the room. Like his shirt, some surfaces would permanently bear the scar of this fateful afternoon. But then he remembered the look on the faces of Ginny and George – the two girls he'd been paired with – when they'd wrestled him down with paint and glitter. It had been pure unfiltered joy.

He met her eyes as he answered her question, wanting to clear up any confusion. "I did. I really did, but...it's growing on me. It's grown on me."

His reward was a small smile which compelled him to confess to her. "*You've* grown on me."

Her smile grew bigger, and Owen continued, "If it's alright with you, I'd like to stick around, and see how both things progress."

A silent nod was all he received. But that was all the encouragement Owen needed.

❧ 31 ❧

Over the next six days the camp became the central focus of the two households. Annika and Olivia led the campers through one planned activity after the other, with varying degrees of success. Most of them turned out nothing like the sisters had planned, but the campers had fun with each event so no one really minded.

Lacey essentially moved next door for the week, telling Owen that it was all hands on deck and she was desperately needed. And despite his early grumblings, Luke seemed to have taken to the camp himself and was spending a good portion of his days next door as well. It seemed he enjoyed the activities just as much as all the other kids.

This was clear on their drive to town on Wednesday morning when Owen took the two of them shopping for school supplies. Even though he'd pre-arranged it with Annika and Olivia, he'd practically had to drag the twins away from the camp. Phillip was bringing over a bubble machine from his hardware store, and he was going to attempt to make the world's largest bubble. And Luke and Lacey were going to miss it. Luke was incensed. Lacey was inconsolable. But Owen put his foot down. They would be starting school on Monday and neither of them had as much as a pencil to their name. School took priority over super cool bubble machines.

"But it's a super cool bubble machine," Luke said on the drive to town for what must have been the thousandth time. Then he moaned and leaned his head against the window. Next to him, Lacey sniffled her agreement with his statement, wiped away a tear and leaned against the opposite window.

"Stop being melodramatic." Owen shook his head. This was why he and Natasha never had children.

Thankfully, they all survived the shopping trip and left town with enough supplies to last them until college, including several new clothing items for Luke as well as a pair of shoes for Lacey that she'd chosen off the clearance rack. Both Luke and Owen had urged her to get a few clothing pieces, but she'd only shrugged them off, stating that she didn't see anything that she liked and then snatched up the shoes from clearance. Owen decided to let the matter go for the moment and purchased the shoes. He figured he still had the weekend to address the situation. He just hoped she'd come to her senses soon.

By Saturday afternoon, everyone was all camped out, but in a good way. It had been a busy, hectic, fun-filled week and everyone was exhausted, including the campers. So naturally, Annika and Olivia had planned a big party. Well, Annika had called it a cookout when she'd informed Owen just the night before. They'd invited everyone who'd helped out at the camp in some way throughout the week. This guest list included Phillip, his family, and a few members from their church. It sounded exactly like a party to Owen.

And to top it off, Owen was scheduled to do the grilling. According to Annika, the job had initially been given to Phillip, but he was prone to burning the food until it took on the same appearance and texture as the charcoal used to light the fire. After Annika had tasted Owen's perfectly cooked fish last week, she and Olivia had both decided that Owen was better suited for the position of grill master. She'd just forgotten to tell him about it.

Truthfully, Owen didn't mind being handed the job at the last minute. Cooking in all forms was a passion of his, and he did enjoy showing off his skills. (He'd even brought his own grill from home, not trusting a foreign machine to treat his food properly.) Plus, it pleased him that Annika was so confident in his abilities that she'd booked him for her cookout. Not to mention that it would be a crime against humanity to make those kids ingest burnt food. A shudder went through Owen at the thought of letting Phillip near the grill. Not on his watch.

"Wait. You're grilling? But I'm supposed to be grilling."

Owen looked up from the meat he was carefully laying across the grill to see Phillip in a bright orange apron that said, 'King of the Grill', holding a pair of tongs and wearing a very confused expression on his face. It was at that moment that Owen discovered that he wasn't the only one Annika forgot to inform about the schedule change.

"I'm doing the grilling," Phillip repeated, pointing the tongs at himself. "So, what are you doing?" He pointed the tongs at Owen.

"Grilling?" Owen shrugged. He didn't know what else to say to the guy who was looking more perplexed by the minute.

"I see that. But why?"

Thankfully, Annika and Olivia appeared on either side of Phillip before Owen had to answer him.

"Phillip, can we have a word with you?" Olivia asked sweetly.

They didn't wait for his response. They just grabbed one arm each and began walking away from the grill with Phillip as their captive. Owen could hear their voices receding as they walked back toward the cabin.

He breathed a sigh of relief. He certainly didn't want to have to tell the man that he was a terrible cook. Instead, he put his head down and focused on the task at hand. He was hoping to have most of the food ready by the time the children made it outside and came exploring him and the grill.

Speaking of which, where were all the children? He wasn't sure what activities had been planned for the day, but it was midday and this past week's experience had taught Owen that they should be causing enough of a ruckus inside for Owen to hear it outside.

"How's it coming?"

Annika walked over to his side to peer at the grill. Owen poked at the meat laid across the grill with his own set of tongs.

"So far so good," he answered, and then asked, "How's Phillip taking the news?"

"Not good, but I think he'll get over it." She nodded towards the patio area where Phillip was seated with Olivia on a brightly colored picnic bench. He looked devastated, head in his hands and still wearing his apron, but with the tongs tossed onto the table next to him. Olivia was patting his shoulder and looked to be consoling him.

"I kind of feel bad for him," Owen said.

"Don't," Annika cut off his sympathy with quickness. "He would've given us food poisoning for sure, if we even managed to eat it."

"Right," Owen said. Then he asked her, "Where are all the campers? Shouldn't they be out here demanding food by now? And where are my kids?"

My kids?

The words slipped from his mouth of their own accord. But were they his kids? It felt like they were his. He wasn't delusional. He knew they were his niece and nephew. But they were his. And saying it aloud made it feel genuine. He wondered how they would feel about him saying those words. He wondered if they considered themselves as his kids. Maybe it was too soon. He could and would give them all the time that they needed.

Owen had been so lost in his thoughts about his relationship with Lacey and Luke that he almost missed Annika's response. Almost.

"Where are they?" he asked again for clarification.

"On a treasure hunt," she said. "They're exploring the cabin to find the ultimate treasure. They split into two teams and Lacey and Luke are the team captains. I think Nosey is the mascot."

Owen shook his head. "Man, you really commit, don't you. I can't believe you're letting them tear apart your house, going room-to-room rummaging through all your things just to play this game."

Annika rolled her eyes. "What do you mean? The treasure hunt isn't in my house. It's in yours."

"Come again?"

"Yep," she said matter-of-factly. "They headed over a little while ago, but they should be back any minute now, so we'd better get that food ready."

"I...you...they're in my house? Unsupervised? A bunch of kids?" With every question, Owen's voice rose a little higher, along with his blood pressure.

Annika, who didn't seem to notice his growing anxiety, simply nodded yes to each of his questions.

Owen spluttered. "How?" It was the only word his brain managed to push from his mouth.

"Lacey let us in." This came from Olivia, who had now joined them with a seemingly recovered Phillip at her side.

"Lacey?"

"Yep. It was all her idea. I mean we were skeptical at first, but she assured us you wouldn't mind."

Annika nodded again. "I was surprised but impressed with your adaptability."

"Of course, we wouldn't let her watch as we hid all the clues. We couldn't let her have an unfair advantage," Olivia explained.

"You hid clues? In my house?"

They nodded in unison.

"When?"

"Last night," Annika answered, then amended, "well, it was more like this morning. Sometime around 2 or 3 am."

"You were asleep," Olivia offered. Then she asked, "Do you always sleep in those weird-looking pajamas?"

"They're back!" Annika pointed to the path to the woods as the first of the campers came trampling out. She and Olivia rushed over to meet the group and find out the results of the treasure hunt.

Owen watched them leave. After a moment he said, "My pajamas aren't weird-looking." However, he may have been trying to convince himself of this as both women were too far away to hear him when he spoke.

"I think you're going to burn that." Phillip, who'd remained behind, had been forgotten by Owen in light of all the new information he'd just received. Now, he reached for the tongs in Owen's hand. "I'll cook it for you," he offered.

Owen snatched the tongs away from Phillip's reach. "Back off Phillip."

"Got it." Phillip backed away from the grill, hands raised in surrender. "Just trying to help."

Owen may have been frazzled by that conversation, but he hadn't completely lost his senses. There was no way he was letting that man near his grill.

"Not on my watch," Owen grumbled and flipped over the meat.

🦋 32 🦋

By all accounts the cookout was a complete success. To Lacey, the entire week had been a success, and she beamed with pride, knowing that she'd been a part of making that happen. She was sitting in the backyard at the picnic bench that had been erected by Mr. Phillip for the purpose of the cookout. Her stomach was full and her heart content as she thought over the week's events. She decided that although she was sad that camp was over, she was happy that she'd gotten to be a part of it. She'd had so much fun that she already couldn't wait until it opened again in the summer. Maybe she could even convince Miss Annika and Miss Olivia to keep it open for longer than a week. She was pretty good at convincing people to do things.

Looking across the backyard to Miss Olivia and Mr. Phillip, Lacey couldn't help but smile. The meal complete, the two adults had a large store-bought box of sugar-filled popsicles that they were handing out. They were practically being mauled by all the girls, reaching for their share of sugar. (All the girls and Luke, who greedily took two.) But Lacey was focused on the adults. She noticed how they periodically looked at one another and smiled. Every time they smiled at each other, Lacey smiled as well.

Then she looked to the other side of the yard, narrowing in on the other couple. Uncle Owen and Miss Annika were on clean-up duty. A few other guests were cleaning too – Mr. Phillip's mom and sister, as well as a few people Lacey recognized from church. They were clearing the table and packing up leftovers. But Lacey was solely focused on the adults cleaning the grill. Uncle Owen was scrubbing the grill in earnest, while Miss Annika collected the cooking tools and the platters that had held the raw meat. They didn't exchange smiles or glances like Miss Olivia and Mr. Phillip. They were barely even talking to each other as they worked. This was disappointing, but Lacey wasn't deterred. She was sure that she could still make this work. There were several more ideas that she'd recently come up with to push the two of them together.

"Here." Luke plopped down on the bench next to her and shoved a popsicle in her face. "I got one for you."

Lacey took the unopened treat. "Thanks."

"So, what are you doing, moping over here by yourself?"

"I'm not moping. I'm thinking."

"About what?"

"Project Adult Happiness."

"Still with that? You haven't given up yet?"

"No, because it worked." Lacey pointed over to Miss Olivia and Mr. Phillip, who were now organizing a relay race with the hyper-active kids.

"Yeah? Well, what about them?" Luke pointed over to Uncle Owen and Miss Annika. "That failed miserably."

"It did not!" Lacey argued stubbornly. "Besides, I'm not done yet. I have more plans and I need your help."

Luke rolled his eyes. "Of course you do." Then he sighed. "Okay. Fine. Just stay here and plan our next move if you want. I'm gonna go join the race." He got up and did just that.

"You gonna eat that?"

Lacey looked over to see Minerva (who should've been racing along with the other campers) had joined her on the bench as well and was eyeing the unopened popsicle hungrily.

"I'll take it if you don't want it." Minerva held her hand out for the popsicle, like it was a done deal. "Mr. Phillip wouldn't let me get two. He said some junk about too much sugar or whatever, but I could eat it over here and he wouldn't know."

"Well, if Mr. Phillip said no, then the answer is no."

Minerva frowned and retracted her hand.

"I shouldn't have told you that part."

"No, you shouldn't have," agreed Lacey.

.....

As EVENING APPROACHED, ONE AT A TIME, THE GUESTS BEGAN going their separate ways. Once everyone had dispersed, Miss Olivia shooed the girls inside for their nightly ghost stories. Luke and Lacey both moved to follow until Owen grabbed them and put a halt to their plans.

"Not so fast," he said. "We're headed home for the night."

Luke hung his head dejectedly but turned back around. Lacey, however, put up a fight.

"But–"

"Nope."

"They need me."

"They'll get by one night."

She chewed her lip as she quickly worked on a convincing argument to present, but Annika intervened.

"We'll be fine Lacey. Go on home like your uncle said."

"You can come back tomorrow," Owen offered, but Lacey still looked crestfallen.

Annika took her in her arms and gave her a warm embrace.

When she pulled back, she said, "Thank you for this week. We couldn't have gotten through it without you."

This brought a small smile from Lacey, and she joined her uncle and brother obediently. She still wasn't happy about leaving, but she could accept it. Owen whistled for Nosey, who came bounding along, and the family of four left to go home.

When they reached the cabin and went inside, Lacey began to head towards the kitchen for a glass of water, but once again Owen stopped her.

"Hang on," he called. "Come upstairs with me. There's something I want to show you."

Surprised but intrigued, Lacey followed her uncle up the stairs with Luke trailing behind. Nosey, who didn't seem to care, headed towards the kitchen, probably to get the water that Lacey herself wanted. When they reached the hallway on the second floor, Owen walked over to the third room on that floor – the only room in the house that she'd never entered. Now, her curiosity was really piqued. She'd wondered what was in this room but hadn't had a chance to grill Luke about it, who'd undoubtedly searched it during one of his explorations.

As the three of them stood before the closed door, neither Owen nor Luke spoke. They only stood and watched her.

"What's in there?" Lacey asked, perplexed at their odd behavior and a little nervous about what must be inside the room.

Owen answered. "A little of this. A little of that. Come inside and take a look." He turned the knob and stepped inside, flipping the light switch on the wall as he entered. Bursting with curiosity, Lacey followed. Luke came in after. He stood just inside the doorway, arms crossed.

The moment she was inside the room, Lacey felt her curiosity melt into disappointment. With all the secretiveness, she'd expected something amazing to be hidden in this room. She couldn't say exactly what she'd hoped for, but she knew it wasn't what she'd found. "Boxes? It's a bunch of boxes?" Lacey looked up at her uncle with a frown. "But-"

"And storage bins," Luke corrected her.

"Look inside," Owen suggested.

Lacey tore the lid off the bin closest to her and peered inside. The contents did nothing but further add to her confusion. "These are clothes."

Luke walked over to her then. "Lacey, these were mom's clothes. Like from when she was young. Like our age. And also, some of it was his dead wife's stuff."

Owen cringed at Luke's insensitive remark, then turned to Lacey. "I've decided. Well, we've decided," he gestured to Luke, who nodded in agreement, "we've decided that everything inside this room should be given to you."

"Huh?"

Lacey looked back and forth between the two of them, but they both seemed to be serious. She turned her attention back to the container in front of her with fresh eyes. Inside were a stack of clothes. A stack of clothes that her mother had worn and probably loved. She reached inside and pulled out a red Minnie Mouse sweatshirt. She fondled it, held it close to her chest.

Her mother had loved Minnie Mouse, Lacey remembered. She'd briefly forgotten that fact, but it was there now, lying dormant in her memories, just waiting to be brought to the surface. Her mother had been the biggest Minnie Mouse fan in the world. If this sweatshirt were any indication, her fondness for the feminine rodent had begun long before she'd gotten married and had kids.

"Try it on," Luke suggested, pulling Lacey from her reverie.

Lacey didn't hesitate. She pulled the sweater over her old ratty t-shirt. It fit perfectly.

"Thought so," Owen commented, noticing how well it fit. "Natasha was really small, so her clothes should fit you too. If anything's too big we can have it taken in."

Lacey didn't hear a word he'd said though. She was too busy

combing through the box to find what other treasures awaited her.

"There's jewelry too," Luke said. Lacey's head shot up and she looked at him with wide eyes. "Over there somewhere," he pointed at a stack of boxes to the left.

"This container," Owen tapped a bin next to him, "has shoes. They're all a little odd though. Not really my taste."

This time Lacey heard him speak loud and clear. Evidence of this was the way she dropped the clothes in her arms back into the bin and dove toward the bin he'd indicated. Once she'd wrestled it open, she seized a pair of hot pink sneakers from the pile and held them up.

"They're perfect," she whispered. Then she traded them for a pair of lime green ballet flats. These she instantly put on her feet, trading her pink flip-flops for them. They fit. Barely. But she would make them work.

"It's not just clothes," Luke said, coming over to join the two of them. "It's all kinds of stuff. There are stuffed animals somewhere over there." He waved towards a stack of boxes in the right corner.

This distracted Lacey from her new shoe collection. Her eyes got big again and she rushed over to the direction Luke had indicated in search of the promised stuffed animal collection.

"I think she likes her gift," Luke commented.

Owen chuckled. "Then let's tell her the other thing."

Luke shrugged, "May as well."

"Lacey," Owen called to her.

"Hmm," was the only response he got as she was focused on her mission.

"We wanted to tell you about another decision we made."

This time he didn't get a response at all, just the sound of her rummaging through boxes.

"Luke and I decided that we're going to church with you tomorrow."

The rummaging stopped.

Lacey looked up at her uncle and brother with wide hopeful eyes.

"Really?"

Owen nodded.

Luke rolled his eyes, then nodded.

Lacey lunged at them and nearly choked them both in her group hug. They hugged her warmly in return before coming to their senses and pulling away.

Owen cleared his throat. He wasn't choked up or anything. There was just a frog in his throat. Or maybe he was coming down with something.

"Yeah well," he managed after a moment, "looks like we have quite a big project ahead of us – moving all this stuff into your room."

"We?" Luke scoffed. "What do you mean we?"

Owen ignored him. "It's gonna take the three of us days to go through all of this. Maybe weeks."

"Let's get started now," Lacey begged. She was practically bouncing up and down with excitement.

"I don't know," Owen said, but then predictably caved at the expectant look on Lacey's face. "I guess we can work for an hour or two."

Luke, however, held out. Not that he minded sorting through the boxes. In reality, he was almost as excited as Lacey. It was a chance to go through his mother's things from a time before they'd known her. The idea made Luke feel closer to her, like he was getting to meet her again for the first time, only this time it was a version that he'd never known. He really couldn't wait to see what information those boxes held.

But he couldn't just say that. He couldn't give in to Lacey's pleas so easily. He had a reputation to uphold. So, he waited until he felt she'd asked and pouted the appropriate amount before agreeing to help.

"You know," he said to Lacey, "this is a lot of stuff. I don't know if it can all fit in that room we're sharing. Not with my clothes too."

Lacey chewed her lower lip as she thought about what he said. Then she came to a frightening, exciting, monumental conclusion.

"I think we should split up."

"You sure?" Luke asked, because he'd secretly been thinking it as well, but he didn't want to be the one to say it. This would be the first time they'd ever been apart. They'd always shared a room, and assumed that they always would. But as they both had learned, everything changes, sometimes a little, sometimes a lot. And sometimes that wasn't bad.

Lacey nodded vigorously. "Yeah. We can move all this stuff to my new room."

"Okay," Owen said. "Then let's get started."

It only took a few moments of working before they all agreed that a snack of some sort was needed to continue the project. Luke, feeling a little bad about making Lacey beg for his help earlier, volunteered to make a snack run to the kitchen while the other two kept working.

"What do you want?" he asked as he walked to the door. Then inspiration hit. "Oh, I know. I'll make us some brownies. I learned how to make them for school."

Lacey thought about it and then nodded her approval. Owen gave him a thumbs up.

"But hurry back," Lacey said, not trusting that he wasn't taking the opportunity to try and get out of work, which would've been pulling a page from her book.

Luke called over his shoulder as he left the room. "There's no hurry to go through this stuff you know. It's not like we're going anywhere."

"Yeah," Lacey agreed quietly, although Luke had already left. "I guess we do have time."

"All the time in the world," Owen said.

EPILOGUE

"No running in the hallway Mr. Castleman!"

"Sorry Mrs. Driver."

Luke turned his sprint into a brisk walk as he passed his English teacher in the crowded corridor.

"It won't happen again, I promise."

"Oh, I'm sure," the teacher said sarcastically. Then she added, "Enjoy your weekend. Don't forget the quiz next week. And Luke..."

Luke paused to hear her, somewhat afraid of a last minute assignment, which she was known to hand out over weekends.

"Happy birthday," Mrs. Driver said with a rare smile.

Luke grinned back at her. "Thanks Mrs. Driver!" He turned and continued toward the school exit along with the rest of the student body, careful not to run this time.

"Hey Luke!"

A loud bellow came from across the campus the moment Luke was outside. A quick look to his right identified the voice as belonging to Robert, one of Luke's two best friends. Robert ran across the campus, catching up with Luke quickly. He was slightly winded when he reached him, and Luke had to wait a moment for him to catch his breath.

"What's up man?" Luke asked.

"What time are we supposed to come over tomorrow? Cause like, I'm helping set up right?"

"Right. Sorry, I told Josh, but I forgot to tell you. Party starts at 12, so maybe come over around 10."

"Cool."

Luke didn't ask Robert if he needed directions to the cabin. The fact was that both Robert and Josh (Luke's other best friend) had been over to Luke's so many times within the past two months that they could probably find the place blindfolded in the dark. In fact, it was Robert who had hand-drawn the map that Luke and Lacey had included on the back of the invitations for their joint birthday party.

"I think your uncle's tired of waiting," Robert said. He pointed to the pick-up line where Uncle Owen was waving Luke down with an impatient frown on his face.

"Yeah, I better go."

"See you tomorrow," Robert called to Luke as he left.

When he got to the truck, Luke saw that Uncle Owen was indeed tired of waiting for him and Lacey (who was nowhere to be seen). Luke didn't understand why when they made him wait every day of the week. It was for that very reason, in fact, that Uncle Owen closed his medical practice at 4:00 every day. He said to anyone who would listen that he was a doctor from 8am to 4pm, and a chauffeur to late teenagers that didn't respect his time the rest of the day.

Luke climbed into the backseat of the truck and pulled out his phone to check for any messages. Then he got an idea.

"Can we get ice cream?"

Their favorite ice cream shop was along the way home. Sometimes, Uncle Owen would stop and treat them. Considering it was their birthday, Luke could think of no better occasion.

But clearly Uncle Owen didn't see it that way, because he answered with, "Not today."

Luke's first instinct was to push, to fight. He opened his mouth to do just that and then shut it again. He mentally counted to three and then made the choice to accept his uncle's decision, even though he didn't like it. This was a technique he'd learned in therapy. They'd only been going a month, but he had to admit that it was helping – both him and Lacey.

"There she is," Uncle Owen sighed as Lacey appeared at the truck with one of her friends in tow.

Lacey was dressed in a pale pink top and a matching pink skirt. Her hair was pulled back in its customary ponytail, the same way she'd been wearing it since it had grown past her shoulders. Luke had to admit that long hair suited her.

Lacey opened the door and slid into the backseat next to Luke. "Can we take Jamie home? Her mom said it's okay."

"I already got a text from her mom," Uncle Owen said. "Come on. Let's go."

The two girls took this as confirmation and Jamie quickly climbed in next to Lacey. Once she'd shut the door, Uncle Owen pulled away from the curb.

Luke immediately felt grateful that he hadn't fought with Uncle Owen over ice cream. Not only would it have ruined the beginning of what was going to be a great weekend, but he would've felt like a fool right now. Jamie, Luke remembered, was allergic to dairy and couldn't eat ice cream. Uncle Owen, who clearly knew that she would be with them, was only thinking of her when he'd turned Luke down. Luke decided that he would tell his therapist about this moment during their weekly session on Tuesday.

"Lacey," Uncle Owen said, interrupting Luke's thoughts. "I have a surprise for you."

"A birthday surprise?" Lacey asked excitedly.

"I guess you could call it that." Uncle Owen waited an excruciatingly long time to continue, knowing that Lacey was on the edge of her seat with anticipation.

"You are," he said slowly, building the suspense, and then finished in a rush, "going to be a bridesmaid."

"What?!" Lacey screamed.

"You and Miss Annika are finally getting married?" Luke asked, and then had the delight of hearing his uncle stutter.

"What? I? What? Me? No!"

"Isn't that your girlfriend? Or wait, is she your fiancé now?" Jamie asked, much to Luke and Lacey's entertainment.

"No," Uncle Owen said through clenched teeth. "Annika and I are not getting married yet."

The three teenagers pounced on his slip of the tongue.

"Yet?" Jamie asked.

"As in you will get married but not yet?" Lacey added.

"No, that's not what I meant," Uncle Owen said in a clear state of panic.

"But that's what you said," Luke attacked mercilessly.

Uncle Owen turned red before announcing loudly, "I'm not getting married!"

All three teenagers found his reaction hilarious and howled with laughter.

"So, who's getting married?" Luke asked, once the laughing died down.

"Olivia and Phillip are getting married," Uncle Owen said, having regained his composure. "Annika told me that Lacey has been chosen to be a bridesmaid. Olivia is going to officially ask you tomorrow."

"Oooh," Jamie said longingly. "I want to be a bridesmaid. I swear you're the luckiest girl in the world."

Lacey beamed. She was feeling pretty lucky these days.

Once they'd dropped Jamie off and made it home, both twins fell into their usual routines – Luke made a beeline for the kitchen to load up on snacks and Lacey dashed towards the stairs and her bedroom to text her friends about the day's events. Owen, however, called them both back before they'd made it too far.

"Come with me to the den," he ordered. They both followed, confused by this unusual request.

In the den, Owen headed to the coffee table in the center of the room where a boardgame was still spread out and waiting to be cleared away (the remnants of the week's family game night). Next to the board game was a large book with a much smaller package sitting on top of it. Owen pointed to the two items.

"I wanted to give you your birthday present before the party tomorrow," he said. "This is actually for both of you."

They both stared at the gifts in bewilderment, and then looked up at their uncle.

"But I thought that Lacey was getting a bike," Luke said.

"Yeah, and he's getting some kind of fancy expensive flash-light," Lacey chimed in.

Owen's mouth dropped open in shock. "What? When did you? How?"

"Not that we were snooping around every chance we got to try and figure it out," Luke said quickly.

"Yeah, cause we would never do that," Lacey added.

"We just kind of guessed that maybe that's what you got us."

Owen crossed his arms and frowned. "Yeah, well there's still time to take it all back to the store, so don't push your luck. Anyway," he pointed to the package, "this arrived yesterday. I'm not sure who it's from, but it's definitely meant for you two."

Luke grabbed the package from off of the book and tore it open with frenzied enthusiasm. When he pulled out the contents, Lacey gasped and Luke dropped the wrapping to the floor as the hand that held the item began to shake.

"This-" Luke began, but couldn't continue.

Owen looked over and saw for the first time the framed photograph that Luke was holding. Although he'd never met the man in the picture and the woman was at least a decade older than the last time he'd seen her, it wasn't difficult for him to identify the couple in the frame.

"It's mom and dad," Lacey said, crying.

"This was in their bedroom, on the dresser," Luke whispered, unable to hold back his own tears.

Owen retrieved the packaging from the floor and flipped it over, studying it for some clue as to where it came from, but there was no identifying information on it, no return address, nothing.

"I guess whoever sent it wants to remain anonymous," he said.

"I thought, I thought they wouldn't—" Lacey began, but then stopped as the tears became too much for her to continue.

Luke picked up where she left off. "I thought they wouldn't be here for our birthday." He was able to finish her thought either instinctively knowing what she wanted to say, or because he had been feeling the same way.

Owen circled them both and gave them an awkward but sincere hug. It was still new to him, this guardianship role, but he was putting in the effort. There were moments like these when he didn't know what to say or do, so he let his instincts guide him. This time he just stood there with one arm around each of them, and let them cry themselves out, and feel the pain of having their first birthday ever without their parents.

After a while the crying tapered off and faded into sniffles.

Luke retrieved the photograph. He'd placed in back on the book when the worst of the tears began. Now, he picked it up and looked at it through blurry eyes.

"We should put this on display somewhere," Luke said, wiping away his tears with the back of his hand. "Just like mom and dad had it."

Owen took the photograph from Luke and walked it over to the fireplace. He arranged it on the mantle so that it overlooked the entire room.

"There," he said. "Now they'll always be right here with you."

Lacey gave a weak smile as she wiped away her tears. "And they won't miss our birthday," she said in a shaky voice.

"What's this?" Luke picked up the book that both he and Lacey had momentarily forgotten.

"That's from me," Owen said. "I found it way in the back of my closet and I just thought you two might like to have it."

Luke and Lacey took a closer look at the oversized book in Luke's hands. The cover was made of some sort of cloth material. And it was old, the cover worn and the edges frayed. Only it wasn't a book precisely. It was an album, specifically a photo album they discovered as Luke opened it and they got a look at the first page.

Lacey gasped and Luke leaned closer to get a better look.

"Is this-" Luke began but cut off, the sentence left unfinished.

"That's your mother," Owen guessed what he wanted to know. "Actually, they're not just pictures of your mother. They're pictures of your whole family – me, mom, dad, everyone. All the people you're related to but never got the chance to meet."

"Come on, let's sit down." Luke ushered Lacey over to the leather sofa adjacent to the coffee table, and they sat with the photo album between the two of them, examining picture after picture.

Owen's phone rang and he reached into his pocket and pulled it out. He didn't recognize the number, but he didn't hesitate to answer. Since he'd reopened his practice, he sometimes got phone calls with medical emergencies from numbers he didn't recognize. Although he didn't care for after hour calls, Owen understood it to be the price he paid for living in such a small town – everyone seemed to know him and passed his number along freely. As a result, he'd recently bought a second phone with a number only shared with those closest to him.

"This is Doctor Stillwater," he said, answering the phone. He stepped further away from Luke and Lacey as he did so, preparing to give the potential client some privacy.

"Hello. This is Abigail Moore. I'm looking for a Mr. Owen Stillwater."

"This is Doctor Stillwater," Owen repeated, wondering if the woman on the phone was having difficulty hearing him.

"Oh. Mr. Stillwater. It's good to hear from you again."

"I'm sorry, but do I know you?"

"This is Abigail Moore," the woman said, as if that name was supposed to mean something to Owen. "I'm the caseworker for Luke and Lacey Castleman."

"Oh," Owen said, reaching back in time for his memory of the woman he'd met briefly, months ago. "I remember now."

"Right." She sounded pleased that he could recall her. "I'm calling to see if the twins received my package in the mail. It should be arriving any day now."

"Your package?"

"Yes, it's an old photograph. I believe the new tenant of their old apartment found it and turned it in, and well, it made its way across my desk, and I thought they might like to have it. So, I put it in a frame and sent it to them. I really thought it might've arrived by now."

"Yes," Owen said, "the photograph. It arrived yesterday, just in time for their birthday. They're both very appreciative that you sent it."

"Good," Miss Abigail responded. "I'm glad to hear that. But I'm also calling about your money."

"My money?"

"Yes, as a relative caregiver you receive a deposit every month to help you with expenses."

"Yes, I've noticed the deposits."

"Well, I wanted to check with you because it seems about a month ago you changed the account number where the money is to be deposited. Is this correct?"

"Yes, that's right. It's all going into a savings account for the twins. It's their money, so they should be the ones to use it."

Owen smiled to himself, remembering the day that he'd taken Luke and Lacey to the bank, and the surprised but excited looks on their faces when he'd told them what he'd decided to do with the money that came in each month. Owen had explained that the money would be available to them once they became adults to use however they saw fit.

Without hesitation, Luke had blurted out, "Travel. Lacey, we can see the whole world." Lacey had nodded in agreement and then they'd both looked to Owen with eyes full of hope that melted his heart. Then, when Luke asked tentatively if they could travel together, it was an easy decision for Owen. Thus, they'd begun to plan their family trips.

"Alright," said the woman on the phone, pulling Owen's thoughts back to the present. "I just wanted to be sure that everything was okay, and to make sure that things were going well with you and the twins. I wanted to see how you all are adjusting to one another."

"It was a bit challenging at first," Owen admitted, "but I think we're getting along very well now."

"Good. I'm glad to hear that. So, it's a good placement?"

At that moment Lacey squealed and Luke let out a barking laugh. Owen looked over to see what had them so delighted and saw Luke holding up a humiliating picture of Owen himself from his dreaded middle school days. Owen could only turn away from the offensive picture and silently wonder why he hadn't gone through that album on his own before handing it over to them. Who knew what other embarrassing photos were in there?

"Mr. Stillwater? Are you there?"

Another peal of laughter came from the couch. They'd found another photo.

Owen smiled to himself before answering, "Perfect. It's a perfect placement."

ACKNOWLEDGMENTS

This book was born out of a desire to tell Owen's story. He was introduced in I Know the Plans as the grumpy curmudgeon, but I felt compelled to show the full depth of the man behind the misery. His story has been weighing on my heart and mind for years now, and I'm ecstatic that I finally get to share it with all of you.

This would not have been possible without the constant help of Tracy Little. Your knowledge and expertise of Florida's foster care system and the Department of Children and Family Services proved invaluable. Thank you for being available to answer all of my random questions.

To Eileen Diaz-Lizardo, thank you for cheering me on. Your enthusiasm over the first book was a source of motivation for me to keep writing when the plot became muddled and the words were hard to find.

Finally, I want to thank my mom, who has and always will be my biggest fan. Thank you for believing in me.

ABOUT THE AUTHOR

Pamela Brown is a former English teacher and a self-proclaimed bibliophile. Pamela is obsessed with the written word. She has been writing for as long as she can remember and completed her first novel at the age of 11. Sadly, this work of genius has been lost to time, but her current work is still available to read. At the age of 12, Pamela began writing poetry and never looked back.

Follow Pamela on social media: